She wanted the gods to help her in her quest, but not at the expense of her safety...

As soon as Adina saw Shiva's third eye open with fiery sparks, she not only closed her laptop but began to run. She ran and ran, but still she saw the fire behind her when she glanced over her shoulder, a fire so fierce that she began to feel too hot. She was soon panting heavily and nearly too tired to run any longer. Then she thought of the Parvati-Shiva prayer of Kalidasa, and instantly she felt as if being lifted up in the air and beyond the reach of the fire to a high and cold peak of the Himalayas. There was a big courtyard in the middle of a garden. There, she saw Shiva again beating his drum and dancing his destructive *tandava* dance. She kept on repeating her mantra: *Vande Parvatī-Parameśvarau.* "I pray to Parvati and the highest god."

Adina was horrified to now see the highest god chasing her, but she kept on repeating her mantra, her voice growing louder and louder.

Twelve-year-old, US born, East Indian Adina is searching for a lost family jewel. Her nani, maternal grandmother, claims to have offered the jewel to one of the Hindu gods in return for a grandchild, resulting in Adina's birth. The family jewels are an Indian girl's birthright, and should have come to Adina, but her mother secretly sold off the jewels, in defiance of Hindu tradition, after she divorced Adina's father when Adina was two. So the lost "crown" jewel is the only one left…if Adina can only find it.

Her quest for this piece of jewelry takes her on a virtual trip through Hindu cosmology and mythology and Indian history. She uses her laptop to find images of a given god, goddess, or historical figure then mediates on that image while remembering all she knows about the being, thanks to her paternal grandparents' tutelage in her Indian heritage. Adina's meditations are extraordinary, however, in that the figure comes alive, and she can interact with that being—sometimes at her own peril…

KUDOS for *Myth and Punishment*

In *Myth and Punishment* by Anoop Chandola, Adina is a twelve-year-old East Indian/American girl from a broken home. Her mother gained full custody by lying about Adina's father, accusing him of child abuse. Even though the judge knew the mother was lying, he still denied custody or unsupervised visitation to the father. On top of this, Adina's mother secretly sold the family jewels (which were supposed to come to Adina), except for one, a piece of jewelry Adina calls the "crown jewel." This jewel Adina's maternal grandmother gave to one of the deities as payment for getting a grandchild, Adina. Adina searches for this jewel by contacting deities through virtual reality on her computer. Sort of. She meditates on a deity until the deity appears on her computer screen, and then she talks to them and asks them about the jewel. Her search takes her through a number of deities, who all deny any knowledge of the jewel. So how is she ever going to find it? The story line is unique and clever. Chandola has crafted an informative and educational story, wrapped around a young heroine's quest, providing an excellent media to teach young people about the many gods and goddess and the culture of the East Indian people. ~ *Taylor Jones, The Review Team of Taylor Jones & Regan Murphy*

Myth and Punishment by Anoop Chandola is the story of a young girl's quest for knowledge. When American-born East Indian pre-teen, Adina, was two, her mother divorced her father, against East Indian tradition, and lied about him, thus restricting his access to Adina. Denied the love and support of her father and paternal grandparents, due to the illegal ruling of a judge who knew her mother was lying, Adina grows up bitter and angry. To add insult to injury, Adina's mother sold off the family jewels, which were Adina's birthright. All except for one. Adina's maternal grandmother claimed to have offered a "crown jewel" to one of the gods in exchange for a grandchild, which turned out to be Adina. However, the grandmother, conveniently, cannot remember to which god or goddess she gave the jewel. Adina wants this last jewel back, so she appeals to the gods and goddesses by meditating on each one until they appear on her computer screen and she can talk to them about the jewel. As she conducts her interviews, she reviews the stories she has heard about each one, giving the reader an overview of the different deities. And sometimes, the gods have surprises for her, and even threatening her life when she makes them mad with her questions. With an unusual storyline, fascinating characters, and a wealth of information on East Indian culture, traditions, and religions, as well as some timely lessons on equality and justice, *Myth and Punishment* is both an educational and entertaining read. ~ *Regan Murphy, The Review Team of Taylor Jones & Regan Murphy*

ACKNOWLEDGMENTS

My sincere thanks to the team at Black Opal Books, especially to Lauri, Joyce, Faith, LP, and Jack for their invaluable help to bring this novel out.

MYTH AND PUNISHMENT

ANOOP CHANDOLA

A Black Opal Books Publication

GENRE: YA/COMING OF AGE/SELF-ESTEEM AND SELF-RELIANCE

This is a work of fiction. Names, places, characters and incidents are either the product of the author's imagination or are used fictitiously, and any resemblance to any actual persons, living or dead, businesses, organizations, events or locales is entirely coincidental. All trademarks, service marks, registered trademarks, and registered service marks are the property of their respective owners and are used herein for identification purposes only. The publisher does not have any control over or assume any responsibility for author or third-party websites or their contents.

DEDICATION

*For any partners in a relationship, and their children,
who have to battle false allegations by the other partner.*

Q & A of the Wise

Why Human Babies Do Not and Should Not Sleep Alone ~ James J. McKenna, PhD, Professor and Edmund P. Joyce CSC Chair in Anthropology, University of Notre Dame.

Get behind the eyes of your baby and ask yourself, "If I were my baby, where would I want to sleep?" ~ Williams Sears, MD (Dr. Bill), Associate Clinical Professor of Pediatrics, University of California, Irvine, School of Medicine.

Hiraṇmayena pātreṇa satyasyāpihitaṃ mukham "Truth's mouth is shut by a golden pot." ~ *Isha Upanishad*, circa 1,000 BC.

Table of Contents

CHAPTER 1

Agni Ignites: The Fire Within and Without

Agnimiile purohitam "I praise Agni, the Priest."
(The First Vedic Mantra)

As she sat down at her computer, Adina remembered what Dada had told her about Lord Agni, that the first prayer in the *Rig Veda*, the first scripture of the world, contained the mantras for Agni, the fire god. The ancient sages used fire, not just for cooking but to burn evil and to achieve enlightenment. Thus, Lord Agni was the greatest heavenly gift to humankind, both as the messenger between the gods and mortals and the provider of burnt offerings to the gods, even if he could be very dangerous. He was not like someone Prometheus stole from heaven.

That priests held Lord Agni in the highest regard and invoked Agni with this mantra, "Rise, O Agni! Wake up!"

Agni then rose up with the flames as, one by one, the food offerings were given to the fire and, through the smoke, all gods received the ritual offerings.

As Adina meditated on this glorious description of

Lord Agni rising from the flames, a terrible forest fire appeared on Adina's computer screen. She gazed steadily upon it and heard thunder as lightning flashed in her peripheral vision.

Suddenly the scene changed to a clear sky filled with bright sunlight, and Adina felt hot. Then the scene changed abruptly again, this time to a night scene with thousands of lamps, candles, and electric bulbs of various colors all dazzlingly bright. Still, Adina didn't alter her steady gaze, for she remembered Dada's description of the Vedic fire ceremony, *homa* or *havana*.

Then the scene changed yet again. A pot with flames rising in it was now on the screen before her, and a human voice came from the pot. "Dear little girl, I am Agni. You have seen my various forms, and indeed I have countless other forms of which you are not aware, but you have invoked my simplest and sacred form. I bless you."

Adina folded her hands to show her respect to the fire god. "Namaste, Lord Agni."

"I am very much pleased with you. What is your name?"

"My name is Adina…uh…and I am also called Adi."

"A very good Vedic name. You will never be poor. You will live up to your name. Who are your parents?"

"My father is Danin—Dan for short."

"He must donate to good causes. What is his family name?"

"Badoni. It's his Himalayan Brahmin family name. Dada and Dadi are his father and mother. My mother's name is Madhu, and her family name is Hota. Nana and Nani are her father and mother."

"Your mother's names are Vedic too. Madhu is mead for sweet. The Hotas are the priests who invoke deities at a *homa* ceremony. I am the first to be invoked as I am the *purohita* because I sit in the front. Now tell me very briefly why you have invoked me."

"Briefly, I am looking for a lost crown jewel."

"That jewel is on the crown of Queen Elizabeth. It's not lost."

"No, that is not the crown jewel I want. I am not a queen. Queen Elizabeth—I mean Her Majesty of Great Britain deserves that great crown jewel. My crown jewel is very small...uh...uh...and inexpensive, but means a lot to me for it will reveal the answer to a mystery."

"What mystery?"

"I have no details, but I can tell you, I know surely, I can tell you now why I am so keen to get my crown jewel back. That is, back with me as soon as possible—with me. Oh, Lord."

"Tell me whatever you have in mind for you appear to be burdened with pain. You and I need to talk to each other, to both open up as much as possible. Are you ready to open up to me? I can enlighten you and bestow on you the fire of eloquence." The flames rose higher and Adina understood clearly that a heated discourse was in the offing.

"Yes, I now feel the ability to fire up my story with unexpected flares and flashes. I am grateful to you as much to Dada and Dadi." She paused for a few seconds. "Do you see my laptop?"

"Yes. It runs with my power."

"Using this computer, I found out the records of my parents' divorce case. I was barely two years old in 2002, the year of their divorce, and now I am almost thirteen years old and know how to get information from the Internet. I found that my mother claimed that I said something against my father, and her parents supported her accusations. As a result, my father was kicked out of our home three days after my mother filed for divorce—"

"What about the accusations?" Lord Agni interrupted.

"The court found the accusations of child abuse false. But my father was allowed only minimum visitation rights and could only be with me under the strict watch of court-approved supervisors. My mother had complete custody, and when my father requested more time, equal time, the judge refused. As if this was not enough punishment of an innocent party, the judge further limited my father's parents' visitation to one day a week while my mother's parents had no such constraint. The judge supported his ruling using a psychologist's report—"

"Was the psychologist a court-appointed official?" Lord Agni inquired.

"Yes. But she should not have been the court's psychologist, however, because of a conflict of interest. My mother had written a good review for this psychologist's book, but the judge refused to declare this a conflict of interest—"

The god interrupted Adina again. "I understand the psychologist knowingly ignored her professional duty to never marginalize an innocent parent. Unfortunately, she is still working for the system!" Agni's tone was somewhat angry, and Adina heard crackling coming from the firepot. "Yes, and she is still making good money, which is her priority, not doing what is right."

Adina nodded. "I was told that Nani offered a small crown jewel to a god or goddess, one of the temple deities where she lived, requesting to have a grandchild. And the next year I was born. I am the only grandchild on both sides, and Nani claims I was born because of her offering and prayer."

"Did your dada and dadi consider her claim seriously?"

"Dada and Dadi laughed at her claim, and Nani accused them of ridiculing her religion. But they all come from one and the same spiritual background, and you are the first god to be worshipped in their common religion. In fact, Dada started the naming ceremony on Nani's request. Through a clay lamp you were invoked first in the ceremony and then the worship of Ganapati started. Dada told me that you are the first of all heavenly deities, and since it is you who carry our offerings to the other gods, which deity did Nani's priest select for the offering of the crown jewel?"

"That is the only jewelry you can have?"

"By Hindu tradition, my parents' jewelry would have been my inheritance but the rest of it was secretly sold by my mom just before she filed for divorce. Dad didn't know what else was happening behind his back."

"All right," Lord Agni said. "I understand your problem, but the priest who made the offering for your nani did not come to me through *havana*. He must have performed the non-Vedic ceremony, the *Puja*. And so I do not know to which deity that offering was made."

"Dada has told me the history of *homa* and *Puja*, and the two differ in their origin and practice. For your *homa,* a few spoonfuls of clarified butter dropped with Vedic mantras over a sacred fireplace are enough to make you happy. The more grease the more fire!"

"You are too smart for your age. I understand you have suffered a lot because of false accusations, but you should be happy that your father was deemed innocent by the court. Your personal doctor's report does not show any of the abuse that your mother and her lawyer claimed happened. The judge should have understood your mother's reason for such extreme charges—complete control of your life. Indeed, the judge was most incompetent not to recognize an obvious fraud. Your mother claimed you had accused him of being an abusive father, but a twenty-two-month old baby has no such understanding of human evil, let alone the speaking ability to convey it. All child specialists know this. I know this. Even illiterate mothers know this. One has to be either an idiot or a crook to believe such impossible things."

"Dad's lawyers call what she did *malicious intent*," Adina added.

"This world would have been much better if there were no malicious liars, but they are among us. However, those who support such liars are more guilty because they have harmed innocent people even more. The judge was in power to correct this fraud. He cannot say, 'Oh, the wife was unhappy with her marriage, and the fact that she made such terrible allegations to get out of this marriage is not a big deal.' Just as he cannot say, 'Oh, it is not a big deal that the husband slapped his wife once a week to show his unhappiness with his marriage.' Just as he cannot say, 'Oh, Osama bin Laden wanted to vent his anger against America and claimed it was God's will, so no big deal.' There is something wrong with this judge. He doesn't realize how much destruction her lies have done to her daughter and husband. She is using an innocent child to get out of this marriage. Some day that child, you, will become an adult and realize what a stigma she got for her inheritance. Instead, your mother sold the family jewelry in a cowardly fashion—"

"Lord, I don't care for that jewelry, but the crown jewel is very important."

Although Adina again highlighted her desire to find the crown jewel, the fire god was still angry about the poor decision of the judge. "The judge ignored Nani's poor understanding of religion. His biggest fault is that he grossly ignored the American ideals of *justice* and *equality*. He has sent a message that, in the land where there are more literate people than in any other, one can lie and be rewarded no matter how the lie destroys others. This is not right. This is a national disgrace. Anything else the judge or others missed on purpose?" Lord Agni now seemed to be interested in hearing more. The flames flared up and thick smoke poured forth. "Claiming to be just without the fire of accountability is not justice," the fire god said, fuming. "Your story sounds hot. A burning tale is true hot stuff, not a smoking gun event shown for sensation. I hope you are not making it up. Are you?"

"Not at all, my lord! My story is not just mine. I will say it again and again. My story represents thousands of innocent victims, not just from the USA but from many other countries. Humans have failed to stop these stories. Some, men and women, vigorously support the villains of these stories. They don't care about the huge number of suicides committed every year by the accused innocent victims. Human efforts have failed to stop the defenders of the villains. So I am seeking divine intervention."

"Then continue your story, dear Adi."

Emboldened by the fiery god's affectionate command, Adi continued to disclose a dark secret which had been hushed. "Lord, my father mentioned that my mother was upset one evening and said that she had a gun. Nani and Dad got scared. Nani slapped Mom, but Mom denied in her testimony that such an incident ever happened. Dad told the court that this proves that she has a serious problem with lying, but in truth so does Nani, for Nani supported Mom's version that the incident never occurred. Those false things, including saying that I made such a terrible allegation against my father when I was less than two-years old, Mom and Nani consider plain truth even today."

"Did you say that she had a gun and the court did not take this allegation seriously?"

"That's what Dad says."

"Your state's corrupt legal system desperately needs

immediate corrections. His testimony about the gun should not have been ignored. Husbands have been shot dead by disgruntled wives. Such murders were feared even at the time of the *Rig* Veda, about three thousand years ago. This is why, in a Vedic wedding, the bride-groom requires a vow from the bride in my presence that she will 'never be a malicious seer and murderer' of her husband, except in self-defense. Did your nana and nani really arrange for a Vedic wedding?"

"Yes, we have evidence of that." Adina was a little baffled. The Vedic fire god had just explained the mean-ing of *Hota*. Maybe he was asking because many Brah-mins now considered themselves liberated from the old ways, she reasoned.

"The Vedic wedding of your parents included the sev-en-step ceremony wherein the bride accepts the last step as the bridegroom says, 'Take the seventh step for our friendship.' If she takes the seventh step, then this is ac-ceptance of her permanent journey with this husband. All these vows are taken in front of me. That is why a Vedic marriage ceremony results in what is called a 'fire-tested' marriage."

"Dada and Dadi, as well as Nana and Nani, were mar-ried the way you are describing, Lord. They took the vows as they moved around you seven times."

"Yes, but your nana and nani don't realize how much they have insulted me. They are unable to read the sacred *Veda*. Their family name, Hota, is phony. They have made a mockery of their religion. It is clear that your ma-ternal grandparents didn't teach their daughter the value of speaking truth straightforwardly. They participated in destroying their own daughter's family."

"The judge made no such comments, though." Adina wanted to bring this fact to Agni's attention.

"The judge made a terrible blunder by rewarding a liar. He would be wise to study cases wherein family members were murdered by a wife in his own jurisdiction. He will find out that a deranged wife isn't so stupid as to tell her husband what she is plotting behind his back. Did you ever hear a terrorist disclosing his plot before the attack? All kinds of terrorists, the domestic variety included, those who destroy families, are cowards. They put all responsibility for their destructive acts on God's will. According to the Nine/Eleven terrorists, God granted their wish to destroy the World Trade Center in New York, and your mother, no doubt, imagines such impossible commands of God to justify her terror too."

Adina heard big crackling sounds from the firepot as much smoke and flares rose upward.

She broke the brief pause. "If I had been big enough, like I am now, I would have told the judge that I always loved my dad and he has always loved me. He has been the most gentle and kind man to me. His witnesses said this. Some witnesses of my mother supported her, common friends of my parents, but they were moved because my mother cried before them. She cried before the judge too, several times. The judge didn't say a word about her conflicting statements. In one place she would say how I loved my father, and then later she would say how I was afraid of him. Her lawyers had the same problem of giving conflicting statements."

"Clearly, the judge is incompetent. Your father may not be as good at the art of crying, which liars use to gain mercy."

"Yes, my mother's witnesses believed her planned tears. How can decent people sit with their children around the dinner table with no thought of *my* true tears!"

"Your mother must have coached her witnesses, but now they and any other friends she shares in common with your father know that the court found her claims to be baseless. They won't trust her anymore, though they may only say such things behind her back. Your mother's name may be Madhu, but she turned out to be utterly bitter for her own husband and daughter. She couldn't live up to her name. She couldn't extend even common civility and courtesy to her loved ones, and so how can this court-proven liar love her friends? They will speak this way about her, and indeed, such backbiting will be common. Losing the trust of friends will cause my heat to rise within her in the form of unusually high anxiety. She may try to extinguish my fire with her false tears, but the heat will remain with her. You will also feel my heat, but in a positive way for I have burned your guilt. You are pure. This is my promise to you. Now you promise me that you will bring the facts to light."

"I will. You are my light. Dada told me that your name is *Pavaka,* the purifier. You have made me feel much better about myself. Thank you, my lord!"

Suddenly, the flames disappeared and so did the pot. Adina waited to hear the faceless voice for a few moments, for she thought Agni would continue. Instead, she heard the sudden thunder of an approaching storm marching toward her with blinding dust. The lightning looked as if it might ignite a great fire to make the Earth a big *homa*, but she was not frightened. Agni's unexpected harsh criticism of malicious liars and their supporters was like a tranquilizer for her, and she felt absolutely no fright at all. Only Agni could be so fiery within and without.

Adi quietly shut the computer down and left her desk. Outside, she saw beautiful sunshine, but there was a great storm brewing on the horizon.

CHAPTER 2

Ganesha's Mouse: The Master of Computing

Shrigaṇeshaaya namaḥ "Salutation to Lord Ganesha"
(A Sanskrit mantra for Ganesha)

Adina's grandmothers had taught her about Ganesha, commonly the first god who was worshipped to remove future obstacles. So she suspected Ganesha was the god her grandmother had offered the jewel, Ganesha whose icon was kept in a cupboard by her mother. There were also other sacred icons in the cupboard, but Adi knew that the crown jewel was offered to a powerful deity elsewhere and with the help from a priest. However, she still suspected Ganesha was the deity in question because every priest knew that Lord Ganesha had to be remembered, even if another god was to receive a gift.

She recalled that Ganesha was the son of Shiva and Parvati, and she remembered the story that her dadi had related to her. Once, when Parvati was alone in her Himalayan home, she felt very cold and decided to take a hot bath. Before going to bathe, she created a child figure from her skin's sweaty dirt that she had rubbed away.

The figure looked so handsome that she decided to give it life. She transferred her *shakti,* or energy, to the figure, which immediately grew into a boy. "Ma, what can I do for you?" he asked Parvati.

Parvati was moved by her son's caring nature. "Son, I want to take bath. You stay at the main door and don't let anyone enter until I come out of my bath. I give you all the energy required to do as I ask."

The boy told his mother he would be happy to honor her request, and, as he headed toward the main door, he grew strong with his mother's blessing. In the middle of Parvati's bath, Shiva appeared at the door, home unexpectedly soon. Ganesha blocked Shiva's entry. Shiva shouted, "Who are you to stop me from entering my own home?"

"I am Parvati's son. I take orders only from my mother. She is taking a bath. When she is through, I will ask her if you are allowed to enter."

"What? She has no son like you claim. Let me in."

"No, sir." The boy became bigger and stronger before Shiva's eyes.

"Let me go in or I will kill you," Shiva insisted.

"No, sir."

Shiva shoved the boy, who merely shoved him back. The all-powerful Shiva felt humiliated by this shouting and shoving match with a mere boy and pulled his weapon, a trident. With it he cut off the head of the boy. The boy died instantly.

As Shiva entered his house, Parvati came out of her bath. "How did you come in the house? I told my boy not to let in anyone."

"*Your* boy?"

"*Our* boy."

"How was he our boy?"

Parvati told him how she created the boy and ordered

him not allow anyone in the house until she finished the bath. "What do you mean when you say, 'How *was* he our boy?' He *is* our boy forever."

"No, no, my dear Parvati. I have killed him since he stopped me and started a bad fight. His dead body is lying at the door."

Parvati went to the body of her son and began to wail as soon as she saw the dead boy.

Shiva claimed to be kind and good, which Adi remembered was the meaning of his name. He felt sorry for his anger at his own son and asked for forgiveness of Parvati. In his shame, he quickly replaced the head of the dead boy with a live elephant's head.

The boy got up, as if from a bad dream. Parvati was elated to see him alive and introduced Shiva as his father. The boy touched his father out of respect and love, and Shiva was so moved that he named him Ganesha.

"One's name should be meaningful," Adi remembered her grandmother saying.

Shiva made his new son the ruler of the community of the gods and gave him his own troops. He rode on a mouse.

Thus Ganesha became the symbol of an ideally successful child. With this awareness, Adina gazed at the picture of Ganesha, a mouse by his side. This was her meditation technique she learned from her Internet search upon her little laptop computer—to gaze at the images she located during her search. Suddenly, she heard a drum and a conch sounding, and the sound was coming closer to her. A faint dancing figure began to emerge out of that picture, and the picture slowly began to shine with bright light. And then she saw the god Ganesha, his divine figure very scary, due to his elephant head with a human torso and a big fat tummy. In one of his four hands she saw an ax, too. She saw a mouse ahead of

Ganesha, and she wondered how he could be expected to ride that mouse, as he looked so bulky.

"Dear Adina, fear not. I am a vegetarian. I am fat, but from the offerings of sweets. A sweet thing could ruin your health, but I am a god. My name is Ganapati and worship starts with me. That little mouse is not just my vehicle. He leads me to any uncharted territory. When he takes me to rich devotees down in the Indian plains then I have to eat a lot. They offer so much. Before this I was slim and trim when my beautiful Pahari mother, Parvati, created me. Like any Himalayan boy I used to walk up and down in the hills then. I appeared like no elephant in any part of my body then. I had no big belly then. Nevertheless, I used my oddities to aid myself and others. A little oddity can be your vehicle to reach big notoriety."

"Namaste, God Ganesha." Adina folded her hands in greeting, wondering how the god knew she was thinking about his girth and the fact that Dadi had told her he rides upon a mouse. "How do you know my name already?" she asked him.

"Adi, your naming ceremony started with my formal worship. Are you familiar with *Puja*?"

"Yes, I have seen your simple worship. First, a bow to your icon to invite you. Then several offerings to your icon with Sanskrit mantras: sprinkling water on your feet, hands, head, and mouth—a complete bath. Then offering you water, sandal paste, sacred thread, rice grains, incense, lamp, flowers, fruits, and sweets with a gift, plus sacred cash called *dakshina*. In the end, a bow again to see you off. Bow to bow equals your highest *puja*, Lord."

"Good. At the request of your nani, your dada performed my *Puja* and it was he who chose your name, Adina. You looked as beautiful as your mother."

"Thanks, God. Yes, Dada, Dadi, Nana, and Nani call me Adi more often than Adina."

"Do you know the meaning of your name?" the god asked.

"My dada and dadi explained it to me in detail. They both have PhD degrees. Dada taught Sanskrit and Dadi taught mythology at a university. Adina means 'rich.'"

"I know why your nana, nani, and parents needed an explanation. Even though they have Brahmin ancestry, they don't know Sanskrit, the sacred language of their religion. Did your Dadi tell you the meaning of my name?"

"Yes. Lord of the Community."

"Any name has several meanings. Only I can tell you the better meaning. Ganapati or Ganesha means Master of Computing. The Sanskrit root *gan* means to compute, to calculate, and *pati* means master, lord. People worship me in their homes for success and security. However, remember that success and security do not have the same home, but it's good to keep them together. In reality, my job is to compute, mainly in order to solve the problems of others. With the help of my mouse, I can guide you to success. Tell me what your problem is."

"Using this laptop, I found out all about my parents' divorce case." She then told Ganesha what she had told Agni earlier.

Lord Ganesha reacted immediately after Adina stopped. "Your case is a good example of taxpayers' money being wasted. The justice system of your state is behaving like a gang, but far less efficiently, of course. They do a job in one year that could be done in a week. If the doctor says right in the beginning that no abuse took place, the case should be closed and divorce granted. But listen, we don't have to discuss the case history. I understand your problem. First, let me inform you that I am not that deity who received the gift of your nani's crown jewel."

Ganesha and Adina looked at each other intently.

"Now, my solution," Lord Ganesha continued. "Go to the congress."

"Yes, God, I understand you want me to go to the congress, but tell me how I am to proceed."

"When you grow more mature, go to your lawmakers with a community or organization of victims like you. The congress can make it a law that a hurtful lie would be punishable crime in every context, including when that lie is used by one member of a family against another as your mother lied about your father. Do you understand?"

"Yes, yes. Your instructions are very clear. Thanks."

"Now about your mother's trickery. She could have sought a hassle-free way of getting a divorce: mediation, arbitration, a no-contest divorce, or simple marriage dissolution. Any of these options would have cost less in time and money."

"That's correct. Some lawyers advertise a quick divorce for two-hundred-ninety-nine dollars, but my parents are lawyers and fought a costly legal battle. Dad was forced to spend over two hundred thousand dollars— money that could have helped me get a college education. Some of my friends tease me, saying, 'Oh, you are a daughter of lawyers. Lawyers are liars. You will be a liar, too. College or no college education.'"

"Anybody can be a damn liar regardless of who their parents are. No, my dear Adi, you can develop a powerful conscience, which means understanding how lying hurts. Lying can, in fact, be so dangerous that it is terrorism. That is why all major religions of the world insist that we must live by truth and not by falsehood. Hinduism forbids, not only lying generally, but slander and abandonment of the husband. I have two wives, and they praise me. This is how a wife is to behave."

"You have two wives? Bigamy is punishable under American law. The solution is divorce."

"Adina, I spoke the truth to you and you seem to take it so lightly," Ganesha said loudly.

Then Adina saw Ganesha raising his ax, and he appeared to be moving closer to her. She heard an ear-piercing male voice say, "Ganesha will not solve your problem. Do you hear me? I, Ganapati, will not solve your problems."

She didn't want to hear that voice anymore, so she shut her computer down. Instead of being afraid, however, she felt fearless and happy as she shouted, "I have heard your message. It's so loud and clear. I am not afraid."

Adina believed in the honesty of Ganesha. She knew he would have told her even if it were one of his wives who possessed the crown jewel she was seeking. She was also happy that the two gods she had interviewed were of very similar opinions.

CHAPTER 3

Sarasvati's Wise Advice

Sarasvatyai namaḥ "Salutation to Sarasvati"
(A Sanskrit mantra for Sarasvati)

Dadi had told Adina about the origins of Brahma, the creator, and other deities, including Sarasvati. There were several stories of her origin. Adina remembered one in particular.

After Brahma created many sons out of his body, he decided to have a daughter, Sarasvati, the goddess of learning and music.

"I am meditating on your picture, Ma Sarasvati. You are as beautiful as my mother and so I call you Ma. I can see a crown on your head, and I can see your four hands. You have a sitar-like vina. I don't see clearly any clothing on your body, which looks to be covered by jewelry. There must be some wisdom underlying this divine fashion, for you are the goddess of wisdom."

Sarasvati appeared then, and she was seated on a throne. Beside the throne was an enormous white swan, her vehicle.

"*Pranam*, Ma," Adina said, offering homage. "I am Adina."

"My *ashish* to you," the goddess said, giving her blessings with a smile. "You look nervous and sad. Make it a general rule to smile before you speak. You can break this rule, only occasionally. Don't be afraid of stumbling. Keep stumbling. Stumbling is the way to learn, discover, and rise. I am the Goddess of Speech and Learning. What can I do for you, dear?"

"I am looking for my crown jewel, and because you control knowledge, I assume you would know where I can find it."

"What crown jewel, Adina, are you talking about?" Sarasvati said with a stern face.

"My nani claims that I was born because she offered a crown jewel to a deity. I want to meet that deity. Are you perhaps that deity?"

"Why do you think that I am that deity? There are thousands of gods and goddesses. Check with other big deities. Don't meditate on me alone."

"But you are the goddess of wisdom and the first female child of your father, the creator, Brahma. You are his wife, too. All later female deities must be familiar to you, and even though you have no child of your own, you might have blessed my parents."

"If you think I could not have a child of my own, then how can I create you?"

"You are right. I should think with wisdom. How can I have wisdom?"

"Everybody has wisdom, but some use it and others misuse it. Don't misuse your wisdom or people will make jokes about you behind your back. Children are born because they have parents and grandparents, great-grandparents and great-great-grandparents, going back to the beginning."

"In the beginning, were your father Brahma and his father Vishnu. Who is the creator of Vishnu?"

"Who told you all this mythology?"

"My dadi. She taught a university course on mythology."

"Dear Adina, mythology is fun. Did you enjoy it when your dadi taught you?"

"Very much. Dadi is a great story teller. She is a published writer."

"You are very lucky."

"I will not feel lucky until I become wiser myself. Now that I have seen you, will I be wiser?"

"You look very wise already. Your interest in inquiry is a clear sign. What else do you want to know?"

"Who created Vishnu?"

"Vishnu is the creation of the artists of words. The real creator's name is *Karma*."

"Who is Karma?"

"It's not a 'who' but a 'what,' a neuter noun. In the beginning some sort of action happened by itself. Every action has a reaction. That reaction is action for another action. That makes a chain—the karmic chain. This cosmos is created by karmic action, not by a god or by gods and goddesses."

"Is this law of karma 'action to reaction' perfect?"

"Always."

"If our world is created by the karmic law, then why do they say 'the world is not perfect'?"

"The world appears imperfect because every being looks at it with his or her imperfect ways."

"So Vishnu is not the creator of the universe. Then why do many Hindu temples show him as the creator?"

"Views of different sects, cults, and religions—they all blur the real knowledge. Those temples may be Vishnu temples, and indeed some say his wife Lakshmi is the creator. But if you go to a Shiva temple, there Shiva is said to be the creator and some say Shiva's wife Uma is the creator. None of them are the creator, however. You are created by karma, actions and reactions of evolution. Certainly not by your granny's crown jewel. Not by any old religious gimmick. Karma and creation are related, technically and linguistically."

"See my laptop? It's new technology, not old religious stuff."

"Very good. Technology came much earlier than religion."

"Yes, Dada told me we humans became modern because our ancestors were tool makers."

"And your crown jewel is also fashioned by tools. Check it with other gods. Maybe they can unravel the mystery of your crown jewel. You will enjoy talking to them."

"Yes, I want to have fun, and certainly I *am* interested in recovering my crown jewel." Adi was a bit despondent that she had not yet found the deity to whom the crown jewel was given, but then she thought on the fun-part of this investigation and she smiled. "Before I leave, I would like to see you playing the vina."

"Sure. Here is a *raga* that is named after me. It's called *Vagishvari* or the goddess of speech. Many musicians who don't know Sanskrit call it *Bagesri*!.This *raga* has become internationally famous because of the Beatles."

"So, you know the Beatles?"

"I am the goddess of music. I should know the Beatles."

After the gorgeous raga was over, Adina said, "That is so sweet sounding." She smiled and asked, "Can I have one more question?"

"You can."

"When you lifted the vina, I didn't see any clothing underneath. Why?"

"It is the way the artists show me. They are right. They think with wisdom. How can the early gods and goddesses have clothes? There were no clothes then. Clothing is a very recent invention."

Adina laughed. "Yes, I have seen the pictures of old temples where gods and goddesses don't look properly dressed-up."

"There is nothing improper about that."

"Then why does my nana think that MF Hussain was a duffer? He hates not just Hussain but all local Muslims of his native place. He would like to use kerosene oil to burn them. A friend heard him saying that. Did Hussain really paint you un-Indian?"

"I know Hussain imagined me as shown in great sacred temples."

"Nana thinks he was taking this liberty because he was a Muslim rather than a Hindu. Why doesn't Hussain make pictures of his own religious leaders without clothes?"

"The answer is very simple. I was created in the beginning. Then there were no Hindus, no Jains, no Buddhists, no Jews, no Christians, and no Muslims in the beginning. I didn't create any religion. Gods don't create religion. Humans do. Have you heard any god saying in any Sanskrit scripture, 'I am the creator of Hinduism'? The word *Hindu* is not a divine word. I know this. I am the goddess of knowledge.

"The devotees of knowledge have no religious boundaries," the goddess contiued. "Don't try to block me in by your religion. I flow everywhere. I change course everywhere. That is what my name means, Sarasvati. Nobody owns Sarasvati."

"But you are worshipped as the Hindu goddess of

speech, arts, and music. Didn't MF Hussain offend you and all Hindus?"

"Those who ban books and arts are the worst offenders. Hussain didn't offend me. He was born into a family whose religion was Islam, but the adherents of Islam do not believe in idol worship. Thus no mosque shows any pictures of the founder of Islam. Those ancient Hindu temple artists didn't call themselves Hindu or their religion Hinduism. Their dharma was art. They believed in the Indian tradition of free expression. MF Hussain followed his own national tradition. That's his right."

"My mother believes not only in the right of free expression but also in the right of free movement. She came to see my dad at his home, not the other way around. You move all around freely and no veil. I never watch veiled men in the Indian TV news, just only women, unless they show some masked male terrorists. Why are there veiled women in this day and age?"

Adina waited momentarily hoping for an answer. "It concerns my family history, Ma Sarasvati," she continued, "My dada's mother covered her face with a veil when facing senior male in-laws. As Dada says, she was not afraid of hyenas as much as her Hindu male relatives. How come you couldn't teach those educated males not to enslave women like my great-grandmother? Like them, she also worshipped you, but she remained uneducated, homebound. At my age she was forced to accept the arranged engagement with a teenager—my great-grandfather. You couldn't stop their marriage which took place just a few months after the engagement ceremony. The boy was not required to be present at the ceremony. They saw each other after the marriage. Other senior male in-laws knew the faces of every farm animal they had, but not hers. She continued her own veil but successfully convinced her daughter-in-law to dump it forever.

Grandma went all the way to get her PhD degree. Did you hear my ancestral story, Ma?"

Suddenly Sarasvati looked very angry. "Don't ask me any other questions." And the goddess disappeared instantly.

"Come back, Ma Sarasvati! I am not going to ask you the other questions I have. I just want to elaborate my question and your historical record. The majority of people in a country where you are respected as the goddess of learning could not read and write until now. In that country, since ancient times, women were not allowed to study the Vedic literature. Dada told me that Sanskrit plays are not really Sanskrit plays. In them, just a few elite men speak Sanskrit and all women and low castes speak the Prakrit vernaculars. They are Prakrit plays with a small sprinkling of Sanskrit here and there. You understand now why your raga is *bagesri* for the majority and *vagishvari* for Dada?" Adina began to pant. She took a few deep breaths.

The screen showed no Sarasvati. But it was clear to Adina that even in anger Sarasvati taught her something very important. Right of expression was not the right to lie.

Dada heard from an Indian friend about a new literacy slogan, not just for India, but the entire globe: Literate globe, capable globe. On his request, Dada translated it in Hindi as *saakshar lok, saksham lok*. He wanted to hang Dada's translation on his living room's wall with his words—*Veils blurr letters*. The slogan should make Sarasvati very happy, even though this friend, unlike MF Hussain, was not a Sarasvati idolater.

CHAPTER 4

Vishnu's Maya Movement

Vishnave namah "Salutation to Vishnu"
(A Sanskrit mantra for Vishnu)

Adina sat, once again, thinking about the creation and avatar stories that her dadi had told her.

In her dadi's version, Vishnu created Prajapati, or Brahma, who created the rest. Prajapati was the father of three kinds of beings: good, bad, and moderate. The good were gods; the bad, demons; and the moderate beings, humans. The demons were liars and terrorists, and to protect innocent gods and humans, Vishnu descended to punish the criminal demons as an *avatar*. Vishnu accomplished the *avatar* form with his Maya power.

There were many avatars of Vishnu, ten of which were very well known. Adina had heard several stories of these avatars, but not all of them played well in her understanding.

The first avatar came as a little fish in a water pot of Manu. The fish spoke in a human voice, and, in the story Adi heard, the fish spoke Sanskrit. Adina ruled out the use of Sanskrit at that early time, as her dada had told her, but the Hotas, Adina's mother's parents, were devout Hindus and believed Vishnu's stories. They knew the *Matsya* or fish story, which claimed that the conversation took place in Sanskrit, but there were other stories they did not care for, only because they were not Hindu. They didn't care for the Bible's Noah, for example, even though Noah's story was much like Manu's.

Noah's common sense was as great as Manu's, as far as Adina was concerned. Noah collected many male and female pairs of many different kinds of animals in his ark. Adina was impressed very much that a male and a female parent were saved by Noah, and she admired his compassionate understanding. Adi thought that the judge in her parents' case could have learned so much from this Biblical story.

The Hotas could have used Manu's compassion and commonsense as well. That little fish requested Manu to save him. Otherwise, the bigger fish would devour him in the open water. Manu took that fish to his retreat and, after a few days, the fish requested that Manu drop him in a well, for the fish was growing bigger and the water pot was too small for him to move around with ease. Manu dropped him into a well, but after a while the fish requested that Manu drop him in a river. The fish became much larger, an unbelievable size, and so the fish requested that Manu guide it to the sea. The fish was very pleased with Manu's care.

"You saved me, and I will save you from the forthcoming big flood. Prepare a big boat right away."

Manu was totally confused by this demand, but he did prepare a boat. Soon the predicted deluge came and there was a horrible destruction of life. At that time, a giant fish arose from the sea and speedily swam toward Manu. The sage was ready with his boat. The giant fish dragged the boat to the top of a Himalayan peak. Dada had told

Adina that a peak near his ancestral district was worshipped as the place where Manu survived and met a woman. They became the parents of a new human race. This race of man was called Manava, Manu's progeny. If Noah were born in India, he would be a perfect avatar of Vishnu, Adi thought.

Adina wasn't thrilled by two of the avatars, the tortoise and the boar, but she recognized the evolution from water to land that they represented. The most outlandish was the *Nṛsimha* avatar in which Vishnu's head was a lion's and the torso human. Its nails, however, were like those in the paws of a lion.

This kind of body was necessary because the demon king Hiranyakashipu was granted a boon by Brahma. The demon could not be killed by any animal or by any human, and so Vishnu became part human and part lion—or *nṛ* and *simha*. Vishnu was mad as hell at the demon king.

This demon had a son Prahlada, who believed in Vishnu as God, and the demon tried hard to convince his son that there was no such thing as Vishnu or, indeed, God. Against his father's warnings, Prahlada even started to teach his peers that Vishnu was God, which made Hiranyakashipu even madder. He asked his sister Holika to kill Prahlada. She arranged for a dance around a bonfire and invited Prahlada. Prahlada trusted his aunt. The aunt was delighted by her brother's request, for she was jealous that Hiranyakashipu had a child and she did not.

When Prahlada was dancing with other dancers near the bonfire, Holika came close to him. She was ready to push him into the fire, but Vishnu's power of Maya caused her to feel a big jolt that threw her into the bonfire and she was burned to death.

This news should have convinced Hiranyakashipu that Prahlada's belief in Vishnu as the protector of the innocent was evident, but instead he took the punishment of his son into his own hands. He asked his servants to prepare a hot iron pillar. When the iron pillar was ready and became red hot, Hiranyakashipu asked his son, "Prahlada! Suppose you hug this pillar. Do you believe that your God would save you?"

Prahlada smiled and hugged the pillar, which burst apart. A man-lion figure emerged from it. The figure roared, grabbed Hiranyakashipu, and tore at his guts. The demon was killed instantly but the son of the demon was safe.

Then Adina remembered the part of the story about the *Vamana,* or Dwarf avatar, after Prahlada's heir became the king. Now God fully evolved as a human. Prahlada was a very pious ruler of the demons, and later his grandson Bali became even more pious. Indra felt threatened by Bali's charitable performances and worried that Bali could replace Indra as the king of heaven. He was performing an unprecedented mega-charity *yajña*. This sort of *yajña* could be compared to a mega-fund raiser for a presidential candidate to defeat the incumbent president of the USA. Indra prayed to Vishnu for the protection of his throne in heaven, and Vishnu guaranteed Indra full protection. He didn't need any matching *yajña* from Indra, however, but planned a little hoax instead.

Near the end of Bali's charity performance, a dwarf Brahmin came to attend it. Bali was very happy to see this little poor Brahmin and asked him very respectfully if he would like to receive any charity. The dwarf Brahmin asked for a piece of space that he could cover by his three steps. Bali laughed, "But you are a dwarf. Your three steps would cover nothing. Ask for more land, sir!"

"No. I will not ask for more than that," replied the dwarf.

"Fine, sir! Go ahead and measure the space with your first step!"

The dwarf took the first step that covered the whole earth, and then he took the second step that covered the entire sky. There was no space left for his third step, and so he asked Bali, "Where do I place my third step?"

The pious demon king instantly realized that the dwarf was none other than Vishnu. He was overwhelmed with devotion. "Lord! Place your almighty foot on my head!"

The lord placed his third step on Bali's head. The step was indeed mighty and pushed the unsuspecting Bali down. Due to that push, Bali reached the lowest level of the space from whence heaven was completely inaccessible. Indra remained safe on his throne in the heaven, highly impressed by the trick Vishnu had played upon Bali.

Before Adina could think of another Vishnu story, she heard a big conch shell sound and wondered where this sound was coming from. As the sound came closer and closer, she saw a shadowy figure slowly moving toward her on the computer screen, until the figure could be clearly seen.

"Oh, it's Vishnu blowing his conch. My meditation is working." She addressed Vishnu. "I see your four hands moving. In one hand you have a conch and in another hand the *chakra*. It's your famous disk weapon. It's definitely you. Namaste. Dadi told me that your name means Pervader. You pervade everything by your power, *Maya*. Namaste, Lord."

Vishnu raised one of his hands to give her his blessing. "*Ashish*. You look inquisitive, my little girl. What do you have in your head?"

"What does *Maya* mean to you?"

"My maya and I are one and the same thing: movement, motion, measure. She is in me. I am in her."

"Many say that you are the first cause of creation, but Sarasvati told me that creation is from the action-reaction chain. If karmic action creates, then what do you do?"

"Sarasvati is right. Karma moves to another karma, cause and effect, which then becomes a cause that moves on to another effect, and so on. Put simply: Step A moves to Step B and Maya and I are that motion or process between A and B. I am the measurement of time and space, but I cannot be measured. Indeed, I look different to different beings in different spaces and times. Such an illusion is the Maya Effect. Am I to understand that you have heard of it before?"

"Dada and Dadi think that Maya has merely become a very popular name for girls, even in America. Everything we think we know turns out to be confusing and needs further search."

"Now tell me what is confusing you."

She moved her eyes upward. "I see a crown on your head, a big crown with large jewels. If you have small crown jewels, one of them might have come from my nani as a gift to you."

"What was the requested gift in return for this jewel?"

"A child for my parents."

"Adina, you are your parents' gift, not my gift. I have no such crown jewel you mention, and indeed no crown has the power to create a child. You can check with any doctor. Now, do you have any other questions? I have to move on. That is why I am walking around you and still talking to you. Just ask me quickly whatever you want to ask."

"You are walking like a human, and your figure is as handsome as my father's. But he feels fine with his two hands. Why do you need four hands? You can keep your chakra and conch in a bag that you can carry with you all the time."

"My figure is imagined by artists. They are free to imagine as they wish. Otherwise, I have no image. I don't create anything just like Brahma, nor does he create cosmos."

"But many worshippers see you as True God. You grant them health and wealth. So Dada and Dadi tell me that your name is Satya Narayana. Do you think that Nani gave the crown jewel to your priest?"

"That is not possible. Note that *Satya* in my name means truth. I punish those people who seek my favor by lying. Read more about me."

"I don't think that you really punish liars!"

"Adina, I sense that you doubt me and Maya. I know you have suffered so much due to the Maya Effect, one illusion after another, but you are not alone. There are many religious fools everywhere. Be ready to fight forthcoming illusions of Maya."

Vishnu disappeared from the screen and was replaced by a middle-aged woman, who was yelling at her, "Why did your father beat you during your last visit? You should have told me. You are now mature enough to say—"

Adina instantly shut her laptop and ran away. As she ran she tried to recollect the word for religious fools. She vaguely remembered that the word started with the letter F. She tried hard but remembered only a joke that she heard from her father. Actually, he also heard this from a doctor. "If a doctor's treatment is good, the religious fool says, 'Thank you God. I am better now because of your kind favor.' The fool never asks why God couldn't hear him before he saw the doctor. If the doctor's treatment fails, the fool sues the doctor. You sue someone because he truly exists. You can't sue someone who doesn't exist."

Adina felt confused about Maya's legitimacy. If Bali was an American demon, he would have sued Vishnu for damages. Instead, he accepted his degradation.

CHAPTER 5

Shiva, the Healer and Killer

Namaḥ Shivaaya "Salutation to Shiva"
(A Sanskrit mantra for Shiva)

It was not easy for Adina to decide on her meditation of Shiva. Her Internet search revealed that Shiva was the most popular deity to meditate upon. She tried many options, tried again and again, but she could not achieve the meditation she desired. So she thought of trying Shiva's figure as Ganapati's father or Parvati's husband. She knew this was successful because she heard a drum. The lord appeared on the screen.

"Namaste," she said.

He blessed her. "*Shivaas te panthaanaḥ santu.*" She remembered this Sanskrit blessing from weddings, where her dada, as their priest, would use this blessing for the bride and bridegroom. He would translate it to the bride and bridegroom this way: "May your paths be good."

Adi knew that Shiva meant "Good."

Unfortunately, Adina's parents had chosen wrong paths. Dada was not their priest anyway.

But Dada said one had to find his or her own good or

else your Shiva may turn out to be Rudra. As Rudra, or Fierce, Lord Shiva could be ferocious and punish those who chose wrong paths. His sons, Karttikeya and Ganesha, and also his wife Parvati, helped him punish wrongdoers.

But Nani might have offered Lord Shiva the crown jewel, Adina thought, expecting "good" from him in the form of Adi's birth.

"Dear child," the lord said very kindly. "What good can I do for you? Don't ask me about the crown jewel. We have open communication in the family, and so you should remember what Ganesha has told you."

"In that case, can I ask you a few other questions?" Adina had some idea of the answers he would give, but she wanted to hear Shiva's confirmation.

The lord's face lit up with happiness. "Sure, go ahead. Ask your questions."

"Why do you and your family members have odd vehicles? You ride a bull. Ganesha rides a mouse. Karttikeya rides a peacock. Parvati rides a lion. How do these animals live together in a family? Aren't they enemies?"

The lord smiled, but then he became serious. "Adina, my name is Pashupati, Lord of the Beings. I treat all animals, including humans, with love. Those who sacrifice animals for me or my family members are ignorant and cruel. My message to them is to love each other, to love all beings, for when there is true love, no jealousy or greed can occur. All must learn the value of living in harmony without hate."

"And why have these animals become your family vehicles?"

"Our respective selections are based on our respective needs. For example, Ganapati is the master of computing and so needs a mouse to accomplish his task. Parvati needs a lion; he helps her approach cruel persons whom he scares or even devours. And so on. What is your next question?"

"Are Uma, Sati, and Parvati one and the same female goddess?"

"Yes. The goddess is the same. She merely has many colorful names."

"But I was told that Sati and Parvati are not one and the same, that they have different parents."

"There are lots of stories about us, some of those stories misinterpretations of our being that can have dire consequences. The Sati story is an example."

Adina remembered the Sati story. Sati was the daughter of Daksha Prajapati, who performed a *yajña*, the Sanskrit name for the sacred fire ceremony. Prajapati invited all the gods except his own son-in-law, Shiva. The gods thought Prajapati was very mean to hate his daughter's husband for a son-in-law is treated like a son in every good family. Sati became completely depressed not to see her husband Shiva at the fire ceremony. Indeed, she could not bear his absence but was also deeply upset that her father had dishonored his own son-in-law. She jumped into the fire and burned herself. When Shiva heard the news, he became fierce and immediately came to the fire ceremony and destroyed it. His father-in-law begged him not to destroy more, but Shiva picked up his trident and, with one strike, beheaded Daksha Prajapati. Even in his rage, however, he spared his mother-in-law for there was no clear evidence of her participation in the conspiracy.

The gods were totally shocked by the beheading and begged that Daksha's life be restored. Shiva took some time to calm down then restored life to Daksha. He put a ram's head on the torso of his father-in-law, who was still able to speak Sanskrit, the language of the gods. A goat had never spoken Sanskrit before. Daksha asked Shiva for forgiveness, and because it had been always easy to please Shiva, he forgave his father-in-law. Then he left for the Himalayas and became an ascetic. Later Parvati was born and raised in the Himalayas. That is why her name is Parvati, Mountain-Born.

"You know the Himalayas," asked Lord Shiva, "the holy and high mountains? After Sati's demise, my best stories are the Himalayan stories. "

"Yes, Lord. I am a Himalayan Indian from my father's side. In fact, many in America notice my Himalayan features. I tell them that is why my last name is Badoni, Adina Badoni. I know what Parvati means to you."

Adina already knew that, when the beautiful Parvati reached adulthood, she chose Shiva, the most primitive god, as her husband. She remembered that in her past life she was Sati, Shiva's wife who burned herself to death. Many times, ignorant Indians burned a widow at the funeral pyre of her husband. They called the burned woman a "Sati" to indicate that she was as pious as Shiva's wife, Sati. These liars distorted the story, however. Shiva objected to the burning of his wife and that is why he destroyed the entire fire ceremony.

Dadi had told Adina that the British spelled Sati as Suttee, and they had banned this human sacrifice. After independence from the British Raj, women in India got more freedom. Now they can divorce, remarry, or just remain single, and they can own property and/or pursue an education.

Adina wanted to know more than what Dadi had told her. "Lord, I have a related question. If you say that some liars distorted the Sati story when they burned their women, then why didn't you chop their heads with your trident? Or are you powerless?"

Adina saw Shiva's third eye opening between his eyebrows. Before she might have been burned by the fiery sparks emitting from his eye, she shut down the comput-

er. She was not interested in the *darshan* of his transformed image, Rudra the fierce. She liked his Adam-like
image, primitive and closer to nature, almost naked. She
wondered how he lived like that in the coldest mountains
in the world. There was no Garden of Eden in the Himalayas. Not a single tree at that altitude. They said Shiva
could live anywhere, she then remembered, for he was
the lord of yogis, Yogishvara, and yogis were immune to
weather. All weathers and all places were fine for them.
No wonder the Shiva mantra was the most used for meditation.

But she also remembered that Dada had given her another Sanskrit mantra: *Vande Parvatī-Parameśvarau.* "I
pray to Parvati and the highest god." This was actually a
prayer from Kalidasa, who was a popular poet in the ancient Gupta Empire. Kalidasa believed the ancient Indian
mythology of the holy trinity: Brahma, Vishnu, and Shiva. He knew their jobs: Brahma created the cosmos,
Vishnu expanded and protected it, and Shiva dissolved it.

However, Adina remembered Dad telling her that
there is always a catch to what else Shiva did to save the
universe. Shiva as Rudra angrily danced, beating his
drum while burning the universe with his third eye. His
consort Parvati wanted to stop the lord and so began to
dance in front of him. Shiva was enchanted by her beauty
and dancing, and so he embraced her and forgot the destruction, and the universe kept expanding.

As soon as Adina saw Shiva's third eye open with
fiery sparks, she not only closed her laptop but began to
run. She ran and ran, but still she saw the fire behind her
when she glanced over her shoulder, a fire so fierce that
she began to feel too hot. She was soon panting heavily
and nearly too tired to run any longer. Then she thought
of the Parvati-Shiva prayer of Kalidasa, and instantly she
felt as if being lifted up in the air and beyond the reach of

the fire to a high and cold peak of the Himalayas. There was a big courtyard in the middle of a garden. There, she saw Shiva again beating his drum and dancing his destructive *tandava* dance. She kept on repeating her mantra: *Vande Parvatī-Parameśvarau.* "I pray to Parvati and the highest god."

Adina was horrified to now see the highest god chasing her, but she kept on repeating her mantra, her voice growing louder and louder. She noticed an extremely beautiful female figure emerging from behind the courtyard. The garden suddenly bloomed with new flowers, bees hovering around them. *It must be Goddess Parvati*, Adina thought.

Yes, the goddess was dancing her *lasya,* the charming—lusty—dance as the myth says. The angry lord embraced his wife, Goddess Parvati, under the only tree in the garden. His third eye was shut now, and there was no fire any more, not a single ember particle. Adina felt safe. She timidly moved toward the couple and stood behind Parvati. The goddess turned around and saw Adina.

"What can I do for you, my child?" asked the kind mother of all as she hugged Adina.

"Mother, I am a Himalayan girl like you." Adina looked into her eyes. "See my Himalayan face, Ma."

"It does not matter. I am Uma, ma of all beings," Parvati said softly as she put her hand gently over Adina's head.

"Ma, protect me!" Adina raised her hands and folded them to sign *Namaste*, the "I pray to you," pose. Her computer bag fell at her feet.

"You are your own protector, my child. You forgot to shut down your laptop completely. It's open. See? It's lying down at your feet."

Adina looked down to check her bag. The little computer screen was indeed still on and, with a click, Adina shut it down and instantly found herself in her room.

She then got ready to go to a soccer game where her father was going to meet her.

CHAPTER 6

Heaven's Reality

Svasti na Indraḥ "Indra is good to us."
(A Vedic prayer to Indra)

Today, Adina meditated on Indra. She saw him exactly as she had visualized him.

"Namaste," she uttered immediately. "Are you really King Indra?"

"Indeed, I am. See my crown and my royal robes?"

"Where are you coming from right now, your majesty?"

"From heaven."

"Many wise people don't believe there is really a heaven."

"They are fools, not wise."

"But why are they respected by highly educated people?"

"Give me examples of such people."

"My dada and dadi, just for quick examples. Both have PhD degrees and taught at several universities."

"Your dada and dadi are big fools. They don't understand higher things."

"Are you under the influence of your favorite *soma* drink? There is really no heaven."

No sooner had Adina said this than she felt a terrible jolt as if from a lightning strike. She fainted. After a few seconds, she regained consciousness and found herself in a big beautiful royal court. In the middle of the court was seated a very handsome man in royal robes. He had a large crown on his head. In one hand, he held a royal scepter and, in the other, a weapon. She remembered that weapon from stories her grandparents had told her, the thunderbolt *vajra*. Beside the king was seated a beautiful woman, whom Adi thought must be Queen Shachi, Indra's wife.

Adina became convinced that she was in heaven as she was greeted by some very beautiful women. Their chat was very friendly.

"My name is Rambha, my dear child. What's your name?"

"Adina, madam. Namaste."

"Welcome, Adina. My name is Tilottama."

"Namaste, madam."

"I am Urvashi, Adina. Welcome."

Adina greeted her the same way.

"I am Menaka, Adina," said another beautiful woman.

"Namaste, madam Menaka. May I ask you a couple of questions?"

"Sure, my child."

"Are you still an *apsara* here? I ask because you are so famous for your beauty on Earth. I thought you may not like to return."

"Not only am I Indra's *apsara* here, but these beautiful ladies are too. There are many other *apsaras*. They are dancing with other sinless men who have come here after their lives on Earth were over. Since you are from Earth, I will give a tour of the big court of heaven."

"Before the tour, may I ask you one more question?"

"Ask any questions you like."

"Did you really dance with sage Vishvamitra? He too was a sinless sage."

"He was so sinless that Lord Indra became scared, for the most sinless man on Earth can dethrone Lord Indra in heaven. So Indra sent me to meet Vishvamitra, who was in meditation at that time. I swam in his pond and sang a sweet song. He opened his eyes and saw me. He kept on looking at me for a few minutes, and I remained quiet. Finally, he proposed to me and I accepted his proposal to be his wife. When I was pregnant with my daughter, Shakuntala, I decided to leave her in a hermitage and return to heaven. Her real father Vishvamitra was not interested in claiming Shakuntala. Have you heard the story of Shakuntala?"

"Yes, my dadi told me a lot of Indian stories. I know that Shakuntala was secretly married to Dushyanta in that hermitage, which is in the district where Dada was born. So I am a Himalayan Indian, too."

"Yes, I can see by your features. You know that Shakuntala and Dushyanta had a son named Bharata. That son is my grandson, Vishvamitra's grandson. Bharata became an emperor, in spite of the sad separation from his father."

"I know that story. Dadi told me." Adina remembered what her dadi had told her about the story in the Kalidasa's famous Sanskrit drama *Abhijñanashakuntalam*, "The recognition of Shakuntala's."

The story flashed before Adina's mind's eye. Dushyanta left the pregnant Shakuntala in the Himalayan hermitage. Then, with a friend's help, Menaka secretly transferred her daughter and grandson to another hermitage far away. One day Dushyanta visited that hermitage, not knowing they were there, and in the garden he saw the little Bharata playing with a lion cub. He was dumbfounded. He asked the six-year-old brave boy who his father and mother were. The boy quickly replied, "Dushyanta and Shakuntala." The king then saw a woman sitting nearby and recognized his wife. Shakuntala was wearing the ring he had given to her during their secret marriage in the Himalayan hermitage.

"I know the great Bharata. India is called Bharat after his name."

"Yes, Bharata didn't turn out like his delinquent father. A loving father doesn't abandon his child in a hermitage with his mother. The child needs both parents. Shame on Dushyanta."

Adina could have said, "Shame on Vishvamitra, whose name means Friend of All. The exception was his own child, whom he abandoned." Adina could have added Menaka's name to this list of the shameful as well, but she knew that Menaka was ordered by Indra to return to heaven after corrupting the sage Vishvamitra. She had to leave Shakuntala on Earth or Indra would be mad at her. Males were masters of females everywhere, Adina knew.

"Good! You already know a lot about my story on Earth. Now let me give a short tour of heaven's court," Menaka said while caressing Adina's head.

Menaka took her to a section of heaven where the *Katthak* dance was going on. "The Katthak in heaven!" declared Adina happily.

Menaka pointed out a man amongst the dancers. "That man dancing in the middle of the apsaras is the Nawab of Avadh. Lucknow was his capital, and in that city he staged plays in Hindi. He was quite revolutionary. He was a Muslim, and yet he had more than four wives, about seventy-four, plus many courtesans. He believed that women's roles must be played by women, not by young men, in these dramatic performances. He thus broke with tradition. He himself would act as Indra and his courtesans would act as *apsaras*, and, thus, he introduced having a realistic cast on an actual stage. When the British dethroned him, the Indian citizens didn't like the British committing such illegal acts. That was why, a few years later, in 1857, the first freedom revolt against the British Raj occurred. Unlike the British ruler, Lord Indra was pleased with the Nawab. So, after his Earthly life was over, he started dancing here with real *apsaras*."

"I have a question. I don't see some of the greatest among men here. Why?"

"To whom do you refer?"

"Buddha, Christ, and Mohammad. And where are the two great men Mahatma Gandhi and Dr. Martin Luther King?"

"Adina, you have to believe in Indra to come to heaven. It's not enough to say his Vedic prayer, *svasti na Indraḥ* or 'May Indra be good to us.' You have to believe in dance and music, especially with women like us. The Nawab believed in Indra and beautiful women, and he drank like Indra. I understand he violated the Islamic code of conduct by doing so, but he also created his own song for each stage performance and some of his songs are popular even today. He was a very unusual king in history. Check with the Bollywood singers."

"Fine. Then where is Lord Krishna? He danced with many beautiful women and played the flute. No king can match Krishna's record. He is far more popular than the Nawab, even in America. How many in America know about the Nawab?"

Menaka laughed again. Adina was puzzled. "Did I say something funny?"

"No, my dear. You didn't say any such thing. I warn you that you should not mention Krishna to our lord of heaven, the great Indra. It was Krishna who wanted to ban Lord Indra's prayers, like 'May Indra be good to us.' Don't even utter Krishna's name around here."

"My dadi and dada don't believe in Indra's heaven. Have they any chance to come here?"

"No. If they don't believe, then they are doomed to go to hell and rot there after their death. Sorry to tell you this so bluntly, but that's the way of heaven and hell."

"You are not the only person to think like that about Dada and Dadi. Even the American judge didn't want them to see me more than a day per week."

"That judge may be allowed in heaven if you tell Indra about him. Maybe he will welcome the judge and arrange a dance with us for him. Now let me take you to another interesting section of heaven."

They moved toward the section where many beings were dancing about joyously.

"Adina, do you understand that dance?"

"Yes, that's Bollywood's fusion of African, European, and South American music and dance. I know because Nani loves to watch those Hindi movies. In America, all the major Indian TV channels are available."

"Very interesting achievements, indeed. We also include all dances in heaven that the good men of Earth engaged in when living there. We dance with them so that they don't need their women."

"Gender discrimination in heaven!"

"I agree, but we have no voice. Men design our heavenly rules in a secret heavenly language, and we women obey those rules like slaves. For example, we dress 'properly' as men want us to. This is slavery. We are told 'Lord Indra is the supreme godhead and his words are God's words.' Linguistic lies are the foundation of religion, whether in heaven or on Earth."

Adina really felt disgusted. "I don't believe in such a heaven. I want to go back home."

"Before going home, wouldn't you like to meet Sha-chi, our queen?" Menaka smiled.

Adina sighed. *Not really.* "Okay."

Menaka and Adina moved toward Shachi, who was seated beside her husband, Lord Indra. "Let me ask the queen if she can meet you privately."

The beautiful *apsara* went behind the throne and whispered to Queen Shachi. The queen was so gracious that she quietly came down and saw Adina where she waited in a quiet corner.

Adina bowed to the queen with folded hands. "My *pranam* to your majesty."

"*Ashish* to you, my child," the queen said, using the blessing word *ashish* in response to her greeting of higher salutation *pranam*. "What brings you here?"

"In truth, I was not ready to come here so soon, your majesty. But I am here, anyway. May I know if any woman of this court has the crown jewel that my nani offered to a deity? Nani claims that I was born because of a heavenly deity and her gift to that deity of that jewel."

"My lovely Adina, you are your parents' child, not any deity's. You don't look like any deity. You must look like just your parents. Moreover, we don't allow anyone here to receive any such gifts."

"I believe you, your majesty. May I know why you allow these *apsaras* to dance with your husband?"

"Oh dear! Dancing is not that a big deal. Indra drinks beakers and beakers of *soma*. Then he feels exhilaration. Then he goes to other places, including Earth, where he deceives women. Many on Earth know he told Ahalya that he was her husband. Poor Ahalya treated my husband as her husband, and when Ahalya's husband returned suddenly, he was enraged by Indra's deception. The sage put a harsh curse on him and made him pay a heavy price for that deception. The sage did the right thing. Lying is a cruel crime."

"I have heard that story from my dadi. But if Indra is so deceptive, then why are so many men on Earth named Indra?"

"All people admire is Indra's power, his position as the king of heaven. Do you think that, in Indian democracy, someone's son has a chance to be a king? You should have a name that you can prove."

"Your name is true, your majesty. You are a dazzling beauty. You should have the same power as your husband."

The queen smiled at Adi then. "You must eat something. How about some fruit?" Shachi signaled to an attendant. He quickly approached and took her order.

"You are right," she told Adina. "In a fair society, we expect equal power for spouses. My husband has all the power here, but how long will he enjoy this power? There will be a day when he will lose this power. He will be an ant crawling with the other ants like him."

Adina was not interested in the "parade of ants" story. She wanted to ask the queen of heaven another important question. She opened her mouth halfway but closed it quickly, not sure if she should ask this question. Shachi observed her mouth. "You wanted to say something?"

"Yes, your majesty. You said 'Poor Ahalya' as if she were innocent. You sound as if you are in sympathy with her, or am I misunderstanding?"

"She also had to pay a very heavy price. I believe men and women should have equal rights and receive equal treatment. Nobody should be discriminated against. Fairness requires freedom. You know that I have a son, Jayanta. I believe he and his wife must have freedom of speech. Indeed, every being must be free to speak the truth, especially when that person suffers from someone's lying. Even a child like you must have that freedom. Otherwise, how will people understand your suffering? Friends want to share your pain, and you want to share your pain with them. You unload your pain by talking to them or you might commit suicide. A fair society gives you freedom to share your story of suffering, which is human. But here I cannot express my pain. Indra lies to me, and Ahalya's case is just one piece of evidence. I am saying all this to you because you are young. Adina, you must learn early on to be on truth's side. That's what ethical parents teach their children."

The attendant delivered some fresh fruit.

"Too much fruit," Adina declared. "Let me save some. Thank you, mister." She opened her bag. "Oh, my computer screen is still on. She quickly shut it down and immediately Adina was alone upon her meditating mat. There was no fruit, no queen before her.

She muttered Shachi's instructions to her: "Adina, you must learn early on to be on truth's side." She then muttered, "I will. The congress will."

Then she wrote a note on a piece of paper: *Sharing one's story of suffering is human. I will tell my story. My father didn't want to abandon me, even for one day. He fought to gain his share of time with me. This is the truth of my story. He is not a Dushyanta or a Vishvamitra. These two men didn't show any common sense. Both parents must share their child's suffering. They were not facing a dumb court like ours.*

CHAPTER 7

Rendezvous with Radha

Raadhe Raadhe "Radha! Radha!"
(A Sanskrit mantra for Radha)

*Haririha sarasavasante/ Nṛtyati yuvatijanena
samam sakhi virahijanasya durante*
"Here Krishna in the juicy spring/
dances with the youthful girls. O my friend,
during the separated beloved's bad period."
(Radha's accusation against Krishna
from the *Gitagovinda* by Jayadeva)

The *Katthak* dance was associated with the Muslim Nawab in heaven? Adina found that something akin to miraculous. She was grateful for what she had learned while visiting heaven.

She now decided to meditate on Radha, who might know what happened to the crown jewel. Lord Krishna decorated her with the most beautiful things.

It wasn't easy for Adina to select the real powerful stories of Radha. In the popular dance, such as the *Katthak*, the use of these stories was secular. In religion, these stories were held in the greatest reverence. Adina's father Danin had a personal experience with the power of the Radha name, for he visited a prominent temple of Krishna in Mathura when he was only eight years old.

Adi knew from what her father told her that the town of Mathura, on the banks of Yamuna, was as important as the town of Ayodhya, on the banks of Sarayu. Mathura was about Krishna and Ayodhya was about Rama, and thus every devout Hindu wished to visit these two holy towns of India to have the *darshan* of these two avatars of Lord Vishnu. But Mathura's lure and lore were unbeatable, Danin had told her. Even its sweets were famous. The word Mathura was "sweet," Madhura, in Sanskrit. Adina's mother was named Madhu.

Danin told her that he was behind his parents near the gate of the Krishna temple, and the moment he entered the front yard of the temple, a host of monkeys chased them. Dan was frightened when a big male rhesus grabbed a garland meant for the temple statue of Radha, or Krishna, from his hand. Another male monkey jumped on him to grab the packet of sweets meant as an offering to the statues. Danin was scared to death, he told Adi, but suddenly the priest shouted from the entrance door, "Son! Utter the mantra *Radhe Radhe*." Dan did exactly that and the ferocious monkey quietly retreated.

Dada waited in a corner and kept watching. Within a few minutes, another family entered the same front yard. The children were subjected to the same monkey business as her father. Danin told her he then understood that it was a regular feature of the temple.

"What a powerful deity," he told Adina. "Her very name makes you fearless." Danin loved to tell others this personal observation about priests. "Priests and monkeys use stunts to get rewards."

But there were stories of Radha and Krishna that didn't show Radha as a powerful deity, even though she had been identified with Lakshmi, the wife of Vishnu. In her early youth she was a cowgirl, or *gopi*. Among many other cowgirls, Krishna loved her most. Was she Krishna's mistress? Adi wondered. One view was that she had a husband she would leave secretly in the middle of night. Close to her home was the forest of Vrindavana, also called Madhuvana or just Madhuban in popular Hindi. There Krishna would play his flute to attract other cowgirls, too. So, sometimes Radha had to wait for Krishna in Madhuban. The wait might have been short, but for Radha every minute was long.

Jayadeva described her situation in his long Sanskrit poem *Gitagovinda* like this: *Radha tells her girlfriend, "Krishna is here in the juicy spring/O my friend, he dances with the youthful girls, during the separated beloved's bad period."* The beloved was Radha, who was impatiently waiting for Krishna.

Some stories said Radha was already married to Krishna before he left his village of Vraja for Mathura. He was obliged to go to Mathura in order to kill Kamsa, the evil king of Mathura. Kamsa was Krishna's uncle who had imprisoned Vasudeva and Devaki, Krishna's father and mother. After Krishna killed Kamsa and freed his parents, he never came back to Radha, and later he married Satyabhama, a beautiful princess. Then he married Rukmini, another beautiful woman. The two women didn't feel very comfortable with each other, even though they were often depicted as very happy co-wives. This was a very simple case of bigamy, but then the marriage became more and more complex, as Krishna collected six more wives. In the Krishna cult, he was an avatar of Vishnu and, thus, beyond reproach, unlike other men with many wives.

Many felt sorry for Radha for she had no place in this crowded harem, but some considered her lucky. Had she abandoned her husband for Krishna, then many would have viewed her as an unfaithful wife, a punishable crime. She could even possibly have received a sentence of death by slow torture. Male avatars were praised and elevated even higher for their holy polygamy, but women were forbidden the practice. Radha had to leave her husband before marrying Krishna, which made this story much more than a myth, Adina knew. It was about gender inequality and the abuse of women.

Danin's story was not a myth. It really happened in Mathura on the bank of Yamuna, which originated, like the holy Ganga, in Adina's ancestral Himalayas. The mantra *Radhe Radhe* sounded very holy for *darshan*. At the same time, she remembered the *katthak* and the Muslim Nawab of Lucknow.

Nobody considered the Nawab, who had eight times more wives than Krishna, an avatar, and the Nawab undoubtedly had other women in his life.

Women are women, Adi thought. *It hardly matters if some were called queens and some were concubines of the Nawab. Nobody can be sure whether those women were faithful to the Nawab, but supposedly the good Nawab never mistreated anyone of them. In fact, it is said that he used them like Indra's nymphs. No wonder Indra might have granted him his heaven.*

Adina meditated and meditated while uttering *Radhe Radhe*. She was also aware of the *katthak* dances and songs that she heard from Dada and Dadi.

Ah, she thought, *the sounds of the tabla drums and sitar and other musical sounds, especially the dance bols or speech syllables echoed by the drums and the "ghunghru" ankle bells: tiṭa kiṭa dhum tiṭa kiṭa dhum ta ta...ta thei ta thei. All this following the Hindi katthak song: "Madhuban me Radhika nache re"*

"Hey, Radha is dancing in Madhuban." This was Da-

da's favorite classical song and dance as shown in the old
Hindi movie *Kohinoor*, which also was the name for the
famous Indian crown jewel, now used occasionally by the
British monarch.

The young Radha appeared before Adi in the forest of
Vrindavana. What a dazzling beauty.

She came closer and closer until the music and dance
stopped. Radha looked at the meditating Adina in a corner.

"Namaste, Mother." Adina folded her hands as she
said these greeting words.

Radha smiled and raised her hand toward her for
blessing.

"Mother, my name is Adina."

"A beautiful name. I bless you that you will prove
your name."

"Mother, what is the meaning of *your* name?"

"It has many meanings. The original meaning is
'achievement or success.' It also means 'prosperity.' It
depends how you see me."

"You have proved your name, too. Dadi told me, and I
can see Dadi's point. People of India with different faiths
adore you. There are no religious boundaries when you
dance. Look at this film song for proof. The poet is a
Muslim. The music director is a Muslim. The singer is a
Muslim. And the Nawab advanced the dance, of which
you are the queen. Mother, how do you judge a successful person?"

"The highest respect is reserved for anyone who rises
against all odds." Radha looked serious.

"Your example is the right one. You were a simple
cowgirl, and look at the fame you have achieved."

"You are so quick to understand. How can I help you
to rise above the odds you face?"

"My grandmother offered a crown jewel to a deity.

She doesn't know what happened to it after the priest offered it on her behalf."

"There are hundreds of thousands of deities. It's hard to know who received that gift. What is behind the offering and your request?"

Adina told the same story that she told the other gods and goddesses upon whom she had meditated. She understood clearly that Radha did not have that jewel, but Adina had included some other aspects of Radha's story in her meditation. She wanted to check with her directly.

"Dear Adina, what is holy and what is unholy is decided by men. It is men who created the scriptures and told the simpleton followers that those books were divine revelations. Those men lied, but were given the greatest honor."

"So lying is rewarding. Is that what you are saying?"

"Yes. But you have to be careful. Later, other liars will propose their books and try to oust the previous liars, precipitating a clash of liars. This is what happened in my case. All the stories you have heard about me are men's fantasies, absurdly wishful stories. What Krishna is doing with Radha and other *gopi* girls in such tales actually are impossible things to happen. But men would like to have those funny things for them in an unreal world."

"You mean the love of Radha and Krishna is a myth?"

"Yes. Those are the myths of women's slavery. Now, women are not willing to remain the slaves of men. The harem of Krishna is a myth, but what is not a myth is that men would like to abuse women like that. Women have to fight their abuse, but not with the use of lies. That glorified model of men is a bad thing, and women need to declare that all are entitled to equal rights. Remember I said 'equal rights.' If you are not for equal rights, you will fail eventually."

"In America, we say no one should try to get the

whole pie. We should share it equally. I understand your point. You are not a feminist, but rather, you are for gender equality."

"I am happy with you. I engaged in this long discourse to hear you say these two words: gender equality. It's unfortunate that some women are lying to gain the larger share of the pie. You suffered just because of that unfair greed. That was the mistake of men that should not be repeated by women. Just fight to stop violence against women."

"I will—"

"But let me add a warning when seeking a compatible partner. Accept full equality of sexes, reject *painful equality of stupids*. If the boy hurts the girl, then it is clear he is stupid. But then the girl is equally stupid if she still wants to marry him." The beautiful Radha looked depressed as she shared the blame for her failed married life.

Adina wanted to react to her guilt, but she heard another Hindi song in the background: "Leave, leave my arm, you enchanter. My soft wrist is hurting." Radha disappeared, and Adina wondered why she became invisible without any warning.

Moments later, Adina understood how Krishna's twisting Radha's hand has been celebrated as love. Like Radha, Adina felt no interest in the glorification of the bully and shut the computer down.

CHAPTER 8

Hanuman's Miracle

Hanumate namaḥ "Salutation to Hanuman."
(A Sanskrit mantra for Hanuman)

O n the screen appeared an orchard full of fruit trees, and sitting in an orange tree was a monkey peeling oranges and eating them. She could smell the oranges but was not interested in them. It was quite hard for her to get Hanuman down from that tree, but she kept on gazing at him. Finally, Hanuman jumped down with a thud.

"Namaste," Adina said, greeting Hanuman.

"Good morning, my dear!"

"I was not sure you could speak English."

"Many mistake me for a monkey. I am a monkey god, and all deities speak all languages."

Adina understood his point. Many in India thought that the ancient Hanuman understood even the modern Avadhi language. The *Hanuman Chalisa*, a miraculous Hanuman prayer of forty verses in Avadhi, was offered as proof. The Europeans had already discovered India when this work was authored by Tulsidas.

"I was going to see Lord Rama, your boss, but then I thought that I should first go through his representative," Adina said. "You can persuade him to find my crown jewel."

"Don't disturb him," Hanuman said. "He cannot locate lost things or persons if they are out of the country. You know because I had to locate his wife Sita in Lanka across the sea."

"I wish he and Sita had a computer like the one I have. Sita could have been located in a click. But let me ask another question. Are you happy with Rama?"

"I am very happy with everything he did."

"He doubted Sita's character."

"It was very unfair to doubt an innocent wife, but husbands take this liberty, to falsely accuse their wives."

"Would you approve this liberty of wives?"

"I believe in equality, but a wife of good character would never take such a liberty."

"Oh, then you don't know about America where many wives have accused their innocent husbands. They bring witnesses, even experts like psychologists and judges, who side with these wives. But I appreciate your sense of fairness. Some don't have as high a level of intelligence as you have. What do you suggest to a woman who destroys her own family?"

"Read the great ancient story of the *Ramayana* by the great poet Valmiki. He teaches that every family member should give priority to the needs of other members. Kaikeyi was an idiot who put her own vicious interests first. Do you know what she did in the *Ramayana* story?"

"Kaikeyi's selfish decision destroyed the family of Dasharatha. Rama, Sita, and Lakshmana went into exile in a forest. Her husband Dasharatha died of a heart attack when Kaikeyi forced him to exile Rama. Kaikeyi's son Bharata refused to replace Rama as king of Ayodhya.

Then, one day in exile, Sita was kidnapped by Ravana, the demon king of Lanka. You finally found Sita in Lanka. "

"Who taught you this *Ramayana* story in America?"

"My dadi."

"So Kaikeyi is cursed by everyone who knew how she plotted the destruction of her own great family. How many family members suffered because one stupid woman wanted complete control of the kingdom. Every wife should learn about this domestic terrorist Kaikeyi."

"You said you liked everything that Lord Rama did. Out of curiosity, Rama ate meat and you didn't. How do you explain that difference?"

"That is a good inquiry. Lord Rama is an Aryan Kshatriya, an avatar of Lord Vishnu who is a Vedic god. Vedic religion allows meat-eating. Indeed, the Vedas consider some meats sacred. The Vedic people regularly killed more than fifty kinds of animals for meat. My kind, monkeys, don't eat meat, which is decided by nature and not by scriptures. I have killed many demons, terrorists. I am in favor of killing terrorists but not for their meat. "

"Your picture must be put in our country's White House with a caption 'Hanuman against terrorists.' Something like that. I am serious."

"No, thanks. I am now old. I can't help."

"Yes, you can, but then you are known for your humility."

"You can see if my friend Ganesha, another vegetarian deity, can help you—"

"I have already checked with him."

"Good enough. I would like to offer you some fruit. I have Lucknow's famous colorful melons and delicious dashhari mangoes right now."

"How do you get them here?"

"Transportation is no problem for me. I am sure you

know my flying tale in the *Ramayana* story. I brought medicinal plants from the Himalayas by flying there and back to Lanka. First, I could not recognize the specific plant the Lankan doctor had recommended for the wounded Lakshamana, Rama's brother. So I wrapped the whole chunk of the land where those plants grow assuming that the specific plant was among them."

"How did you wrap the large chunk of land?"

"By my long tail. I wrapped it around the necks of many demons and choked them to death too, but I never tried it on a demoness."

"Wow! I want to feel your tail. Can I touch it?"

"No, you can't. You are such a nice beautiful girl."

"Please, please show me your tail. I will believe your *Ramayana* tale only if I see how long and strong your tail is."

Hanuman jumped up on the tree. "You are too smart for your age." He wrapped his tail around Adina's neck, and she began to choke. She quickly shut her computer down and Hanuman was gone.

She was not comfortable with his tail at her throat, but she admired the intelligence of that monkey. He understood that literary joke and let her feel the choking sensation on request. Some had difficulty understanding literary jokes, Adina knew, for her dada and dadi had such problems with some of their friends.

CHAPTER 9

Kali, the Dark Energy

Jayantii maŋgalaa Kaalii, bhadrakaalii kapaalinii
"Victorious auspicious Kali,
Benevolent Kali the skull-wearer."
(A prayer mantra for Kali, the Black Goddess)

Kali was wearing a garland of skulls when Adina saw her on the screen just after she meditated upon her presence.

Adina paid her respects instantly. "*Pranam Ma.*"

"I bless you. Fear not, my child. It's a dead garland I am wearing."

"How old is your garland of skulls?"

"Since the advent of humans, I have been crushing the brains of the bullies and keeping their skulls in dark places. A few special ones I use on my garland. I keep replacing them with new ones."

"How do you decide on the replacements?"

"That is quite easy. You may not know the old ones' names, but some bullies you would know. I am waiting for the skulls of Hitler, Stalin, Mao, Idi Amin, and Osama bin Laden."

"You are known as Kali the black goddess, but you make no color discrimination."

"My color has no color. No one can find my true identity. I will always remain dark, but I will also continue to have skulls of evil men of any color: white, black, brown, or whatever."

"How about women?"

"I believe in gender equality. There, in that corner, you can see some women in pain."

Kali first pointed and then picked up a white woman. She cut off her head and sucked her blood with her long tongue.

"Oh, no! Ma, stop that. Please stop that, Ma!"

"She killed her three children, and then she lied that a black man had kidnapped them. That man was lynched."

"So you will punish every liar?"

"I will suck the blood of any liar who inflicts pain on innocent people. Right now, I am waiting for a black woman who encouraged her daughter to falsely accuse her son-in-law of hurting their child. He had never abused his little daughter, but their white neighbors supported the allegations. The court psychologist didn't care for the pain of the little child and recommended full custody be granted to the mother, who was found a big liar by the court. The baby girl suffered from trauma because she could not see her father regularly. The father committed suicide. I will get the mother-in-law first."

"What you are saying is not very different from my story, Ma."

"Tell me your story."

Adina told Kali the entire story just as she had to the other deities she had meditated upon.

"Adina, I have no use for a crown jewel and thus was not the one to receive it, but your story is the tale of thousands of liars and their victims. Such stories will continue if you don't blow the whistle on the perpetrators."

"I want to tell the world the truth, but many would not believe me. Some think that I am a daughter of lawyers and, like them, I am a liar. I have overheard some say, 'Like mother like daughter.' Is it true that a boy is a liar if his father is a liar or a girl is a liar if her mother is a liar?"

"No. It's not true. It could be the other way round, too. Gandhi was a lawyer, and only a lunatic would believe that Gandhi was a liar. But one of his sons was known for not respecting his father's honesty."

"I get your message, Ma. So how do I start whistle-blowing?"

"Adina, everyone has to find his or her own solutions. You are a very intelligent girl. You will find your way. Now I am thirsty and you must get out of my way. I have told you what I like to drink."

Adina thought the goddess was joking until she disappeared from the screen, and Adina heard loud screams and scolding.

"You dumb woman! How dare you plot against your son-in-law? The psychologist showed on TV how you lied to him, and yet you screamed at him. Your skull and your neighbor's skull—"

Adina lost no time shutting down her computer to extinguish the painful cries.

CHAPTER 10

The Solver of Suffering

Buddham saranam gacchaami
"I take refuge in the Buddha."
(The first vow to enter Buddhism)

Adina's dada and dadi had told her that, unlike God or gods, the Buddha was real, and she reasoned that a real person could give real answers to real questions. So she discarded all the myths about his birth and death as she held the Buddha in her awareness. *Simple facts about him should be enough*, she thought.

She remembered the tale of the Buddha's life as her grandparents had told it to her numerous times. Gautama was an Indian prince who lived about 500 years before Christ. In the prime of his youth he left his beautiful young wife Yashodhara and infant son Rahula to seek the truth, but he eventually came home again. Some Brahmins ridiculed him for giving up his ascetic's life because they couldn't appreciate the fact that he had accepted his family and the family accepted him. \

He wanted to help his immediate family, but the entire world became his family. The cause, that united him with the bigger family, was suffering. In his service to the world, the Buddha relied on his own intelligence, or *buddhi*, and thus people began to honor Gautama as the Buddha, the man with an intellectual enlightenment. As an intellectual person, he tried to be as honest as possible. He said such things as: "Be your own lamp. Take refuge in you." And with his sermons, he empowered humans to take charge of their *sukha,* or happiness.

Adina had wanted to take the matters of her life into her own control, and, indeed, she began to feel empowered when she started meditating. She decided that she would not be fooled by religious leaders who said, "Take refuge in God."

Adina could not forget some of such leaders' unproven claims of contacting an almighty deity, such as: "Oh, I was given this instruction by God's postman when I was attacked."

"Oh, I found His divine writings when I fell in a narrow dark cave."

"Oh, I heard His divine voice when I was drowning."

"Oh, my heavenly father revealed these truths in my nightmare."

Most of these claimers were illiterate, and some were very violent. They justified killing humans for the sake of their imagined almighty.

Adina kept gazing at the Buddha on her computer screen. He was sitting in the lotus posture while preaching at Sarnath, telling those present of compassion, not only for all human life, but any life. She remembered that he taught that the sanctity of life knew no species boundaries. All of the living pursued happiness. This simple fact led the Buddha to want to eliminate all suffering. These thoughts enveloped Adina's consciousness as she saw his right hand raised in blessing.

She remembered that the Buddha declared four noble

truths, all of which are about *dukha,* or suffering. There was suffering. The cause of suffering was craving, but there was a solution, which was the path of moderation, the middle path. Adina was very much aware of the four truths as well as of her parents' failure to take the path of moderation. Instead, they went to extremes. One clear extreme was lying, and its consequences were severe. So she was now taking refuge in the Buddha, his *darshan.* She gazed at his image on her laptop screen for some time without blinking.

Her meditation worked. She saw Gautama the Buddha in the *Mrigadava* Deer Park near Varanasi. He was quiet and looking at her very affectionately.

"Lord, I take refuge in you. Namaste," Adina said with utmost respect to the wise Buddha.

"May you be your own guide," he said, and he blessed her. "There must be a reason for you to see me. What is it?"

"Lord, you came back to your family after you found knowledge. How did you feel when you met your wife and son?" Adina asked, without showing any signs of deprivation on her face.

"Yashodhara cried. She was happy to see me un-harmed. I hugged Rahula. He was excited and filled with joy. I understood, by their reactions, that they welcomed my enlightenment. Those two were the first family members to appreciate what I knew, and that gave me great peace," the Buddha answered with a smile. "To be to-gether with your loved ones is the easiest way to rid your *dukha.*"

Adina wanted to cry but firmly held her tears back.

For a minute, she remained silent until the Buddha reminded her, "Adina! Tell me why you meditated on me in the Deer Park?"

She mentioned briefly her search for the deity and the

crown jewel, but this time when Adina told the story, she included the extremes her parents went to and the resulting pain. "I know you don't believe in those deities. I know you never said that you were an avatar of God. Many think you were merely silent about that. Your silence, they think, does not mean you do not believe in God or that you are not his avatar—"

"My ancestors did not worship one God. Every place I visited had too many deities. No two places had the same deities, or, indeed, the same number or kind of deities. People keep imagining one God or many gods, but a truth is not truth if it is not transparent. I had to remain silent or people would keep asking me about countless fictional divine figures. Know this, Adina, nature creates us. No divine figure can create you or me or the cosmos. If that deity's grace was the cause for your birth, then every other childless believer in that deity should receive the same effect. Since that is not the case, the question becomes: why does the deity discriminate against some believers? There would be no suffering of the believers if there was something like God to help them. Human action alone is the way to end human suffering. Suffering, or *dukha,* is, in fact, not to be taken negatively. It motivates you. This is why *dukha* is a noble truth."

"Lord, I want to hear from you if there is any hope to end my suffering."

The Buddha smiled gently. "First, understand the cause of your suffering, and then deal with it in your own way. While achieving understanding of the cause, remember that whatever took place at that time in your life has passed anyway. The chain effect of those initial actions by others continues in your life, but that too shall pass. Remember my major sermon: All things pass. But you can speed up the passage of an effect that bothers you. Your first step is to keep the truth of both cause and effect transparent."

"How do I do that?"

"You already know. You are your own guru."

"But I want you to tell me if making a terrible truth known is always right."

"Yes. Your intention is to end, not only your suffering, but also the suffering of countless other innocent victims worldwide. Keep the bigger picture in focus. A cause becomes noble when it helps the helpless everywhere and all the time," answered the kind Buddha.

"You mean it's okay for me to go forward with my search for the solution?" Adina wanted the clear approval of the wise Buddha.

"For a faster end to your problem, you need a *sangha,* or a group movement. Be in touch with other victims. Unite them. Ask them to raise their voices against such false allegations. Displaying the ideals of equality and justice on postage stamps is not enough. I also encountered this duality in my searching after the truth: Display versus doing. My holy ancestors gave many fantastic sermons in the holy *Upanishads*. One sermon is highly questionable, however. It says this: 'All beings are one and the same, self or *Brahman*.' Then why have they continued discriminating against their own low-caste people? The ideals are phony if they are not practiced. Your complaint is that your country failed to give the smaller fishes the privileges that the big alligators have been given. Assemble the small fishes to show their plight to the lawmakers. You will succeed in ending their suffering as well as yours. Did you understand the meaning of Buddha's sermons?"

"I take refuge in my intelligence, I take refuge in fairness, and I take refuge in people's power," Adina answered spontaneously.

"You are an intelligent girl. Remember to work for faster passage of this problem that has beset you. Anything can be changed, nothing is permanent. Will you strive to change?"

"I will, Lord. I have one more question. May I ask?"

"Questioning is very important. Enlightenment comes only to them who ask the right questions. You will get answers, which are sometimes received in silence. Don't wait for the words of an answer to receive that answer, and keep questioning. This is the way to be a Buddha. Anyone can become a Buddha. My name is Gautama. Gautama asked question after question until he found the answers in words or silence. Don't worry what people call you, dear Adi. Ask Gautama your question."

"Did Gautama pass to nothingness, achieve his goal of *nirvana*?" Adina strived to show no emotion on her face.

She heard no words as the Buddha had predicted. She gazed at the screen and saw these sentences:

Only people, not dead deities, can eliminate suffering of people. Be kind! Thus, the Buddha passed away in peace.

Suddenly her computer screen went blank. A plain white screen was before her. She waited and waited with anxiety and tried, in vain, to restore the screen. She was not sure if her choice of words was correct, but she kept on questioning for a while. She wondered if she should have said *Buddha* instead of *Gautama*. But then she laughed as she repeated his words: "Don't worry what people call you."

She then closed her computer and wrote a note for Dada.

Dear Dada, you have said to me 'Humans have caused more suffering for humans.' I see your point. Last year, you signed a petition to save Muslims from the Buddhist fanatics of Myanmar. The country Myanmar is the next neighbor of Buddha's birthplace. These poor Muslims came in Myanmar from the neighboring country. Treating neighbors with love is a true testimony of humanity. It is equally true that neighborly love can be neighborly victimizer. Dad told me how neighborly love exacerbated his suffering. I know who caused my suffering. Once you said, 'The closest to you can cause the costliest suffering for you. The Buddha should have highlighted that as an Ignoble Truth, because his cousin Devadatta was a pain in the neck for him. And I lost my jewelry. On top of that, add over two hundred thousand dollars from Dad. Not to mention Mom's. And that loss happened when I was less than five-years-old. She was a girl called Adina, not a poor girl. And—Okay, I will tell you more when we meet and have fun together, as usual.

CHAPTER 11

Bargaining with the Cheap True God

Satyanaaraayaṇaaya namaḥ
"Salutation to Satya Narayana"
(A mantra for True God)

The Buddha's way to seek happiness was not easy, as her dada had warned her. Adi also knew, even at her tender age of thirteen, that people kept looking for faster and easier ways.

One of the easier ways to remain hopeful was to bargain with god, and not with just any god, but the True God. One convenience the True God offered those who sought such a bargain was that He ignored the shortcomings of His devotees. Just for one hour's service, He could help them, no matter what their wish might be. Adina thought that perhaps her nani might have thought of this bargain. Dada had told Adina that the bargaining chip with True God was *devotion*, whereby the dishonest devotee could cry and the True God would believe his tears.

According to Dada, peddling devotion was one of the oldest human businesses. The gurus of this business were

known as shamans and priests. The oldest human ancestors in Africa might have started consulting shamans to
get rid of their obstacles and, maybe that long ago, they
might have used animals as shamans. Some people, including some people in India, worshiped animals even
today. Millions of temples were built to serve these ven-
erable animals, who in return protected humans. On the
other extreme, some of the cousins of these very animals
were offered for sacrifice or served as food, and poachers
even sold the organs of some animals internationally.

The priests of the Satya Narayana, or the True God,
had simplified the old ways of devotion. There was no
need for any temples, shamans, or animals. In fact, the
priest's services cost practically nothing, in the monetary
sense, but one could offer gifts to the True God through
the officiating priest. The priests, invoking the authority
of some scriptures, claimed that the name of the True
God was *Narayana*, the same as Vishnu. When Narayana
fulfilled the wish of His devotee, then He was known as
Satya Narayana. He punished the devotees if they paid
Him no respect.

Adina wondered what happened if the devotee paid respect to the True God and then He did not fulfill the devotee's wish. Was the bargain with the True God then a
lie?

Dada told Adina a story of a ritual that took place in
Lucknow during his days as a young student. Dada's
roommate informed him that a friend of their soccer
coach was organizing a big Satya Narayana ritual at his
residence in Lucknow, the capital of Uttar Pradesh. Dada's Lucknow college faced an Agra college in the finals,
and winning that match was a matter of pride for these
two major Indian cities.

The ritual worship, or *puja,* was open to anyone interested in having his or her wish granted. For this purpose,

any attendee could offer *dakshina,* or a cash gift, at the end of the worship. The *dakshina* was collected on a big plate that had one or more candles. The burning candles represented the sacred fire called *arti.* The *dakshina* was shared by the priest and the organizers. Part of it covered the cost of the free sweets and punch that were distributed as sacred food called *Prasad.* The community cause here was to win the soccer championship and the cash gift was for the college's sports fund.

A well-known local *pandit*, a Brahmin priest, was to perform the ritual, and lots of local Lucknow folks were in attendance. Even though the host's house was quite big, many had to sit in the front yard, from where they could see the worship inside the house. Many students attended the ceremony, and Dada and his roommate brought a dozen classmates along. He told them that his high school hockey team had won in the local finals game because of this ritual in his Himalayan village. Nobody questioned him, even though Dada was not serious. It was true that his hockey team had won but there had been no *Puja.*

The worship started on time, a miracle in itself, her dada told Adi. The priest blew on a conch shell and told the audience to remain quiet until the end of the sacred food distribution. The first god of the worship was Lord Ganesha. After the priest put the sacred food in the elephant mouth of Ganesha, a man shouted, "*Jay Ganesh ji,*" Victory, Lord Ganesha—a victory wish for the Lucknow team.

After the Sanskrit part of the ritual was over, the priest began to recite the stories of some ancient devotees who succeeded in their lives, due to this ritual. He then retold those stories, about a half dozen, in Hindi because nobody would understand the original texts in Sanskrit. Be-

fore starting the first story, the priest blew on a conch
shell and rang a bell.

The effect of the sacred noise of the conch and bell
was seen clearly. Many who dozed off during the Sanskrit part of the ritual woke up now. Dada said that, at
this point, many men and women began to arrive, joining
the invited devotees, and some looked very poor. Some
didn't have shoes, and a couple of women wore torn sa-
ris. In the Satya Narayana ritual, a person's gender, caste,
wealth, education, age, etc., did not matter and so the un-
invited knew that they would receive the same sacred
food as all the others, for the lord treated them as equals.
But the ritual favored only those who performed it. The
priest told stories that indicated as much.

The wood-seller story was one such proof. Once, a
low-caste wood-seller saw a high-caste Brahmin doing
this ritual. The Brahmin told him how he changed his
luck from rags to riches with this ritual. The wood-seller
became rich after he learned the ritual from the Brahmin
and performed it. But the worshipper must be sincere and
truthful. The devotee who lied about the vow of doing
this ritual would face terrible times.

In another story, a merchant saw a king doing this ritual. The king told him how he had no heir, but after doing
this simple and short ritual, he had a son. The merchant
was highly impressed as he too was childless. When he
returned home, he told his wife, Lilavati, that he had tak-
en a vow to do this ritual for having a child. In a year, the
merchant couple was blessed with a daughter, Kalavati.
When the merchant forgot to do the ritual, his wife reminded him of the vow he had taken, and so the merchant
promised to do it on the occasion of Kalavati's wedding.

Kalavati grew up to be a beautiful woman and got
married to a very handsome young man. The merchant

forgot to do the ritual again, however, and Lord Satya Narayana put a curse on the merchant.

Soon after Kalavati's marriage, the merchant and his young son-in-law went to the sea coast for trade. One day a thief, who was being chased by the guards of the king, left all his stolen items near the boat of these two merchants and disappeared. The guards thought that the merchants were behind the burglary and arrested them. By the order of the king, the guards placed them in a bad prison and all their merchandise and money was taken away.

Back home Lilavati and Kalavati also faced tough times. Their home was burglarized. One evening Kalavati attended the Satya Narayana ritual in a neighbor's home. She told her mother Lilavati about the ritual she saw, and, inspired, they then performed it together. Lord Satya Narayana became very pleased with their devotion and granted them their wish for the safe return of the two merchants, their husbands. He appeared in the king's dreams and ordered him to release the two merchants or face His wrath. The king followed His order and compensated the men generously, returning their boat and filling it with merchandise and money.

Lord Satya Narayana wanted to test their honesty. When their boat landed, He approached them as a monk and asked them very humbly, "O, merchants. What is in your boat?"

They laughed while looking at him with suspicion. "Our boat is full of grass and plants," they answered.

The monk left them immediately and sat at a distance. The merchants saw their boat raised up in the water, and there was no money or merchandise in it any longer, just heaps of worthless grass. The senior merchant began to wail.

Then the junior merchant consoled his father-in-law as

he requested him to do the ritual of Lord Satya Narayana.

His request made the crying merchant realize that the monk was Lord Satya Narayana, and he approached the monk where He was sitting not far from the boat. The merchant touched the monk's feet and cried, "Lord, I am a fool. How could I understand your maya when even Brahma the Creator doesn't understand? But I will worship you." The lord forgave him for lying and restored all the wealth to the boat that it had carried before. Lilavati and Kalavati also experienced happiness back home.

When the priest wanted to continue this story further, he saw a young man smoking pot near the entrance door. "Lord Satya Narayana forgives bad behavior," the priest said loudly. "Right from a young age we should learn to speak truth. To speak truth, we must be in our senses. These days, young students smoke pot and cheat on their exams. Lord Satya Narayana punishes them for the use of bhang. They fail in their school tests because they can't—"

Before the priest could finish his sermon, the young man got up and walked toward the priest. He inhaled the pot deeply. The members of the audience laughed when they saw a flame rising from the pot.

The young man grabbed the Satya Narayana manual from the priest's hand and raised it to his eye level. "Show me where it is written that smoking bhang causes failure," he yelled. "Why can't you read the holy manual with honesty?"

Before he got an answer from the priest, the pot smoker was dragged out by a couple of young men.

The rest of the ritual went as planned and was very successful as the *dakshina* plate became filled with rupees several times over. Many parents thanked the priest for his sermons and gave him additional *dakshina*. The hosts were very apologetic to him for that young man's bad behavior. They told the priest that his sermon-giving was justified in such a context, and the priest, in turn, assured them of the imminent win of the Lucknow soccer team in the final match against the Agra team.

A few days later, the priest was admitted to a local hospital in serious condition. A newspaper gave a long story of the cause of this condition. Many people read the news and felt entertained, even though the Lucknow soccer team lost to the Agra team by a single goal. The rumor was that the goalie of the Lucknow team was an Agra native and let the ball inside the goalpost while falling down with a pretention of a slip. The occupants of his native city of Taj Mahal, were overjoyed by this last-second goal—another Taj "crown" for Agra. Some Lucknow college students beat their goalie later, but the priest became the worst victim of their beating. The police suspected the same pot smoker was the ringleader of the beaters. In fact, it was Dada's roommate who identified the ringleader.

Adina began to doubt that it was the Satya Narayana ritual that was the cause of her birth. The ritual demanded too much sincerity and truth-speaking from the worshipper praying for the fulfillment of a wish.

CHAPTER 12

Hunting with Divine Vehicles

Sarvebhyo devebhyo namo namaḥ
"Salutations and salutations to all the deities"
(A mantra for all deities)

Adina did not understand how it happened that she found herself in a park full of green plants and trees. Something must have gone wrong with her meditation. She also found herself surrounded by wild animals, and she watched a cobra chasing a mouse as a peacock was trying to catch the snake. The peacock obviously didn't care for another bird nearby—a white swan—which was busy picking up some things from the green surface of the park. Then she saw a lion trying to grab the neck of a bull.

"No," Adina shouted.

She heard two gun shots. The animals got scared, especially the lion and the peacock. Adina looked about for the source of the shots and saw a man with a hunting rifle in his hand.

"Ah. Hey, sir. You are the shooter?"

"Yes, Adina."

"How do you know my name, sir?"

"I am Shri Ram Sharma of Agra. Your dada and dadi know my writings about hunting. After my death, I became the guard of these divine animals."

"Pranam. I bow to you, sir. Dadi has met you, and your daughter was Dadi's classmate. Dadi has told me so many tiger stories. You killed man-eating tigers and saved so many lives. But you are a vegetarian. Dadi told me that you personally knew Mahatma Gandhi. He liked you very much. But why? He knew you were a hunter? Dadi calls you the second James Corbett of India."

"Jim Corbett and I were friends, which is ironic. I was fighting underground against the British for India's independence and Jim, the British hunter, was my model. In fact, by birth, he was Indian. He was born in Nainital, near your dadi's ancestral home. What a great hunter of man-eating tigers he was! Some of the worst man-eaters he killed were in your ancestral region of the Himalayas. Jim saved hundreds of lives. He wrote those stories in his language, English, and films were made of his stories. So the whole world knows about him. He inspired me. I could not resist my ambition to become like him. So I became a hunter and wrote my stories in my language, Hindi."

"Dadi told me that many Indian children know those Hindi stories."

"And India honored Jim with an animal sanctuary, which was established in 1957 as Jim Corbett National Park in your ancestral region. One hundred years before, some Indians started to hunt the British in India. In 1857, India's first country-wide freedom fight took place to achieve that goal. Most thought that Indians hated the British, but history loves to change. Later Jim Corbett was considered a sadhu-saint by Indians. His later life was dedicated to the welfare of animals. Jay, jay Jim!"

Shri Ram Sharma was so euphoric about Corbett that suddenly the lion roared.

Adina became frightened. "Oh, no. Is he going to attack that bull again?"

"No, that's his way of saying, 'I want some food.'"

"Why are these animals here, sir?"

"Do you see that big green house over there?"

"Yes, and I see a big crowd sitting in the yard."

"A Sarvadeva *Puja* is taking place. Since it is the All Gods Worship, it will take time. Many gods and goddesses have come as invited guests and these animals are their vehicles. This lion is Durga's vehicle. The bull is Shiva's Nandin. The mouse is Ganesha's vehicle. The peacock is his brother Karttikeya's vehicle. And so on."

"What about that deadly snake?"

"That cobra is not a vehicle, just Shiva's garland. Deadly or not deadly, these animals are very patient. The *Puja* may go on for hours while nobody is here to look after their feeding. They keep waiting and waiting. This park is not their natural habitat for their food. In desperation, they resort to violence. That's when hunters like us have to keep their violent behavior in check. Everybody in that crowd wants to have his or her wish fulfilled. So the *Puja* will take hours. Let me go in and find out how long it will take."

"I never thought of the slavery of these animals, but I know that it is a myth that a horse loves its rider. Every rider is a pain in every horse's neck. How come humans, who are also animals, are not any divine's vehicle? And if humans can use planes for quick visits, why can't these super-intelligent gods?"

"This is one of the reasons that 'All Gods Worship' was replaced by 'All Life Love' in two religions of India. It's incredible that five hundred years before Christ, two religions of India stood for the sanctity of life," the vegetarian Brahman hunter said. "Jainism and Buddhism started the movement to prevent cruelty to animals. Mahavira and Buddha dedicated these religions to the cause of *ahimsa*."

"I know you mean the concept of 'non-injury.' Thanks for saving these animals, sir," Adina cried loudly.

"It's good that you are meditating on these animals. I bless you. May you become a hunter of man-eating animals. Don't let other animals injure your life." The hunter then disappeared.

Adina was confused by what she had just learned: Jim Corbett and Shri Ram Sharma were both hunters and animal lovers. She never expected such a thing. Then her thoughts returned to her goal for meditation, finding the crown jewel. She wondered: what if Nani attended a big *Puja* session of All Gods Worship. She understood now how difficult it would be for her to approach so many gods who were being honored in the big *Puja* in that green house.

A list of deities who might be present there flashed before her mind's eye. This *Puja* started with Ganesha, and then a number of deities entered, most commonly Brahma, Vishnu, Shiva, sixteen holy mothers like Lakshmi, Sarasvati, Durga, Bhavani, Nirriti, etc., and then cosmic protectors like Agni, Indra, Varuna, Vayu, Nirriti—the only female protector, etc. Then heavenly bodies like the Sun, Moon, Mars, Mercury, Jupiter, Saturn, etc., entered. Even witches, known as Dakini and Shakini, were invited because they could also fulfill the worshippers' wishes. Every invited god or goddess came on a personal vehicle, which was always an animal. Daunting though she now realized her task to be, Adina continued her meditation.

She was startled when she heard more gunshots. They were from the green house. She thought that Sharma ji might have used his gun again. But for what reason in a

Puja? She never had heard of the use of guns in a *Puja*. Then she saw Sharma ji coming out again. This time he was accompanied by two rams, which took Adina by surprise.

Before she opened her mouth to ask about them, Sharma ji addressed Adina very affectionately. "Adina, it was not me who used the gun this time. I won't try to shoot that priest. His trouble started when he uttered the mantras to sacrifice two rams. As soon as these two rams were dragged onto the sacrificial ramp, a shot rang out, the bullet hitting the priest's turban. The gunman then said, 'The next shot can be a little lower if you touch the rams.' The gunman was nobody other than Jim Corbe—"

"James Corbett, the hunter from Nanital?" Adina interrupted with surprise.

"Yes, the priest is also a Brahmin from that area. That Brahmin could be your dadi's relative. Jim knows many Brahmins of your dadi's native place. This priest began to argue with Jim, but Jim is too smart. He told the priest very politely, 'You are a Pahari Pundit. You may believe in animal sacrifice, but *Puja* does not require animal sacrifice. This is not a Vedic yajña where animals are brutally sacrificed. I warn you that you'd better abandon your Pahari way of performing Vedic rituals.'"

"Dadi has told me many stories of animal sacrifice in Garhwal and Kumaon hills. Not only Vedic but other rituals also included cruel animal killing in that Pahari region. I am ashamed that my ancestral region practiced sacred slaughter."

"I feel the same way. Jim Corbett is really a *sadhu* compared to this Pahari priest. Let me find out if he and the priest have settled their disagreement with no injuries." The hunter then disappeared again and the two rams joined the other animals in the park.

The violent animals in the park looked impatient

again. The lion didn't roar but opened his mouth a couple of times while looking at those two rams. *Maybe he was yawning*, Adi thought. The peacock screamed loudly and hovered around the cobra. Then, seemingly out of nowhere, came an eagle.

"Oh, it is Vishnu's vehicle,"Adina said. "So Vishnu is late. A typical Indian god, boasting of his fast movement."

The two birds began to fight over that snake. The cobra quietly slithered under the sitting bull, taking the advantage of the birds' feuding. That move of the cobra compelled the bull to get up and roar in fear. Then the lion ran toward those rams.

"Help! Help!" Adina cried.

She expected Sharma or Corbett to come out and scare the violent animals. Instead, she saw a saintly figure emerging from the void. She quickly recognized him as Mahavira, one of the founders of Jainism.

Adina was awed. "My pranams to you, Lord," she said with respect. "I bow to you. I know that you and Buddha didn't believe in God. God is useless if He can't save these helpless creatures. Those deities—"

Before she could say more, all the animals looked calm and disengaged, with no fear of each other. Adina was speechless. She saw the saint raising his hand up to bless her, and her eyes closed, as she absorbed the compassion flowing from his blessing.

After a couple of minutes, she opened her eyes to find nothing on her computer screen.

CHAPTER 13

Buffalo Demon's Brutal Revenge

Durgaayai namaḥ "Salutation to Durga"
(A Sanskrit mantra for Durga's prayer)

Thoughts of animal torture for divine miracles kept reverberating in Adina's head. In fact, her dadi had told her that some gods were well known for granting a wish sooner if the offerings for them were soaked in the oozing blood of a dying animal. The Durga *Puja* was perhaps the most powerful example.

Nani believed in Durga's power to grant wishes, but she and Nana were vegetarians and could not be associated with any animal sacrifice. Dada and Dadi were also vegetarians but they were Paharis, and, in their Himalayan culture, this puja was presumed more effective if a male buffalo was offered to the wish-granting Mother Goddess, Durga. Her most popular festival of India, the Durga *Puja*, could last up to ten days during the Dashhara holidays. Most devout Hindus considered it mandatory to visit the holiest Himalayan places of Adina's ancestral region. Many were vegetarians and respected the right of animals to live, and they seldom knew that the local

Himalayan people, the Paharis, celebrated the Durga *Puja* in a way that they would consider demonic.

Dadi had told Adina why the Mother Goddess Durga had to fight to save *suras,* or gods, from an *asura,* or demon. Her fight with demon Mahisha, or Buffalo, was celebrated in Dadi's native Himalayan area.

"What if Nana and Nani offered their homage, including the crown jewel, in a Himalayan temple without knowing the details of the Pahari culture's Durga *Puja?*" Adi wondered. In fact, she remembered, it was not necessary to visit a Himalayan temple. Durga was the Goddess of Mountains, the highest Himalayas, which were closer to heaven where the deities resided permanently. Not everyone could reach those altitudes, and it was no wonder the goddess was named Durga, meaning Difficult to Reach. Thus the devotee could request his or her local priest to offer the gift to Durga in the Himalayas. Adi knew the wish-gift rule: The higher the gift reached, the easier to attain the wish. But every rule had an exception. The *aṭhwaar* story Dadi told Adina was proof.

The eighth day of the ten-day Dashhara festival in the Garhwal Himalayas was for the buffalo sacrifice. The sacrifice was called *aṭhwaar,* "the eighth-day," or the day to run a male buffalo to represent a demon for the pleasure of Durga Devi. Could it be a game enacting a male-female power battle? she wondered.

The main thing Adina remembered from Dadi's stories on the subject was that the goddess loved jewelry, so much so that she was covered with the best jewels, and she needed no clothes to cover her stunningly beautiful body. At one time, the demon fell in love with her, which Adi found very strange. The buffalo demon she wanted to kill loved her! Everything about her sounded very surreal to Adina.

Indeed it was. In order to find her divine form, Adina

chose the eighth day of the nine-night *navaratra* worship of the goddess during the Dashhara festival. She meditated in the evening, and, after waiting for a long time, she succeeded in achieving an image of Durga. The goddess initially had two arms, then four arms. She definitely looked capable of killing to Adi. A huge sword in her raised arm meant action. Adi noted that her whole body was covered in jewelry and she wore no clothes. Her naked feet stood atop a downed body, which Adina at first thought was the body of the demon she fought. But then she saw that the body was a human. Was he alive or dead? Adina bowed to the goddess.

"Namaste, Mother, I bow to you."

"I bless you, my dear daughter. May you have all the *shakti* to fight for your cause." The Mother raised one of her right arms as she said the blessing. "I know you are looking for the crown jewel, but I have no such a jewel."

"Your name is *Shakti.* What does this mean to you? And why is that man lying under your naked feet? Is he that infamous demon that you wanted to punish?"

"My name means synergy, for many gods together created and empowered me with their energies. But this man under my feet is worse than a demon. He is a greedy terrorist who approved of the killing of animals in the name of the Goddess. He is a Pahari priest and so may be your relative."

"My dada says that all Pahari priests are our relatives. But why are you prolonging his torture? He is not completely dead yet."

"Adina, he falsified the established facts and incited his folks to torture a defenseless male buffalo."

"Mother, I thought you also killed a buffalo. All buffalos, male or female, are innocent creatures."

"I never killed any buffalo. I killed a demon that *looked* like a male buffalo. I am called *Mahishasuramar-*

dini or Mahisha demon's murderer. He and his fellow demons had tortured gods and goddesses for no reason. But this Brahmin under my feet put a spin on Mahisha because it means 'buffalo.' He told his people that I killed a real male buffalo. You don't demonize an innocent life."

"But is that enough reason for his torture, Mother?"

"Yes, it is. The priest did say all that was mentioned in the books. It is true that synergy, or Shakti, is fabricated by the major divinities."

"You are saying that you are fabricated? How?"

"It's a long story. But here is a brief summary for you."

What the goddess told her was not new. The two wives of Prajapati, the creator of beings, had always been in conflict. The gods were Aditi's children and the demons were Diti's offspring. A beautiful daughter of Diti did penance to obtain a son that could kill all the children of Aditi, and her wish was fulfilled. The demon was named Mahisha, and he looked like a male buffalo. Shiva gave him such strength that no god could kill him. The gods were very unhappy with Shiva's blessings.

When Mahisha became an adult, he tested his strength. He chased Aditi's children, and many were killed by the demon. Some deities fled to the earth, some to heaven, and some hid underground.

Then the major gods assembled in front of Brahma. The lord of the creation requested Vishnu and Shiva to produce Shakti with their combined energies. Other major deities joined Vishnu and Shiva. Shiva empowered Shakti's brain, Vishnu her arms, Brahma her feet, Agni her eyes, Vayu her ears, the two Dusks her brows, Kubera her nose, the Prajapati team her fingers, the Sun her toes, Indra her waist, Varuna her thighs, the Moon her breasts, Yama her hair, and so on.

The result was the goddess Durga, more powerful than all the deities and demons combined. They gave her their weapons to fight the demon, and she grew up with many arms so that she could use all the deadly weapons at once. They gave her a lion to ride, and as she rode the lion for the first time, all the gods surrounded her with cupped palms.

"You are now Durga the woman who shall slay that buffalo demon," they said.

"Dadi has told me how you became Durga."

"The gods sent me out to challenge the demon. When he saw me the first time, he was awed by my beauty and wanted to marry me. I refused, and he requested that I be his bride again. 'Durga! You will be my *mahishi*. Marry me.' I knew he had many beautiful nymphs in his palace. I laughed. 'I don't want to be your queen. You already have those nymphs. You are despicable.' That made him very mad and he wanted to kill my lion, but I scared him away. After a while he came back to fight me. We had a long fight, during which he played many magical tricks. He transformed into a giant buffalo and attacked my lion. I threw my noose around his neck and dragged him down the hill. But he loosened the noose and changed into a lion, and so I attacked him with my dagger and cut his throat. But then he changed into a man and attacked me with a dagger. I shot his hand with an arrow and he dropped his dagger. Then he transformed himself into an elephant and grabbed my lion with his trunk. I pierced his trunk with my trident. He came back to his buffalo body, this time more fierce. I took a shot of wine, then another, then another until I became intoxicated and felt no pain. I laughed at the buffalo demon. He yelled at me and said foul words. I pierced his tongue with my trident, which made him speechless. He leaped up in the air to attack me, and I cut off his head and crushed him under my feet, just like I am doing to this priest. That enemy of gods was dead. A woman finally was able to kill the demon. The terrorist of gods, humans, and other animals lay dead under my feet."

"But this priest was not an enemy of the gods. He worshipped them." Adina wanted to understand the difference between a priest and a terrorist.

"I don't forgive liars, whether priests or terrorists, anybody who hurts innocent beings by lies. The liar may benefit in the beginning, but in the long battle he will be punished, no matter how many tricks he uses to win. This priest was a born liar. He must have learned lying form his parents. He lied even about my birthplace. He said that Vishnu came from Badrinath and Shiva came from Kedarnath and met at the Rajarajeshvari temple where I was created. These temples of Vishnu, Shiva, and Durga in the Garhwal Himalayas were not there when I was born. He told another lie by stating that the demon was from Bhainswara village. This Garhwali village does mean the 'place of the buffalo.' The demon was not born there. He did look like a buffalo, but he was not a buffalo. Buffalos don't kill any creatures. Then this priest added more lies about the buffalo killing every year during the Dashhara festival. Thus, every year there is brutal bloodshed, the death of an innocent creature."

No sooner had Durga said this than she disappeared from the screen. A documentary followed just after her disappearance:

The Brahmin priest was doing the Durga *Puja* on the eighth day. "Now Durga is ready to chase the demon buffalo," he proclaimed after he finished reciting the seven hundred Sanskrit verses of Durga from the holy book *Devii-Maahaatmya*. As soon as he sprinkled holy water over the beast, he whipped him. "*Jaya Durge, Mahi-*

shasuramardini," he shouted, Victory to Durga, the slay-
er of Mahisha demon.

Two drummers started playing *damau* and *dhol* loudly
and others played conchs and rang bells. Some beat metal
plates with the drummers. Everyone moved with their
dance behind the buffalo. The beast moved a little farther
away due to pain, and as soon as the buffalo came out in
the open, the priest signaled to stab him with a *khunkhri*,
a Himalayan dagger. A man caused a wound on the buffalo's back with the blade. Then others joined him in that
act. The beast began to run faster on the trail. The crowd
gave chase. They crossed a small stream where another
group of people was waiting. Drummers welcomed the
bleeding buffalo. For a while, the buffalo stood over the
cool water, the blood flowing from his body swirling in
the stream. Then the new group took over the torture.
They began to hit him with whips and cut him with dag-
gers. The animal got up and began to move again. After
crossing the stream, the crowd ran the buffalo uphill, inflicting more dagger wounds upon his body. From the
hilltop, they forced him to jump into a ravine, and, within
a few minutes, the beast died writhing in excruciating
pain.

When the participants in this ceremony of death
reached the ravine, the priest asked a man to collect fresh
blood in a pot as part of *Prasad*. The priest recited a few
mantras while the blood was collected. Then he dipped
his finger into the bloody pot and put a blood mark on his
own head. The man who collected the blood went around
and put a blood mark on each person's forehead, and
each recipient shouted, *"Jaya Durga Ma,"* Victory to
Durga Ma. Two low-caste attendees began to butcher the
buffalo. For them, it was all meat to enjoy in the evening.

At that point, Adina screamed and covered her eyes
with her hands. When she opened her eyes, there was

nothing on the computer screen. Remembering that the practice of *aṭhwaṛ* in Garhwal was banned long before she was born made her feel better.

CHAPTER 14

The Joint Power of Two Gods

Jai Jai Kamalesur Mahaadeb
"Hail! Hail! Kamaleshvara and Mahadeva."
(The local Garhwali greeting for Vishnu and Shiva)

T he other Himalayan temple, the Kamleshwar Mahadev, was famous for fulfilling the wishes of childless women, and countless childless women of India visited this temple. The temple was the symbol of Kamaleshvara and Mahadeva sharing the same residence, as if the two gods were one. Kamaleshvara was "lord of the lotuses" or Vishnu, and Shiva was "higher god" or Maha Deva.

Dadi had told Adina that the small temple made of stone was located in the town of Srinagar on the banks of the Alaknanda in Garhwal. *Maybe Nani's gift reached here,* Adina speculated, especially given the temple's fame for providing women with children. And so Adina meditated on the lord of that temple, but she could only achieve a very blurred picture. Sometimes the lord looked like Vishnu and sometimes Shiva. Then Vishnu transformed into Lord Rama, which made Adina more interested in him. She meditated on Lord Rama, and his image became clearly visible. She greeted him. "Lord, I bow to you. Pranam."

The lord raised his hand and blessed her. "May you succeed in your search."

"People come here and offer their prayers to Vishnu and Shiva. That is why this temple is called Kamleshwar Mahadev. Am I right?"

"You are right," Lord Rama replied.

"Dadi told me a tale of how a childless couple was blessed with a son by visiting your temple. As the tale goes, Vishnu worshipped Lord Shiva with one thousand lotuses of Manasarovar, but Shiva wanted to test Vishnu's devotion to him and hid one lotus. When Vishnu realized that he had offered Shiva 999 lotuses, he was baffled by the loss of one lotus, and to compensate, he offered his lotus-like eye. Shiva now believed Vishnu's devotion to him was deep indeed. Vishnu wanted a very powerful weapon to kill demons, and so Shiva gave him a gift, the famous *Sudarshana Chakra*. That disc weapon was deadly. A childless couple witnessed this gift-giving, and the compassionate Parvati requested that her husband Shiva give the couple the kind of gift they were looking for. The kind lord granted them their wish. Since then, any childless couple can come to this temple and be blessed with a child. But how is it that you are in this story, Lord Rama?"

"Everyone here knows me as an avatar of Vishnu. I fought Ravana, who had abducted my wife Sita. I regained my wife after many lost their lives in the fight. For the *moksha* of those dead, I came to this temple and offered one thousand lotuses so that all the dead went to heaven. The story your dadi gave you is mine."

"Did you really come here for the salvation of those dead? Dadi told me that the Alakananda and rivers like

Ganga, Yamuna, Mandakini and other Garhwal rivers have nothing to do with Rama or his ancestors. Your ancestor Bhagiratha may not have ever seen Gomukh from where the Ganga emerges. How could he bring the Ganga from heaven? They say Lord Vishnu and Lord Shiva granted Bhagiratha his wish to purify his ancestors' souls and released the river on the earth for him. The Ganga, therefore, is called the Bhagirathi after his name. Bhagiratha led the Ganges from Gomukh, and when it met Alakananda a few miles from Srinagar at Dev Prayag, it became the Ganga. Ultimately, the Ganges reached the Bay of Bengal. But this is not due to Bhagiratha's effort. All Himalayan rivers were already formed before humans arrived."

"Well, your dadi is a scholar. What can I say?"

Suddenly, three women appeared in the picture on Adi's laptop screen. They were shouting. "Where is Kamleshwar Mahadev? You Vishnu, you Shiva, come out! Come out! Come out! Explain to us what you did with our babies! Don't hide! Come out!"

Adina was dismayed by their protest. "Lord, why are they shouting?" she asked Rama. "You are lucky they are not saying your name. Some say that you and Sita returned to Ayodhya after killing Ravana. Then Sita gave birth to your first son, Lava. After his birth, you exiled Sita, and she lived with Lava in a forest retreat. She had another son, Kusha. Dadi thinks that Sita must have used some sort of technology for Kusha's birth like is used in modern hospitals. She didn't visit any temple, but then, a *darshan* of any temple or holy place cannot give you a baby, says my dadi. But my nani believed in miracles."

"That is why these women came to this temple. What happened to them was not what they came for. Other miracles than what they asked for took place instead."

The screen changed as soon as Lord Rama finished his

sentence. Adina saw three episodes, one for each woman. Adina called them T for the tallest woman, M for the medium-height woman, and S for the shortest woman. But Rama used their real names as Adina heard his voice behind each documentary-like episode.

"In the evening, the big moon was shining outside and Tara entered this temple to pray along with the big crowd of worshippers. It was the fourteenth day of the bright half of the holy month of Karttik. The gentle noise of the slow-flowing river Alaknanda was audible, even inside the temple. Every entrant bowed or touched the big sitting bull statue at the temple entrance, Shiva's bull, the Nandin. The local people called him just Nandi. Tara touched the bull and bowed to him. Then she went inside where she saw many devotees who had surrounded the *Linga*, a cylindrical stone that is the sacred symbol of Shiva. The lord created the entire universe with this *Linga*. The head priest and the devotees poured ghee, clarified butter, over the *Linga*. It was covered completely by the ghee offerings.

"Other childless women joined Tara to worship the *Linga*. They all stood in the designated area outside the temple in the night. Each woman had to remain standing the whole night, praying the Kamleshwar Mahadev, and no food or drink was allowed. Fasting the whole night was essential to their prayer, and each woman held two clay lamps filled with ghee. The lamps were constantly lit throughout the night. If one lamp was extinguished, the other would be used to light it again to keep the prayer in light throughout the night. The prayer was not in words. The awareness of the *Linga* and the wish to have a child constituted the silent prayer of every woman.

"Around midnight, the lamp in Tara's left hand was extinguished by the wind and she used the other lamp on her right hand to light it. In her haste, she allowed the lit lamp to come in contact with her sari and she was enveloped in fire. She cried out, but no woman came to help her. Obviously, no woman would like to disturb her sacred vigil, but some men who were inside came out and doused the fire. She had to be rushed to the local hospital. Her burns, fortunately, were not very serious. She never had a child of her own, but she adopted an orphan boy."

Then the second woman's episode started. "Kummi was not exactly a childless woman. She already had three daughters, but she desperately wanted a son. Her worship went very smoothly the entire night, and in a year she had a child. She wept for days, but not for joy. She wept with dejection, for the baby was a girl. Her mother-in-law was disgusted, but her mother consoled her. Two years later she had another girl. This girl's birth had no connection with the Kamleshwar Mahadev temple. After the birth of her third daughter, Kummi developed an angry feeling for the ghee-soaked *Linga* worship."

The next woman's documentary then began and Adi thought it was scary. "Chhama felt very hungry and thirsty after midnight. She knew that the temple would not allow her any food or drink for she was a worshipper looking forward to having a son, and a worshipper must sacrifice in order to show true devotion to the *Linga*-worship. Chhama could not bear the pains of hunger and thirst, however, and she abruptly left the temple and quietly proceeded to her nearby village.

"On her way she was attacked by a tiger. Her cries were heard by some villagers who made a big noise to scare the tiger and it ran away. She was unconscious when the villagers reached her, but later, when she awoke, she was very happy to learn that Shri Ram Sharma killed that man-eating tiger in Rudraprayag a few miles up from Srinagar at the confluence of two holy rivers, Alakananda and Mandakini. She was even happier when she had a son a year later, but she had realized that the temple worship for this purpose was just superstition. She decided to tell other women to disbelieve in such prayers. Once she stood outside that temple when this particular worship was taking place and shouted against this tradition while standing near Nandi, the bull of Shiva. No woman left the vigil. But she was able to contact Tara and Kummi later in her life."

Adina then heard the protests of these three women again. Tara screamed, "Your *Linga* worship is a lie. Come out and tell about this lie!"

Then a male voice was heard. Adina recognized Rama's voice, which became louder as he spoke. "Tara, you are a sick woman, a mentally sick mother. Mental sickness first kills the logical sense. You told your orphan son lies about his birth. For ten years you kept telling him that he was the son of you and your husband. In school his classmates began to ask him why he didn't look like either of his parents in complexion and other features. You told him that that was the way God intended him to be. Then a year after of his constant nagging you told him that he was adopted. Again you lied that his parents died in an accident and none of his relatives were known to you. You know very well that his parents didn't die in any accident. You cooked up the story. Now he is a grown man and still looking for his roots."

Tara became quiet, but Kummi and Chhama shouted.

"You also lied, Lord Rama," Kummi said. "Did the one thousand lotuses really come from Manasarovar?"

"And you are an insensitive husband," Chhama declared angrily. You kicked your innocent wife Sita out of your palace. To humiliate your innocent spouse publicly is insanity."

Rama didn't answer their accusations directly. Instead he said loudly, "Kummi, destroying your own child's future is the most heinous crime of a mother. You were desperate to have a son after your third daughter, and you began to give her a slow-acting poison. Now she is grown woman who will never be able to bear a child. When you had your fourth daughter, you used a poison that stunted her growth, which discouraged boys from marrying her. Your husband began to beat you when you had the third daughter. You are lucky he didn't kick you out of his parental house."

"I was happy with my husband. He never beat me," Kummi tried to claim, but her tone indicated she was lying.

"And you, Chhama. You are Chhaliya the cheater. For years you had no child. Finally, you had a son. His father was not your husband, but you never said so. Now, all three of you crooks get out of here! I have killed demons, but they were all males. You are lucky. Just get lost!"

Adina lost the screen. She couldn't understand why the image disappeared. In this Kamleshwar Mahadev show, she noted one impossible item, which was very entertaining: One thousand lotuses from Tibet's Lake Manasarovar!

CHAPTER 15

Kabir, the True Teacher

Behavior is rizhomatic, not just cladistic.

L ife's influences originated, not just from a single branch, but from several roots. Kabir's life was a simple example. His complex social circumstances made him a formidable champion of social equality. Dada had told Adina quite a lot about Saint Kabir of Varanasi, the bluntest saint-reformer of India. That bluntness came out of his fight for fairness. He was a strict vegetarian and yet he relished roasting Hindu pandits and Muslim mullahs, like kabobs, with his sermons.

But why Muslim mullahs? *His parents must have found more social equality in Islam than in the Hindu caste system*, Adina decided. *Kabir's Arabic name means "The Great One," and, in Islam, that name is used for God, too. His parents were weavers. The weaver community is classified as low caste, untouchables, and this low status might have been responsible for his ancestors converting to Islam.*

But Kabir's teacher was the renowned Swami Ramananda, not only a saint but also a Hindu pandit. One of

Kabir's couplets contains these words: *Sat guru ki mahi-ma ananta*—The greatness of my true teacher is infinite.

A story says that Swami Ramananda was his guru who taught him one word, *Rama,* for God. So Kabir believed in one God with several names, God who was neither Hindu nor Muslim, just an energy.

Kabir was illiterate and could not write even his favorite name for God, *Rama.* His God was everywhere, inside and outside, so there was no need to visit holy places. "Find God in you" was his greatest lesson. The Muslim ruler of India, Sikandar Lodi, tried to punish Kabir for his freedom of expression. After Sikandar Lodi's death in 1517 AD, a sect called the Kabir Panth, or Kabir's Path, was established. His disciples recorded his words in lots of books and founded several temples in his name.

"What if Nani visited one of the Kabir temples for her wish?" Adi wondered while remembering Kabir's legendry miracles. "Maybe Kabir could answer my question about the crown jewel."

For meditation, she needed to be in a good mood, and so she read a couple of Kabir's Hindi songs translated to English by the Nobel Laureate Rabindranath Tagore. Those songs didn't help her mood, however, and so she read more. None of those translated songs helped her mood.

Then she played a Hindi song sung by some Indian singer.

> *Dulahinii gaavahu maŋgalaachaara,*
> *Hama ghari aaye ho raajaa Raama bhartaara.*
> (Bride! Sing auspicious celebration,
>   'You have come to our home,
>   King Rama the bridegroom!)

Just these two lines were enough to bring tears to her

eyes. She stopped the song and wiped her eyes. She failed to do any meditation.

The next day she tried to meditate again. This time she played another song.

> *Kaahe rii nalinii tuu kumhilaanii,*
> *Tere hii naali sarovara paanii.*
> (Why, hey, little lotus, did you wither?
> Your very root is in the lake water.)

Adina understood the metaphor of this Kabir bhajan: *Lovely girl! You are rooted in joy. There is no reason for you to be depressed.*

She felt happiness within and started her meditation. And soon, she began to hear *Rama, Rama.* Then Saint Kabir emerged as he appeared in one of his famous pictures at Kabirchaura in Varanasi.

"Pranam, Your Holiness," Adina said to greet the saint.

"Live long, my dear. Tell me your name."

"Adina, your holiness."

"For what reason did you meditate on me, Adina?"

"In the beginning, I had only one reason, but now I have a couple more because I experienced some difficulty in your meditation."

"Tell me first about your difficulties."

"I read your *bhajans* in English translation by Tagore. None of them put me in the right mood. Why?"

"Adina, I didn't know how to read and write. I composed poems orally and a couple of my disciples recorded them under my name. Then more disciples came, then more, then their disciples, and on and on. They all wrote verses and so not all of the *bhajans* attributed to me are my words. If some songs didn't serve you well, then they are not my words but the words of my devotees dedicated to me. Now whatever I say here you have my permission to record. You can continue now."

"I began to cry when I heard your devotional song: 'Bride! Sing auspicious celebration."

"Explain to me why this song made you cry. This is my song."

"Your song talks of the soul as bride and God Rama as bridegroom. This means spiritual union with celebration. The pictures of my parents' wedding reveal how my nana and nani decorated their home and lit it when my father's party was welcomed. When my parents went near the altar, Nana and Nani looked so overjoyed, so beautiful. Until the last year of their marriage, my parents seemed to live very happily. I have seen many pictures, videos, letters, and gifts that are evidence of my parents' happy married life. My birth added more happiness, too, but a year after my birth, some things did not go well. So I cried." Then Adina told about the ugly divorce that was blessed by her mother's parents.

"Your parents are very fortunate to have you. They must have thought of you as a miracle."

"At least my nani did. She claims that I was born as a miracle, but my father doesn't, and my dada and dadi don't either. Nani offered a crown jewel to a deity to wish for my birth. I thought she might have offered it at one of your temples."

"There is no way to prove or disprove your offering, Adina, but such an offering would not have occurred at my temples. I believe in one God, and my favorite name for God is Rama. But my Rama is not the Rama of the *Ramayana* epic. God is formless. He has no avatars, no idols. He is within everyone. Your nani cannot be a real follower of my Panth. She was mistaken that a deity caused your birth. Your mother gave you birth just like my mother gave me birth. Your nani is still living in Sikandar Lodi's times if she doesn't understand this law of birth."

"How do you know your mother gave you birth? They say you didn't know your parents. You were found abandoned by a weaver couple and they adopted you. Nobody knows if your parents were Hindu or Muslim. Only your name hints that you were raised a Muslim, but no one knows."

"I must have parents, for Maya has that rule, Adina. Maya is nature, not a deity. My weaver parents found me. They never said that some deity was responsible for my birth. They were honest parents. They told me from the beginning that I was adopted and didn't know if I was a Hindu or Muslim. They were victims of being called low-class untouchables.

"You know I believe in equality of all," he continued. "I don't believe that anybody is born as Hindu or Muslim. Nobody is born like that. Only fools think they were born like that. You need human parents. That is why you are human. Your parents, as you say, met as bridegroom and bride. They needed each other, no matter how they met. Just like Vishnu and Lakshmi needed each other. Just like Shiva and Shivani needed each other. That is how Maya plays her game, with a father and a mother."

Adina smiled. She remembered Dada humming the lines of Kabir.

> *Maayaa mahaa ṭhaginii hama jaanii,*
> *Kesaba ke Kamalaa hoi baiṭhii Siva ke*
> *bhavana bhavaanii.*
> (Maya! I know you as the great trickster.
> You sat with Vishnu by being Kamala,
> and in Shiva's house as Bhavani)

"Sir, you also had a wife? Isn't that true?" Adina

asked with no intention of any ridicule, just a query. "Maya tricked you?"

"My wife never abandoned me. We both raised our son Kamal. We believed we were equal parents." The saint looked very grim. He paused and looked into Adina's eyes intently. Then he continued. "Your mother attempted to destroy the family. Ask her what kind of pain she would have felt if her mother had accused her father falsely? Your mother is selfish. She didn't care about your pain. Your legal system needs lots of daylight. The judge couldn't see equal parental rights. What kind of judge is he who knew that the woman lied and yet gave her custody? He demanded no apology for what humiliation your father suffered. How was he appointed as a judge if he has no sense of social equality? What happened to other experts? The psychologist's expertise is worthless if she couldn't see why nature needed two parents. How was she appointed as a behavioral expert? And how did a lawyer support a terrible lie? Such lawyers have darkened the legal profession. It's a crime to separate a child from either parent. It's a crime to reward the lying parent and punish the truthful parent. Those who supported your mother's decision had clouded vision if they couldn't see your tears. Do they have any children?"

"Yes, they do. But none of them went through my kind of pain."

"I hope their children grew up healthy. You should be happy that you could not be destroyed and your father could not be destroyed either. You are indeed a miracle baby."

Adina began to sob. When she opened her eyes, she couldn't see Kabir and yet the screen looked bright. She looked all around. No Kabir anywhere. His couplet made sense.

Herata herata he sakhii, rahaa Kabiira heraai
Bunda samaanii samudra me, so kata herii jaai

(Gazing and gazing, O dear girl, Kabir got lost.
The drop merged into the sea. How can you see that?)

Kabir was not easily followed. It was believed that, at his death, Hindus wanted his cremation while Muslims his burial, and they quarreled over his dead body. Neither religious group understood him but he was loved by both. Dada told Adina often that the naming of children after a person was the best test of that person's popularity, and every year many Hindu and Muslim boys were named after Kabir. Such was the greatness of the word, "Kabir."

The holy *Guru Granth Sahib* was solid proof of Indian respect for Kabir. The Sikh scripture contained many words of Kabir, and yet, unlike Kabir, Guru Nanak was so well-educated that he had read and understood the Vedas, the most difficult scriptures. In his own time, he was revered not only as the founder of Sikhism but also as a Vedi, the knower of the Vedas, and yet his religion respected the illiterate Kabir's words. The guru was larger than life. He was not just a founder of a faith, but a social reformer. "Keep the doors of your house of worship open to all," the guru said. "Guru's door or *Guru-dwar* of Nanak leads every entrant to equal sharing in that house."

Dada heard the extended meaning of the door leading to a view window. If you have a window made of glass, you must clean it often for a better view.

Adina knew how Kabir inspired ordinary folks with his sharp tongue. He might have asked Adina to request her mother to keep the door open for equal sharing and clean the glass window more often. But Adina had already started crying.

CHAPTER 16

The Wishful Thread of the Big Mogul

Do gaz zamiin bhii na milii kuu-e-yaar me
"Not even two yards of ground was granted
to me in my beloved's backyard."
(The last line of a famous poem of Bahadur Shah Zafar)

Adina remembered a quote that she had heard from her dada. "Every thread has a limited length." A descendant of the great Mughal dynasty of India said this when she came to his office seeking a job. Dada could not offer her the teaching assistant position she had sought at his university. The department had some money a year before but that had evaporated quickly among other administrative expenditures. Dada loved to tell her story to other Indian immigrant friends.

When Dada heard first her name, Shab Mughal, from her own mouth, he was surprised. "You couldn't be a true Mughal. Shab, are you really a Mughal?" Shab was young, in her early twenties, and beautiful, but her dark-brown complexion was more like Dada's.

"You expect me to look like a Mongol. Right? Because that's what Mughal means." She laughed. "After Akbar, no Mughal emperor looked like a Mongol. That was because Akbar married a native Hindu Rajput girl, Jodhabai. Salim, her son, ascended to the Mughal throne with the name Jahangir. Tell me. Does he really look like a relative of Genghis Khan, as his great-grandfather Babur claimed to be the case? With Salim Jahangir, all Mughal rulers became like other Indians: Khichri."

Dada told Adi he had laughed, for he appreciated her reference to Indian Khichri: rice cooked with beans, vegetables, and spices. "Just like Khichri advanced into the rich and colorful 'pilaf' dish, the multi-colored Mughal threads made India the most attractive country in the world. The Taj Mahal stands as a solid proof," Dada said.

That's when Shab said, "But every thread has a limited length. The sun rises and eventually comes the dark night. That's what my Persian name Shab means, Night. I see nothing in my future."

"Don't give up! You belong to the greatest dynasty of Indian rulers. You should sue the Government of India. You should say, 'The Taj Mahal is ours! The Fatehpur Sikri capital of Akbar is ours! Give us part of their revenues!' I have seen so many praying at the tomb of Sheikh Chishti in Fatehpur Sikri alone, Shab. Have you seen Fatehpur Sikri?"

"No."

"You should visit. Maybe your wishes will be fulfilled if you pray at the saint's tomb. Some of my relatives say their wishes were fulfilled."

"I, too, have an aunt in Bombay. For years she and uncle waited for a child. Then they heard a story from a Hindu couple about how their prayer at that tomb fulfilled their wish for a son. The couple had heard of Akbar's wish. The emperor desperately wanted an heir to the Mughal throne. He had heard of the miraculous power of Salim Chishti, a simple and kind Muslim Sufi saint who commanded the respect of people of any faith of India.

The emperor then met with him and his wish was fulfilled.

"Akbar honored the saint by naming his first son, Jahangir, Salim after the saint. When the saint died, Akbar built his tomb in his new capital, Fatehpur Sikri. People who go to see the Taj Mahal usually visit the nearby Fatehpur Sikri tomb, too. My aunt and uncle credit their son's birth to their visit to this tomb."

"Do you believe that?" Dada asked the young woman.

"Let me give you the reason why I told you all this. Very soon Akbar abandoned his new capital, for Fatehpur Sikri had a serious water shortage. But maybe he didn't want to reveal the real cause, for it is believed by some that he had many other wishes he sought to have fulfilled. Anyway, his move from Delhi to Fatehpur Sikri was a fiasco, but believers seldom ask why Akbar abandoned the new capital so soon."

"I got it." Dada understood the secret power of the Fatehpur Sikri tomb. Even today it attracted visitors, not because it was Akbar's temporary capital but because of its connection with the saint.

Adina wondered what Akbar's other wishes might be that Shab mentioned. Akbar was not able to read or write. Unlike his last heir, Bahadur Shah "Zafar," he had no talent for composing poems. But Akbar was known as a great speaker, Adi remembered. So why not ask him directly?

She meditated on him until his Mongol face began to slowly emerge on the screen. Adina was thrilled to see the mighty Mughal emperor of India.

"Your Majesty, I salute you," Adina said with respect and curiosity.

"May you live long, my daughter," the figure of Akbar the Great said, blessing her.

Adina was thrilled to see the robust emperor looking

at her with so much tenderness. "I am very grateful for your blessing, your majesty."

"What's your name?

"Adina."

"Adina? That means you have no religion.The word '*din*' means religion like in my religion *Din-e-ilahi*, the religion of truth." He shook his head. "I am just joking."

"I believe in your religion, your majesty. That's *no* joke. Your religion is simple and the best. It respects all beliefs."

"You are a girl of commonsense like I was, but I am not literate like you. Tell me what I can do for you."

"Your majesty, you made the tomb of Sheikh Salim Chishti. Many childless parents pray there. My nani believes in the power of prayers, and she might have come to pray there with her gift of a crown jewel. I am looking for that jewel."

"Dear Adina, the sheikh remained poor. He was not interested in any material possessions. He taught me to love all fellow humans. He understood the true meaning of *din*, kindness. He was our empire's greatest Sufi and so I honored him by building his tomb. People pray there and offer just a colorful thread. If you visit the tomb, you will see countless little colorful thread pieces tied to the tomb's screen, which people believe is sufficient offering to the saint to receive his blessings. Your nani has no reason to offer a jewel there. Ask me for anything else you want to know."

"You got a male heir, just as you wished when you honored the saint. My nani says that she wanted a girl, and so she is happy with my birth. Or did we misunderstand her real wish?"

"In my country, I tried very hard to stop people from wishing only for sons. I was aware of mothers poisoning their infant daughters to death. The whole world knows that widows were burnt alive in my country. I wanted to stop such inhumane practices. But many idiots resented me, hated me for my wish to ban such terrible acts."

"They say that your greatest wish was granted by the saint and so you named your first son after him. What other wishes did he grant? Some say you had one ambitious wish that you kept secret."

"Adina, I tried very hard to get that wish. But every thread has a limited length."

"Now I know the source of that quote. Can you tell me what that wish was?"

"That wish is no secret. The saint wanted me to expand my empire as much as possible, but with love. He believed in 'one world' and I failed to have even 'one India.' I don't want to talk about my biggest failure."

"Your majesty, you didn't fail. You made India a big beautiful country, attracting the whole world to it."

"In order to make 'one India,' I tried to convince those little Muslim and Hindu kings to join my empire. But some didn't care about India's unity, the world's unity. I fought some of them, for I wanted to dissolve all those little kingdoms. But I couldn't realize my dream."

"Your majesty, your dream has been realized by Sardar Patel. He dissolved those kingdoms and created one India—"

"No. Patel failed me. He agreed to the demands of those idiots and let them partition my country. My subjects will never get true happiness by the partition. Here I was thinking of 'one world,' and those narrow-minded leaders couldn't keep the 'one India' I gave them. They killed my dream, and they lied."

"But their dream was to free Bharat Mata. They achieved it."

"I never thought that Bharat could be mother. How could it be? *Bharat* is not a feminine word. My pandit told me that, since ancient times, Indians kept worshipping Prithivi Mata as the first female deity in the Puja. Prithivi is Earth. She is real deity unlike those millions of imaginary deities. Your nani's crown jewel must be found somewhere with her. Because, Earth is the Mata—the mother of all countries. Those who do not consider Mother Earth as the mother of us all humans are narrow-minded. The pandit said. But some are happy with the smaller piece of a longer thread. My dream was my country's ancient ideal: One World, One Mother Earth. I failed my pandit."

His voice sounded choked. She wanted to know the identity of the emperor's Hindu pundit.

"You are not illiterate. Your—" Before she could complete her sentence, the image on the screen disappeared.

Adina felt the load of pain in the voice of the mighty emperor. She also remembered the pain of his last heir, Bahadur Shah, who used his pen-name, Zafar, in his poems. Dada and Dadi love one of his *ghazals*. Its last bleeding line is deadly: *do gaz zamiin bhii na milii kuu-e-yaar me*—Not even two yards of ground was granted to me in my beloved's backyard.

The "ground" in that line refers to the burial place for him, and the "beloved's backyard" to his beloved country India.

He wrote this *ghazal* in his small jail cell in Yangon, Myanmar—formerly Rangoon, Burma. The British had exiled him there for leading the first 1857 Indian Independence War against their rule, the Raj. How painful that the last heir of the great Mughal Empire had no pen to write his poems in that jail! The only writing pad he had was the prison's wall, on which he wrote with his bleeding finger. His Dargah, or tomb, was in Yangon where he died.

Adina stood speechless for a few minutes. Then she closed her computer and decided to tell others that the illiterate Akbar was a visionary emperor, but his unwritten wish was misunderstood.

She remembered the rest of the story her dada had told her about Shab, who took a part-time job in a restaurant, which she thought was below her Mughal dignity. Somehow, she finished her PhD dissertation at Dada's university. Akbar would have been so proud of her for such a literate achievement, Adina thought, and she regretted forgetting to inform the emperor that Shab had realized his dream of 'one world' in her small way. She married an American, one of her classmates, who didn't look like the Mongol Akbar or the Indian *khichri*. She had a small family that looked like a *khichri*, the yellow Indian *"pilaf"* cooked in the USA.

CHAPTER 17

Mira's Miracles

Hari tuma haro jana kii piira
"God! You remove this person's pain."
(The first line of a prayer song of Mirabai)

Who was the greatest female saint of India at the time of Akbar the Great, Mughal emperor?

The question came to Adina as if out of the blue, but she found the answer easily. The name belonged to someone even the emperor respected, someone whose temples had been opened to the low-caste untouchables. Mirabai's guru Saint Raidas—Ravi Das—was an untouchable, and he used to address Princess Mirabai affectionately as Mira.

One Mira story that grew out of Dada's experience was very impressive to Adi. When Dada got his first job teaching in India, he began to look for top music scholars and artists. He found one brilliant elderly musician who had a lot of students in his college town. One of the young female students of this musician became a center of attraction in the town, not because she was very attractive, but because she would go into a trance occasionally, possessed by the spirit of Mira. The proof of her trance was her eyes shedding tears during Mira's song when played by the teacher.

Dada attended one such session. He told Adina he had a difficult time entering the jam-packed living room of the musician, even though the living room was as big as a hall. People sat outside the windows and the doors in the front and back. Dada found that there were people of different faiths among the audience. The tabla drummer was a Sikh and the singer was a Brahmin. Dada was moved. As the teacher sang "*paga ghungharuu baandha miiraa naachii,*" the student got up. Her eyes looked glazed, as if she was in a trance, but she was singing and dancing to her teacher's music. The crowd, too, seemed to be possessed. No one even clapped but remained solemn until the music and her tears stopped!

Dada, however, did not believe in many miracles that are said to be related to Mira. For example, when Mira died, he told Adi that no one could see her dead body. People there believed that her body was merged into Lord Krishna's form. For Dada, Mira was a real human being, a brave Rajput reformer fighting for social justice in her gentle ways and so the story did not ring true for him.

A few minutes before she sat down to meditate, Adina played Mira's most popular dance-song, "*paga ghungharuu baandha miiraa naachii.*" Though the song has several versions, the meaning is always the same. "Mira put ankle-bells on her feet and danced."

Two lines of this song were very moving for Adina. She hummed them.

One line was "*Saasa kahe Kula Naasii*—The mother-in-law calls her the destroyer of the family." The other line was "*Raanaa bhejyo bisa ko pyaalaa*—the Raja sent a cup of poison."

Mira's mother-in-law and brother-in-law, who was

Rana or Raja, decided to kill her. To Mira it was clear that not only men but women, too, supported the humiliating slavery of women.

She refused to commit *sati* when her husband Prince Bhoj Raj died a few years after their marriage. Instead, she began to dance in the streets, singing songs in praise of Krishna. In her poems she called Krishna her lord, lover, and husband. Soon after Rana offered her a sweet drink to honor her, and Mira drank it happily. She didn't die, even though the drink was mixed with poison. Immediately after that incident in her native Rajputana, now Rajasthan, she began to be revered, not because she was a princess of a Rajput dynasty but because she was as a miracle-maker.

Adina had several reasons to meditate on Mira, but mostly because of some similarities to Mira's life and Adina's parents' circumstances.

When, supported by her parents, Madhu sent the divorce notice to Dan, it was the darkest night of his life. The notice was like the poison, or *visha* (*bisa*), for Mira. The divorce notice had almost destroyed the *Kula,* or family, and in fact, at least two lives could have been destroyed utterly by this poison. Many husbands have committed suicide when falsely accused by their wives, and Adina knew her father could have gone to that extreme, especially when he couldn't bear watching his daughter's depression. Dan had told her he understood why Mira's prayer, "*Hari tuma haro jana kii piira*— Lord! You remove this person's pain," has given great hope to many so that they can overcome the pain inflicted by family members. That Adina had survived this long pain was a sort of miracle.

Adina was now wondering if, because Nani believed in the miracles of the saints, she visited the Mirabai temple of Chittorgarh. Adi knew that people pray for their wishes at this temple. What did Nani do at the temple in case she did enter it? Adina would rather check with Mira.

After the song was over, she meditated on Mira, which took considerable time. In the beginning Adina heard the song "*Hari tuma haro jana kii piira*—God, you remove this person's pain."

Adina kept meditating. As soon as the song was over, she heard the ankle-bells. She understood that Mira was coming, dancing. The lovely princess did come dancing while playing an *ektara*, a small string instrument. She came closer and closer to Adina.

Suddenly she stopped dancing. "My little girl. Why are you here alone?"

Adina calmly looked at Mira's bare feet and the ankle-bells tied above them. "Mai, I touch your feet with my eyes."

Mai Mira, or Mother Mira, seemed to be moved by Adina's devotion. "I bless you. What's your name?"

"Adina is my name. You can call me Adi. I feel the power of your blessing, Mai. My pain is gone."

Mira looked curious. "What pain?"

Adina told her story very briefly.

Mira told her that she never believed in such miracles. "Adi, your nani could not have gained anything by visiting my temple. Tell your parents that you are alive because they are alive. They will always be your parents, not some saints or deities."

"But my parents are not together. My mother wanted a divorce, not my father."

"Tell your father that he should feel happy that he is not in the company of the relatives who tried to harm him. My miracle was that I was able to leave my in-laws, but even then they kept lying about me. The court has recorded that your mother lied, and anybody can see that record. No one should believe what your mother and her relatives say about anything, henceforth. I respected my husband Prince Bhoj Raj, but my relatives thought that I didn't love him because I didn't burn myself on his funeral pyre. So they considered me a fallen wife. It is much the same—liars spreading untruths about those they should love and value."

"But in your poems you say that your husband was Lord Krishna. Can a deity be someone's husband? Is there any conflict, Mai?"

"No conflict. I had only one husband and that was Bhoj Raj. I saw Lord Krishna in him. That was my way to respect my husband. That way I became one with my husband forever. Otherwise his premature death would have tormented me throughout my life. In my poems, I did say that my husband was Krishna, but a poetic device can save your life. My times were very bad culturally because relatives didn't care for a widow in her helplessness, but I always said to them, 'How can I be a *sati* when my husband Krishna is alive! How can I be a widow!' The lord is immortal as I call him *abinaasii* in my poems."

"Mai, did you write all those poems?"

"Not all of them. I started first in my own dialect of Rajasthani. Then I went to Mathura. There I wrote in their local dialect, Braj Hindi. When I moved to Dwaraka, I wrote in Gujarati. My admirers keep adding more poems under my name, however, and many even altered what I had written originally. But that goes on. I have no control over that tradition."

"You are known to break traditions, though," Adina reminded her. "You successfully stopped the burning of a live woman on her husband's funeral pyre. You didn't cover your head because, you said, 'If men can go around with uncovered heads, why can't women? If men can

dance in the streets why can't women?' By your own example you opened a new chapter in women's rights. Even
if you had called Krishna your second husband, I would
take it as a widow's right to remarry. If men can have
several wives, why can't a widow have another husband?
Some of your male relatives had several wives at once.
But let me ask you one more question. Why did you
choose an untouchable low-caste man for your spiritual
teacher?"

Mira smiled. "Now you can say that I broke a harmful
tradition. I wanted equal rights. You think that I was for
women's rights, but I was for equal rights for all men and
women. No one should have special favors. My untouchable guru, Raidas, deserves the same treatment as any
learned Brahmin or Rajput man. We don't know how
many wise people we lost because of the criminal caste-
system."

Then Adi told Mira the story of the musician and his
student who was possessed by Mira.

"I don't possess anyone. Her trance is simply my ad-
mirer's extreme attachment to me, which happens for
various reasons. Some consider me a saint, some a sing-
er-dancer-poet, and some just a woman fighting against
the bad traditions of those times. I am just like any other
woman who was victimized by those very relatives
whose dharma was to protect me. Who knows? Perhaps
that possessed girl was a victim, too. I suspect her tears
released her deep-seated pain."

"Mai, Dada says that anyone who knows your story
hates your relatives, and yet you didn't take any personal
revenge. Instead, you chose a career that might inspire
others to do good for humanity. Do you have any message for the world?"

"Fight to protect innocent victims."

Adina looked again at Mira's bare feet, which were

moving rhythmically, as if dancing. Tears forced her to close her eyes.

Strangely, she kept on hearing Mira's voice. "Adi, it's the music and dance that alters consciousness. Read '*pa-ga ghungharuu baandha miiraa naachii*' with no music and dance, no possibility of possession. Then sing the song and dance with it. You and the audience seem to feel my spirit. Anything becomes candy when mixed with sugar. So does *kirtan* or any religious singing when mixed with music and dance. There is no such thing as spiritual experience. I want to tell you again. I, Mira, did not possess that woman. Open your eyes. Open your eyes…"

Adina did open them, but there was nothing on her computer screen. It had shut down when her eyes were closed. Nevertheless, she remembered Mira's last words, which she heard clearly even though they were somewhat faint. "Music and dance came before the origin of words."

CHAPTER 18

The Grabber's Eclipsed Rights

Raahave namaḥ "Salutations to Rahu"
(The mantra for greeting Rahu)

The Hindu Planetary *Puja* had two main purposes. It removed bad *karma* and improved good *karma*. On Dada's birthday, his father performed this *Puja* to brighten Dada's future. Among the nine *grahas,* or planets, two planets were very well-known to darken destiny. They were Saturn and Rahu.

Dada told Adina that Saturn made sense, as anyone could observe it, but he questioned his father if there was any such planet like Rahu. For proof her great-grandpa would resort to the story of Rahu. Adina thought about that story, wondering if Rahu had any connection to her crown jewel, for she knew that Nani too believed in the powers of the planets. And in order to please a planet the believer has to offer a gift. Rahu was the most dangerous *graha* for he could grab your future as his name meant Grabber. Such expressions were commonplace in India: "*Meri kismat me Rahu lag gaya hai*—Rahu has eclipsed my luck."

Adi knew that, according the story, Rahu was the most dangerous, even though he was the least powerful planetary deity because of his foul demon mouth.

Even foul-mouthed demons could be worshipped, which Adi knew the Rahu story revealed. The gods never thought of this possibility. They wanted to destroy all the demons, but the constant battle between the two enemies didn't achieve victory for either party. Finally, both parties decided to churn the cosmic ocean together for their common good. One of the fourteen extraordinary gains that came out of this churning was *amrita*, the immortalizing drink.

That drink became a serious threat to the survival of both gods and demons. The future physician of the gods, Dhanvantari, emerged out of that churning holding the immortalizing ambrosia in a pot. The pot was called *amrita kalasha*. When the gods and demons heard this news, they began to quarrel again. Every one of them wanted to be immortal. The gods were very concerned. They wouldn't tolerate even one demon's immortality. While the two parties were engaged in their battle of words, an extraordinarily beautiful woman appeared in front of them. Some demons were instantly enchanted by her magical beauty. The gods, too, got excited by her charm. There was silence until she addressed them all.

"Gods and demons!" she said in her sweet voice. "Don't fight for the drink. I will distribute that drink equally. Just form two rows, one for demons and one for gods."

So the gods and demons sat in two separate rows facing each other. She started first with the gods' row. At the end, she came close to two gods, the Sun and the Moon. A god was sitting next to them whom they exposed as a demon in disguise, but Mohini had already served the demon a few sips. Nevertheless, she got her concealed disc weapon and beheaded the demon, who was Rahu. His head and torso rolled down dead, but within seconds both parts got up. The head pursued the Sun and the Moon and grabbed them. After some struggle, the two gods managed to shove Rahu away. The head cursed the two deities and promised to take revenge when he got an opportunity. Rahu does get such an opportunity occasionally. Sometimes he grabs the Sun and at others the Moon and temporarily overpowers them, but they soon get up and gradually drive Rahu away. This attack of Rahu causes eclipse of the Sun and the Moon.

No other demon except Rahu received the drink for Mohini disappeared with the pot of *amrita* after the last god was served. But as she was flying away, some drops of the drink fell in four places: Haridwar, Prayag, Ujjain, and Nashik. Each of these holy cities celebrates a "pitcher fair" known as *kumbh mela* every twelfth year. The "mega pitcher fair" known as the *Maha Kumbh Mela* of Prayag—Allahabad—at the confluence of the Ganges and Yamuna rivers held the record for the largest gathering in the world. Pilgrims made the majority of the visitors. They took a holy dip, assuming that some residue of the *amrita* may be in those waters.

Adina thought of this story as the basis for her meditation on Rahu, who has the status of two planets. The head is the Rahu planet and the torso is Ketu. The head has the mouth, which makes it the obvious selection for *darshan*. Adina was not afraid of watching Rahu's head talking. In fact, she thought of Rahu as an animated figure like in the Disney cartoons. But for her this was not entertainment. She was looking for the crown. *Who knows?* she thought, *Nani's gift might have pleased Rahu and he granted her wish! Demon worship can also be fruitful.*

Adina gazed at the head of Rahu as shown in astrological literature until his head slowly rolled toward her. His face was quite pleasant, as he was smiling.

He started talking. "Dear little girl. How are you?"

"Namaste, your holiness. I am thrilled to see you. My name is Adina."

"May you be richer and richer." Rahu seemed to understand the meaning of Adina's name. "What's your need?"

Adina told him about her search for the crown jewel and the story related to it.

"Adina, I do have a crown but not yours. But let me ask you a question. Are you sure that it's a crown? Could it be a necklace or a bracelet or a finger ring? I am asking this because my other half, Ketu, might have a gift like that. You have to check with him."

"No, sir. It is definitely a crown. Since you have given me your honest answer, I am not disappointed. I also wondered why the Sun and the Moon called you dishonest. I hope you are not offended by what I have said."

"Dear Adina, the gods never realize that they are crooks. You know they had a plan to deprive us demons. Our fight was for equal rights. Ethnic equality, I mean. But would you like to know what a liar that sweet good-looking woman was? She charmed us all, but she did not have the ethical guts to tell us that she had changed her sex. She was Vishnu and kept a concealed weapon. That's cowardice. That's cheating. She had no right to behead me and make me divided. I could not stop her. I was defenseless. The Sun and the Moon accused me. I had no complaints against them, but they complained against me. The three wanted to discriminate against me even unto making me non-existent. Yet religious people condemn me but not that violent Mohini. They praise Mohini as an avatar when in truth that enchantress is a thief who ran away with the joint property of gods and demons. It's a shame a liar and a robber is favored. Her dropping of the *amrita* is celebrated at the Maha Kumbh Mela. Now do you understand why I was forced to become a grabber?"

He didn't wait for Adina's answer. The screen became completely dark. Adina tried very hard to see Rahu's head, but she had no luck. She began to feel dizzy as though she were running through the sky at supersonic speed.

Finally, she landed at Allahabad, right at the *sangam*, the confluence of Ganga and Yamuna. These two holy rivers made her happy. They originated in her ancestral Himalayas. Adina saw millions of people were at the confluence and knew it was the Maha Kumbh Mela of Prayag. She watched a huge procession led by the Naga sadhus, these nude, ash-smeared monks. They were raising their hands to give blessings to the people who were following them. The Allahabad winter didn't seem to bother anyone. She thought she might be crushed between them, but she flew through the air again and landed a block away, where women were cooking and distributing free meals.

There she saw white sadhus with Indian sadhus, black sadhus, and Chinese-looking sadhus. A few drummers and dancers were chanting, "*Kare Krishna Hare Krishna.*" She walked across the street where she saw a booth of religious books. In front of the booth, the shopkeeper was talking to a young white man.

"You are from America?" the shopkeeper guessed.

"Yes," the young man said.

"Welcome to our *Mela*. You have joined the biggest 'meeting' of humanity in our city of God. That's what Allahabad stands for. Are you comfortable in such a crowd?"

"Yes. I am delighted to see such a large fair that is so well organized."

"Courtesy of our great mayor Rita Joshi. This is the most prestigious city of India. Six prime ministers of India called it home."

"I know two of them. Nehru and his daughter Indira."

"Did you know that this city is the birthplace of India's greatest film star?"

"Of course. Everybody knows Amitabh Bachchan."

The happy shopkeeper shook hands with the young man. "So, beside the *Mela,* what is your interest in India?"

"I want to learn genuine meditation technique."

"Did you know Maharishi Mahesh Yogi was educated here, at the University of Allahabad?"

"No wonder he was a big believer in God."

The shopkeeper laughed. "The university taught him physics. This university is not a Madrasa or an Ashram."

The American also laughed. "But he mixed physics and religion. Many in America thought that he was converting his TM practitioners to Hinduism."

"I get your point. Here, too, many think of him as a person with a double life. Everybody is the confluence of honesty and lying, just like the water of the Ganga is white and the water of the Yamuna is dark. Whatever might have been the case for the Maharishi, his TM technique is very effective."

"I heard that the *darshan* technique is much easier. My aim is to compare several techniques. I saw many sadhus at this fair who are claiming their techniques are better."

"The *darshan* technique is also of several kinds, but be careful. Anybody charging you for teaching meditation is simply running a business. Let me ask you a different question. Have you taken a dip at the *sangam*?"

"Not yet. There are too many people there. I may have to go a little farther down for a bath in the river."

"No, you must take a dip at the *sangam*. That's where

Mohini dropped the *amrita*. Let me take you through the crowd."

At that point, Adina felt a jerk. She closed her eyes, and, when she looked at the screen a few minutes later, there was nothing.

CHAPTER 19

Lakshmi's Testimony

Lakshmyai namaḥ "Salutations to Lakshmi"
(A mantra for Lakshmi)

Rahu's anger sounded genuine to Adina. He was proof that a god might appear good but could be cruel in his actions. An avatar of Vishnu, Mohini the enchantress turned out to be very unfair. A mediator or judge should remain impartial, but Mohini lied. She pretended to be a woman. A sex-change in order to cheat someone was a crime. She did not distribute the ambrosia equally among gods and demons, though she promised she would. And worse, she beheaded Rahu with a concealed weapon.

That's also a bloody crime, Adina thought. *Now, the more important question is how safe Lakshmi feels with her husband Vishnu. Does he bully his wife? No other goddess has that many jewels. Gods gave them to her as gifts. Human devotees also follow that gift-giving tradition, mainly for their own prosperity for Lakshmi is Prosperity. Does Vishnu steal her jewels and give them to his supporters secretly?*

Adina wanted to know all about these secret acts of Vishnu. The story that Goddess Lakshmi came out of the famous churning was not enough. Adina needed to check with Lakshmi herself, and maybe the goddess might have the crown jewel.

Adina had little trouble meditating on Lakshmi. In the picture before her, the lovely goddess was seated on a lotus, and Adina remembered that she was also known as Kamala, the lotus goddess. She rose up from the lotus and came closer to Adina.

"Dear Adina, I bless you with prosperity."

"*Pranam*, Mother. How do you know my name?"

"My husband Vishnu and I know everything. There is no need to tell me about your case. You have come here to know if I have your nani's gift. There was no such gift left with me."

"I have talked to Vishnu, and he told me all sorts of philosophical things about his reality, very different things. But you are calling him your husband. I believe you. You are his wife. In that case, I have another query. Why were you given to Vishnu by the gods, why not other wonders that came out of the famous churning?"

"Dear Adina, I was not offered. I chose Vishnu of my free will. I went to him after I had seen other gods. They all gave me gifts. With their clothing and ornaments, I looked a real beauty. That's how my name became Lakshmi, the shining beauty. But I didn't care for gods' gifts. Each god thought that I would favor him. None of them was good looking to me. Some gods did not even know how to dress up properly. Shiva had nothing on his body except a tiger skin, and he had a blue mark on his throat. That was because he drank all the black poison from the churning just before I came, thanks to his kindness. Otherwise, all of existence was endangered. He was the first god who cared for a clean environment. But I was looking for a real handsome husband. Brahma had four heads. I would not have had a chance to talk to him. And even worse, he had married his own daughter, Sarasvati. Then I moved toward Vishnu, and I was stunned. He didn't even look at me because he was too busy with other more important matters of the churning."

"Were you not already the best matter from the churning, Ma?"

"The best matter came at the end. It was *amrita*, the 'ambrosia' to make every god immortal."

"Ah, that brings my next point. Ma, I have to tell you about my encounter with Rahu."

"Before you say anything, I can tell you that my husband did the right thing. The demons are violent. They learn only when they face force."

"But what Rahu faced was a charming beauty, claiming to be fair to both parties. Then she killed him with a concealed weapon. Ma, even humans are not punishing murderers with death. Many countries have abolished death penalty. What's wrong with gods?"

"Dear Adina, your concern is understandable. I don't support violence. My goal is to make humans rich."

"There also I see complaints. Some rich people have honored you most. They have built temples to make them look honest. In fact, many of your wealthiest devotees go to the Badrinath temple in my ancestral area. The slum people, whose families are struggling, also worship you during the Diwali festival of lights."

"That's very sad. My message is that to work hard is to perform true worship, but my ideal is to keep family harmony. Both parents must teach their children the value of a good work ethic and honesty. If one parent is unethical, the child can still be vulnerable. As a wife and mother, I maintain these ideals. I support my husband, no matter what Rahu has said. I am with my—"

Adina's eyes were filled with tears as she interrupted. "The rest is clear to me, Ma. How often do you spend time with your family members?"

"Ah, you seem to know my problems. I, too, feel sorry that I don't get enough time to spend with them. The reason is very obvious. My husband and I are dedicated to public service. I have to attend the *Puja* services of my faithful devotees. I am invited even with other deities. The worshippers don't want me to leave their homes when the *Puja* is over. When the *Puja* ends, they bid farewell to all the deities except me, Sarasvati, and Kubera. Sarasvati doesn't care to return but I do. Her husband Brahma is always busy with his children, grandchildren, great-grandchildren, and so on. Brahma's four tongues are enough to entertain his large family. But my family is small. It needs my company most."

"Why does Brahma need such a large family?"

"That's a good question. You will have to find out from him. Why such biodiversity? I found out that Vishnu followed his advice regarding churning the ocean. We all respect him as *Pitamaha*, 'grandpa' of all. So he fulfills the wishes of anyone, even the demons, which is how the demons become powerful and attack gods. His reasoning is funny for favoring demons. He says, 'Oh, they are my spoiled children, and every child needs fatherly care.' No doubt some demons are really nice."

"Did you mention Kubera?"

"Yes, Kubera is worshipped as a *dikpala*, a direction protector. He guards one of the ten cosmic directions. That's a big honor for a demon."

"But Dada and Dadi told me that he was a king of my ancestral area and his Himalayan capital was Alaka."

"What is important for you to know is that all demons are not our adversaries. Gods have been very democratic. They offer key positions to good demons. Kubera doesn't behave like a *rakshasa*. He has a proven record of being a dignified demon. He deserved to be the gods' secretary of treasury. I like him. That demon cooperates with me. We both want everyone to be prosperous."

"You have made it very clear why the worshippers want you and Kubera to stay in their homes together, which is a good example of gender equality and of gender freedom. I have never seen you or any goddess keeping veils while seated beside other gods."

"Adina, don't forget that, among the ten *dikpalas,* one is a demoness, Nirṛti. Don't forget that Rahu is also included in the planetary *Puja* even though he lost his original body—Hold on, Adina, I hear Kubera's call." Lakshmi looked around. "Yes, it's him. I have to go. Some devotees are starting a Puja. I bless you. May you be prosperous." Lakhsmi then disappeared and the white screen had nothing on it anymore.

CHAPTER 20

The Divine Who the First Grandpa

Kasmai devaaya havishaa vidhema
"Which deity do we offer homage?"
(A mantra for the homage of *Ka*, the god of "creation")

A question could become productive without an answer, as Adi had learned. Dada's favorite ancient example was this Vedic mantra: "Who is that god whom we are offering homage?" For many this meant, "We are offering homage to Brahma." They thought the *Ka* "Who?" was the name of Prajapati in the mantra. Brahma could fulfill wishes of all because he was the progenitor of all, the Prajapati. No wonder he was admired as grandpa, *Pitamaha*.

Lakshmi had created even more confusion for Adi because she made fun of Brahma's large family, not to mention his marriage with his own daughter. She also told how her husband Vishnu followed Brahma's advice to churn the ocean, which produced fourteen jewels and Lakshmi was one of them. And she ridiculed his four heads. *Does Brahma really have four heads?* Adina wondered. *That kind of figure would look very scary.*

Nevertheless, Adina became very much interested in knowing why he had such a large family. Lakshmi had suggested that Adina should ask the grandpa of all directly. Maybe he would know where Nani's crown jewel went as well.

So she meditated on Brahma. The first time she failed, and the second time she failed. Then she waited another week. Early on the Sunday morning of that week, she decided not to eat her breakfast. She opened her computer and meditated on the *Puja* picture of the four-headed god of creation.

Very shortly, the god appeared. "Adina, I am Brahma. I bless you, my child."

He was all wet. Adina couldn't believe he was Brahma for he had only one head.

"Salutations to you Pitamaha," she responded humbly. "I was expecting to see you with four heads. You have only one head and you are wet. Was my meditation faulty in any way, Pitamaha?"

"Your meditation was not faulty, but you have been remembering all sorts of stories about my origin."

"I liked one of your stories very much. That one says that you didn't know your origin. You thought that you came out of water, and so you have been searching and searching for your roots in the cosmic ocean. You began to look all around, which is how you evolved four heads. But you did not discover your roots there, and, with much frustration, you started the creation billions of years ago. Gradually, you created all the beings, and thus you are our grandpa, our Pitamaha. You evolved my ancient ancestors from water."

"That is why I am still wet. Had you thought of my primordial origin, then you would not have succeeded in your meditation. Thinkers of ancient times knew who I was, but I left them guessing my name. Actually, they tried to sense my identity. I was the Shining Embryo, the Cosmic Egg, and many other poetic names."

"Can I ask you then how you were created?"

"Nobody created me. All those creation stories are just myths. Brahma's real name is *Svayambhū*, Self-Born. No god created the cosmic egg, which is the only egg that has no chicken first. This self-born egg is rightly called Brahma's Egg, *Brahmaṇḍa*. Thousands of years ago the wise thinkers said that the creation is self-born, *Svayambhū*."

"So you are the chicken and you are the egg!"

"Good. Vishnu is neither the chicken nor the egg. Just ignore what Lakshmi says. I never came out of her husband's navel. Her story is good entertainment for children. Isn't that funny that I am emerging from Vishnu's belly while his wife is doing nothing? She was born when the churning of the ocean was started on my advice. Why did she marry him? Doesn't she love to remain seated in this and that household? That's not public service!"

Adina had a hard time not laughing. Then she told Brahma a story that she had heard from Dada. In his youth, Dada saw smoke rising from a house across his village on the Diwali night. The owners of that house had worshipped Lakshmi. Then they participated in the ceremony of fireworks. These fireworks were very similar to the Fourth of July fireworks on America's Independence Day. After the fireworks, everybody was given sweets as the sacred food. This *Prasad* was considered Lakshmi's blessing of prosperity.

The family of that house suddenly awoke shouting, "Fire! Fire!"

Neighbors came to help, but the whole house burned down and the big beautiful icon of Lakshmi was all charred.

Adina remembered Dada's story of Lakshmi and his

ancestral town, where there was a temple of Lakshmi-Narayana on the highest hilltop. There a Lakshmi Puja was celebrated on the first morning of Diwali. The main attraction of the temple was the beautiful statues of Lakshmi and her husband Narayana—Vishnu. It was believed that they were made of solid gold. The statues could be viewed easily from the wide-open entrance of the temple. The entrance was accessed after climbing dozens of stone steps.

The following year on the morning of Diwali, the *Puja* was once again taking place inside the Lakshmi-Narayana temple. A small bonfire near its first step spread all over, including to the site of the *Puja*. In front of the bonfire stood the head of the family whose house was burned down last year. With other family members he was shouting, "Lakshmi Puja, Hai, hai—Worship of Lakshmi, pain, pain." After each shout he threw a page of the holy book, called *Lakshmi Puja,* into the fire.

When the smoke reached inside the temple, the priest came to where the holy book was being burned page by page and asked the man what he was doing. The man told the priest that he was offering oblations to Goddess Lakshmi. The priest understood and said, with a disgusting look on his face, "You may burn a holy book here. Nobody is going to burn you. Your protest has no value. The government is not going to ban the holy book."

Brahma smiled after he heard this story. "Adina, the priest should have also told the book-burner that Lakshmi was safe in his neighbor's house. You know the other name of Lakshmi?"

"What is it?" Adina looked curious.

"*Chanchalaa*. Flaky. She never stays in one house. Not even with Vishnu. He is happy with his other wife, too. Her Vedic name is Shrī."

"Now I understand why Lakshmi looked slightly uncomfortable when she revealed that you had fulfilled the wishes of all, even the wishes of corrupt and evil ones. You have no hand in fulfilling Vishnu's wish either, I guess."

"I fill no wishes. My job is to evolve life after life, beings and beings. Every being has a limited life, and indeed I will also collapse after billions of years. I have given freedom to every being regarding how to conduct its life. I don't dictate. I don't decide. This is why I have a very few temples whereas Lakshmi is so popular. How many Bollywood movies are inaugurated glorifying me?"

"They should. If the moviemakers are themselves productions of Pitamaha, then they should be thankful to that creator for their movie productions. Don't worry for lay people, Pitamaha. The scientists are dedicated to respecting you. It's very fortunate for me to hear about the truth of creation from our creator. Long life of billions of years to your creation and you! But I am still wondering why you have appeared to me with one head when I was hoping for four heads."

"Seeing me with four heads might have scared you and disturbed your attention. Otherwise, I have countless heads. For one-on-one conversation, I use just one head, but never discount my other heads and their voices."

"Pitamaha, it was nice to see you with one head only on this little screen."

"Make a note. All my heads say this with a unified voice: No gods created your babies ever. If they did, then why do some behave like demons?"

"Is it not true that demons too are your creation?"

Suddenly the screen filled with smoke and Brahma was no longer visible. She heard repeatedly in the background the famous prayer mantra of the *Rig Veda*:

"*Kasmai devaaya havishaa vidhema*—which shining entity are we offering the fiery oblation?"

CHAPTER 21

Karttikeya's Six Mysterious Headlines

Skandaaya namaḥ "Salutations to Skanda."
(A mantra for Karttikeya)

The most important deity in any auspicious Hindu ceremony was Ganesha, but the Lord Karttikeya, the first child of Shiva and Parvati and the god of war, was even more important, though worship of him was not as popular.

Once upon a time, there was complete destruction of heaven. The demon Taraka and his soldiers had stolen and sold some of the heavenly treasures. Indra's horse Uchchaishravas was even grabbed by Taraka. This was a very special horse because he came out of the famous Ocean Churning, the *samudra-manthana*. With his tall antenna-like ears, as his name suggests, he could detect noises coming from miles away and alert Indra of any danger.

Taraka forced Kubera to contribute the gods' wealth for supporting the demon army, and Lord Kubera, a demon himself, was now a helpless treasurer of the gods. Indra was no more the king of heaven.

Adina had asked all of her grandparents this baffling question. "Why does Brahma try to please his bad children, their bad children, and on and on?"

Taraka, like other demons, knew that his first ancestor, Brahma, could fulfill his ambition of ruling heaven, earth, and below the earth, which was *Patala,* nether world. Not only that desire but also the desire of remaining immortal became Taraka's goal. So he decided to fast, which pleased Brahma, the Pitamaha of all. Known as a fair granddaddy, Brahma rewards any of his descendants who give him respect.

"Son, here I am," said Granddaddy Brahma to Taraka when he appeared before him. "What can I do for you, son?"

Taraka asked to grant him those two desires. "I want to be the absolute monarch and I want nobody to be able to kill me. These are my two wishes, Pitamaha."

"Yes, you will be the ruler of the triple world, son." But the tricky granddaddy hesitated to give him immortality. "You cannot be killed," he said to Taraka. "A very powerful being like Shiva's son could be a danger to your life, but you don't need to worry. There is no possibility of Shiva having such a son."

Taraka was happy. Shiva had no wife and would never have any child. Sati, Shiva's wife, had already committed suicide by self-immolation, and, after her death Shiva took a vow not to remarry.

But Taraka didn't realize that all vows were breakable, and even gods were no exception. Brahma understood. The gods understood. They began to wish for a son of Shiva when Taraka raised a war against them and routed them out of heaven. They began to look for a beautiful girl of marriageable age whom Shiva might choose as his wife.

The problem was that Shiva had become a Yogi in the

Himalayas, but exactly where nobody knew because he kept roaming and remembering Sati.

Then, one day, he was passing through the place where an extremely beautiful young Himalayan princess named Parvati was engaged in taking a vow to marry Shiva. He noticed her and felt good about her.

"Why did she look good to a Yogi?" Shiva asked himself. Then he realized that Kama, the god of love, had made Parvati look even better than Sati at that time. Shiva was infuriated by Lord Kama's magical trick and burned Kama to death instantly by emitting fire from his third eye.

The news of Kama's death immediately reached his wife Rati, who came to meet Shiva and began to wail. Shiva found out from her that Kama was requested to play this trick by the gods, and so he forgave Kama and revived him instantly. Rati was very grateful to Lord Shiva.

This event made it clear to Parvati that Shiva didn't want to accept her love, and she went on a hunger-strike. She had abandoned all food, refusing to eat so much as a single fern. So her parents, Himalaya and Mena, began to call her Aparna, one without a *parṇa,* or fern.

Lord Shiva was kind by nature, and when he found out about Parvati's hunger-strike, her devotion moved him. "What if, like Sati, she committed suicide because of her love for me," he asked. So he married her.

Their first son was named Karttikeya, so named because he was raised by the six Pleiades sisters, the *Krittika* nurses. Each nurse gave the little boy such good care that he grew six heads, one in honor of each nurse. So Karttikeya was also called Shaṇmukha, the one with six mouths. When he became an adult, he challenged Taraka and there was a terrible war between gods and demons. Karttikeya routed all the demons out of heaven and the earth and reinstated Indra as the ruler of heaven. The demons had destroyed the heaven, but Karttikeya restored it as it was before. He fulfilled the wish of the gods. Since then, everyone believed that Lord Karttikeya could grant any wish.

Adina was aware of this story and so meditated on Lord Karttikeya. The screen showed Lord Karttikeya seated on a throne. Each of his six heads had a crown and he was scolding a big group of men.

"You liars! Ever thought of getting your heads examined? I will break your heads because you broke six civilized principles of marital life."

Adina heard those six principles from his six mouths, one by one: "Don't take marriage vows if you have any intention to break them. Break the vows decently if you have any intention to break them later. Never lie to break the trust of your family members, especially the trust of your children. If you do, they will have nothing to do with you some day. Respect the equal rights of the falsely accused and abused family members, and keep improving your ethical conduct."

Then the screen changed and Adi saw a queen-like goddess sitting on a throne. Adina recognized her as the powerful commander of Karttikeya, Devasena, the wife of Karttikeya. Adina saw her beating many women who didn't look like demonesses. It bothered Adina that this woman was bullying other helpless women. She would rather see Lord Karttikeya on her screen again.

She heard his voice coming from behind the screen. "Devasena, a case of six liars has come before me just now. I am going to attend to this case."

The lord did appear on the screen, but with only one head. The crowd of men was no longer there. Adina was puzzled about the case of the six liars. Who could they be? She decided to ignore the case altogether. The good thing she felt was that she could now comfortably start one-on-one conversation on her own case.

"Pranam, Lord Subrahmaṇya," Adina said to show her respect.

"Ashish, my baby. You pronounced my difficult name so well. I am impressed." The lord then pronounced his blessing for her in Sanskrit.

"My dada and dadi have taught me many of your names. They told me that in India Karttikeya is more popular in the north and Murugan is more in the south. And one *Purāṇa* scripture is named after your name *Skanda*."

"You are so well-informed. And so am I. Your purpose for meeting with me is already known to me. I have no crown from your nani."

Adi smiled. "How did you know my purpose? I have not given you even my name yet."

"Adina, why do you think I have six brains?" The lord laughed and Adina did too. "Adi, with my six brains, I understood every strategy of the demons and was able to decimate them. Here are some examples."

The picture on the screen changed to that of a war zone and a duel between Taraka and Karttikeya that was full of tricks and fierce strikes. She thought that the lord could be hurt when other demons surrounded him. She didn't want to watch and requested that the lord to stop the war scene. "Lord, did you get hurt? I was scared for you."

Karttikeya laughed. "Those demons had no idea that Devasena was going to surround them. She slaughtered all the demons."

"Lord, why was Ma Devasena beating those women? They were not demons," Adina interrupted.

"Those women were worse than demons, for they falsely accused their husbands and made their lives miserable. I also was mad at those husbands you saw me scolding. They also made their wives miserable. Some used to beat their helpless wives and some gave no child support. Some never cared to meet their children after the divorce. The result was that many fatherless children became hardcore criminals. These men and women destroyed their heavens—the family. The justice system failed to do justice, and so Devasena and I are going to fix these criminals."

Adina's eyes were filled with tears. "I understand what you mean, my lord."

"Adi, these men and women had taken vows as spouses to love each other, to live for each other. Then they lied to destroy each other and also destroyed their children in the process. In spite of being documented liars, they preached ethical conduct to their children. I understand your tears." The lord then remained silent as he saw more tears begin to flow from Adina's eyes.

When Adina managed to compose herself, the lord continued. "Let me give you a story of honest vows. You already know that my father Shiva was not interested in a second marriage, but when he heard of my mother's vow to marry him, he decided to test her honesty. He secretly sent a monk to meet her. The monk saw Parvati, frail and eating nothing, just living on water. He politely began to talk to her, trying to dissuade her from her vow of marrying Shiva. Parvati told him that she was firmly set on her vow. Then the monk exposed Shiva as an improperly dressed man with no money to take care of his wife. Parvati told him that she was not interested in his clothing or wealth, but wanted to marry him out of love. Then that monk uttered some bad words against Shiva, allegations Parvati could not stand. She began to walk away, but she was stopped by the monk who had held her hand firmly, an uncivilized act. Parvati wanted to move ahead but could not move, as she immediately recognized that the monk was Shiva himself. The great poet Kalidasa describes this first meeting in these words, 'The daughter of the mountain king did not move, did not stay.' She was thrilled to be held by the very spouse she had prayed for. My parents were married, vowing to remain together forever. Devasena and I take my parents as our model spouses. Your mother's parents didn't teach your mother our values. They helped her do the opposite. They sought more help from others to do the opposite. All of that is in the records."

Adina had tears in her eyes again as she heard him saying, "You deserved better family care, my dear Adi!"

When she wiped her tears she saw a blank screen. After she composed herself, she began to guess the case of the six liars the lord had mentioned to Devasena.

She also wanted to check with Devasena directly. Childless women did a ritual to please this goddess, she remembered, but Adi was certain she would have told her husband if she had received Nani's gift.

CHAPTER 22

Interviewing Real Arundhati

Arundhatiim pashya
"Look at Arundhati."

The most celebrated wife in the standard Hindu wedding was Arundhati. Her husband was the sage Vasishtha, and the Morning Star represents her. Her husband was represented in the *Saptarshi Mandala,* or the group of seven stars—Big Dipper. Six sages traveled with Vasishtha, but Arundhati was always by her husband's side.

It was mandatory in the performance of traditional Hindu weddings to highlight the stability of marriage. After all the vows taken by the bride and the bridegroom at the altar, the highest vow was not in big words but in high looks. The bridegroom led his bride out in the open, just the two of them under the vast sky, and then the groom scanned the heavens. When he located Arundhati, he requested of his bride, "Look at Arundhati!"

Her gaze followed the direction of his raised index finger and she then fixed her gaze on Arundhati. She promised by her gaze alone that she would be with him forever just as Arundhati was with Vasishtha. This was the highest vow of the wedding ceremony, and Adi always found it very moving.

The sky becomes the limit of the sincere feelings of the two for each other.

Goddess Arundhati had counseled many wives to hold to their marriage vows like she did and stand by their husbands. She also counseled Shiva to marry Parvati after his wife Sati died by self-immolation. For a long time, Shiva carried Sati's dead body along with him. *Unfortunately, Sati had no child, but she could have consulted Arundhati*, Adina mused as she pondered this story. On the other hand, Lord Rama banished his faithful wife Sita from his capital, Ayodhya. Sita was pregnant with Rama's son Lava. Arundhati counseled Rama, too, to bring Sita back with honor.

Adina knew that childless women in India had a special *vrata* ceremony to worship Arundhati, and she thought it possible that Nani's priest offered the crown jewel in a *Puja* of Arundhati.

With this awareness, Adina meditated. Before Goddess Arundhati appeared, the screen began to emit a soft light all around, but Adina steadily kept her eyes open until she saw Arundhati emerge on the screen.

"Pranam, Ma. You are our Morning Star, the best one," Adina said, trying to show happiness through her gaze at the goddess.

"Live long, my dear child. Tell me about you."

Adina slowly but firmly told her who she was and why she wanted to see her. The main question this time was if that women's *vrata* was true.

"Adi, all children come as gifts of nature to their parents. I do not accept such gifts as you have mentioned, and so your nani's gift could not have come to me. She doesn't seem to respect me. If she had, then why didn't she teach her daughter to stand by her husband?" Arundhati asked in a firm voice.

"Not only Nani but Nana also supported her act of filing for divorce, and with false allegations."

"When they say that they have a religion, then they indeed have a religion," Arundhati said in an even-more-strained tone. "It is inhuman when a childless couple has a baby and then a jealous spouse goes on to break the child's bond with the other parent. It is even worse when the justice system rewards the vicious spouse. One should be very careful when choosing a spouse to raise a family."

"Did you encourage Shiva to choose Parvati for a son?"

"The gods wanted him to have a son. I thought that Parvati would be the best mother of his son."

"But Shiva didn't want to marry a second time. Isn't it unfair to change his vow?"

"Shiva had no wife. It was perfectly right for Shiva to have another wife, but not to have wives," Arundhati said.

Adina laughed.

The goddess frowned, as if to be certain that Adina understood her objection to polygamy, "What makes you laugh, Adina?"

"I thought you might like to hear another Shiva story. We have a family friend whose wife died, in spite of the best medical treatment in Texas. We were told that she was a big devotee of Shiva. Why then did Lord Shiva let her die so early? Her husband was not worried about this question. Like Shiva, he also told friends that he would never marry again, and his friends understood his vow to be firm. But then, like Shiva, he remarried a year later. He could have two wives at the same time just like his grandfather had if he were in India, but American law does not allow any man to have two wives at the same time."

The goddess also laughed. "The gods do allow more than one wife, but my husband, sage Vasishtha, has just me. However, several sages are like savages."

"Ma, your husband should also be looked to for a stable marriage," Adina said seriously.

"I agree with you, Adi. There should be equal respect for husband and wife."

Now Adina felt sad. "Respect was the problem in my family. How can others give you respect if one spouse humiliates the other openly?"

"I understand. Such a couple should get out of their marriage before they follow dark ways."

"Ah, so you mean a merely stable marriage is not preferable to a happy marriage. Is that correct?"

"Adi, you are the first one I have told my opinion. When the bride and bridegroom gaze at me, they should be made aware of this opinion."

"Let us call it the 'Arundhati Amendment.'"

Both laughed.

"Add to that: Gaze at yourself, not at the Morning Star, to start a bright day," Arundhati stated.

Now Adina was more eager to understand the real Arundhati. "You said that the gods allow a man to have several wives at the same time. Why can't goddesses rebel against this practice?"

"Most goddesses pretend to be happy wives of one god. In reality, they fear those male bigamists. There is no real democracy in the world of the gods."

Arundhati is for democracy! Dada and Dadi might be surprised, Adina thought so as she asked another question. "Isn't democracy a new concept?"

"Yes, it is. Soon democracy will take over the whole world, and the heavenly kingdom will make for a good

Disney movie. God would look like the Wizard of Oz.
But, in the real world, democracies will have disturbances. It's natural. The creation is full of disturbances."

"Ma, how do you know this?"

"Oh, easy. I watch everything from space all the
time." Then she paused for a minute.

Adina couldn't wait. "Ma, why are you silent?"

"I just wanted to tell you how your justice system is
not a justice system. Here is a case that I watched recently. A father was accused by the mother as she filed for
divorce. They had a daughter. The mother reported that
the father abused the daughter. The court found that the
accusation was fabricated to gain custody of the daughter.
The mother was found to suffer from anxiety, and yet the
psychologist recommended full custody to the mother.
She ignored the traumatic issue of the false accusation.
The court, too, ignored the falsehood and ruled that she
have full custody as recommended by the psychologist.
The father did all he could to fight the system on these
simple grounds—he was found innocent, and the mother
had mental problems, and she lied. A year later, the little
girl disappeared. The father complained to the court,
which now showed sympathy for him and gave him custody of the little girl, whose whereabouts were no longer
known. These idiots gave him full custody of a child who
wasn't there. There are so many stories like this one, stories filled with gender bias for political gain. Adina, do
you understand my point?"

"Yes, I do. Does your husband support the equality of
the parents?"

"Vasishtha believes that a society is a fair society only
when it treats all as equals. He talks like a guru because
he is a guru, not like your TV-guest gurus."

"What's the difference?"

"How many TV-gurus are petitioning the US Congress to grant both parents equal rights to raise their children? Vasishtha wants gender equality. He doesn't want to grant favors to the guilty party. Rewarding any kind of guilty party leads to a worse kind of inequality. You must be aware of Vishvamitra's jealousy. He thought that he and Vasishtha were not equal, that he was higher than Vasishtha in spiritual attainment. He wanted to destroy our family. That's not spiritual attainment. Later, he abandoned his own infant, Shakuntala. Vasishtha never abandoned his children. This was Vasishtha's sage advice to Vishvamitra: 'Your spirituality includes your love for your own child, and any society that deprives you of a permanent bond with your child is far from spiritual. But you were not deprived by society. It was your own decision. You didn't care for your daughter's suffering. She needed you, but you failed as a parent...' Adina, do you understand my position?" Then Arundhati began to soar up and up, leaving a trail of red light.

"You stand by your husband, or don't look up at you at the end of your wedding," Adina shouted.

"What else?"

Adina heard those words from a distance. "Democracy equals equality," she shouted even louder.

"Thank you for allowing me to be on your computer screen. I am very happy to have an interview with a person who represents the new generation."

Adina heard the same faint voice emanating through the red light.

Then she became confused as she noticed several other flashing lights chasing the unstoppable red light. Between them she saw a sentence flashing on the screen: *WE, THE PEOPLE, DEMAND THE RIGHT TO EQUAL TREATMENT.*

CHAPTER 23

The Highest at the Highest

Jai Guru Deva "Victory to Guru the God"
(The Beatles' praise of the TM Founder)

T he famous song composed by John Lennon "*Jai Guru Deva*" attracted Adina's attention. Then she saw a portrait of the four young Beatles seated cross-legged on the floor with their guru, Maharishi Mahesh Yogi. The holy guru, Guru Deva, of all these famous personalities was not there, but his picture was hanging above them on the wall. Then she saw a portrait of the Guru Deva, the late Swami Brahmananda Saraswati.

Adina remembered that this learned swami was persuaded to accept the most prestigious holy title of Shankaracharya of Jyotirmath at Joshimath. He took the last name and orange robes of the Saraswati monks that were descended from one of the ten orders established by Adi Shankara.

It was believed that the founder of this monastery was Shankara, the Adi Shankaracharya, who came there in the eighth century AD from Kerala, the southernmost part of

India. He believed in the oneness of all, the central point of ancient Vedanta beliefs.

A few miles from Joshimath were the twin peaks of Nara and Narayana, and between them sat the Badrinath temple, which also was known as Badarika Ashram. This temple, near Tibet, was the highest holiest place of Hinduism. Even though it was called Narayana's temple, earlier it was a Buddhist temple honored by Indian and Tibetan Buddhists as one of their most sacred places. The Badrinath temple was under the authority of Jyotirmath.

So Swami Brahmananda commanded the highest respect of millions of religious people, Adi's dada had told her, and he was visited by India's first two presidents, Dr. Rajendra Prasad and Dr. Radhakrishnan. The head disciple of this swami also trained Maharishi, who on his advice spread meditation internationally with the brand name "Transcendental Meditation" or TM. Adina thought it interesting that the same disciple and the next Shankaracharya initiated Dada, Dadi, and Daddy into meditation.

Adi also remembered that people often sought a *darshan* of the Shankaracharya, not for meditation but for his blessings. A blessing could be for the fulfillment of the wish that led the worshipper to perform a *Puja* at the temple. Because of Badrinath's Himalayan cold and altitude, many worshippers were unable to make the journey. Nevertheless, they could send their offerings to this temple through other roaming priests called *Panda*, a word derived from Pandit or Pundit.

Maybe Nani's offering reached here through a Panda priest, Adi thought. The holiest Shankaracharya of this holiest temple was Swami Brahmananda. He would know if any successor received Nani's offering at the temple.

Adina gazed at the solo portrait of Swami Brahmananda Saraswati, the Shankaracharya of Jyotirmath, clothed in a monk's orange robes and sitting cross-

legged. She thought about his life. He was born as Raja
Ram in a Mishra family of Brahmins. His birthplace was
near Ayodhya, the capital of the *Ramayana* hero King
Rama, which was the meaning of his name. The moment
she thought of him as Raja Ram, a young monk emerged,
but not at Ayodhya. He was at Prayag Raj, the "king of
the confluences" where the two holiest rivers of India
meet in the city of Allahabad. He wore only an orange
robe, a *dhoti*.

Then he disappeared but emerged again at the bus stop
that had a sign saying *Deva Prayag*. This was the place
where the Alakananda met the Bhagirathi. The Ganga,
the holiest river, was known here as Bhagirathi and originated at Gomukh, located in the Gangotri glacier. The
Alakananda descended from the Satopanth lake in the
Chawkhamba range of the Himalayas. The monk disappeared and reemerged at the Rudra Prayag bus stop,
where Mandakini from Kedarnath joined Alakananda.
This confluence was named after Rudra, which was Shiva's fierce form. The confluence was noisy because of
the Mandakini's fierce flow. The swami jumped into the
waters and disappeared, but a few miles upstream, he appeared at the Karna Prayag bus stop where Alakananda
welcomed its tributary Pindar, originating from the Pin-
dari glacier. The swami took a bath at this confluence,
and then he walked on foot, only to disappear again. He
remerged at Nand Prayag's bus stop. Here was the confluence of the Alakananda and the Nandakini. The Nanda
Devi peak was one of the highest in the world and its
glacier was the headwaters of the Nandakini. The swami
folded his hands and bowed to Goddess Nanda after taking a dip at this confluence. He disappeared again and
reappeared up at the bus stop of Vishnu Prayag. Here he
took a dip where the Alakananda met the Dhauli Ganga
that came from the Niti Pass area.

Adi remembered that Mahatma Gandhi's ashes passed through this area on their way to the holy lake of Manasarovar in Tibet.

Finally, the monk abandoned the long river route at the monastery of Jyotirmath at Joshimath, but now he was an old monk, not the young monk Adina saw at those six confluences. She understood. Now she was looking at him as he was in the portrait.

He raised his hand to bless her and spoke in a gentle voice. "My little child, why have you travelled so far?"

"Jai Guru Dev. My pranams to you. I am Adina. My ancestors are from here, but I live in the USA." Then she told him the purpose of her meditation on him.

"This is very strange to hear what could happen in the land of Lincoln. I always think of the USA as a country of equal treatment. Why is it that, if a highly decorated sportsman lies, his honors are taken away, his money is taken away, and he is publicly humiliated again and again? And why is it that a parent who lies to destroy others in the family is rewarded?"

Adina remained quiet.

"I don't think your crown jewel could have been accepted by the head priest of our Badrinath temple," he continued. "He is a Nambudiri, the same family of Brahmins from which came our founder, the Adi Shankaracharya." The swami laughed loudly. "There is no chance to bribe this head priest. If he lies, then he is a sinner."

Adina also laughed.

When both stopped laughing, Adina cleared her throat. "I have been told that the first Shankaracharya revived Vedanta beliefs. What is Vedanta?"

"Vedanta is not a belief, it is the USA—the United States of All. What is the outer state is the inner state. In short, unity of all is Vedanta. We call this allness Brahman. You are it. Indeed you are from the USA."

Adina smiled. "Swami ji, I found a quote from you in my search on the Internet—'One should always be cautious, so that no sin happens, so that one has no regrets at the time of death.' Is this quote really from you?"

"My native language is Hindi, Adina, but whoever translated it is correct. I thank you and the translator."

"What is the biggest sin in your view?"

"To hurt any being is the biggest sin. Sanctity of life has to be our universal duty. That's what Adi Shankara considers the most basic ethics, considers the Dharma—unity of all. We must meet all as our own self. The smallest meeting point you just saw was Vishnu Prayag, and all meet at the king of the confluences, Allahabad. The Kumbh Mela is the biggest human meeting. The meaning of it is, 'We are all together in a pot, in a *kumbha*.' We can't hurt any fellow human. We all are pot-fellows."

The pain of her lifelong sadness shot through Adina, making her squirm in her seat. "I am hurt. My own parent caused my hurt."

"Others who supported your parent also hurt you." The swami frowned, his grim expression almost frightening. Adi remained quiet until the swami continued again. "Our message of *ahimsa* had been sent to your country by my disciple Mahesh. All his followers understood it."

She nodded. "Swami Vivekananda had already sent that message much, much, earlier. He had also meditated here at Karna Prayag."

"Remember the rule—'The messenger must practice the message.' Dharma is kindness. Mahesh never ate meat, any meat."

"How about the local Brahmins? They perform animal sacrifice regularly."

"The *Bali* sacrifice is a pretext. The Paharis love meat, and therefore Jainism and Buddhism could not flourish here. Mahesh could impress the Beatles but not the Pahari

Brahmins. Our founder, Shankaracharaya, had philosophical debates and defeated all the pandits, all the leading Jaina and Buddhist scholars of India. But he failed to convince the Pahari Brahmins. I know almost all *panda* priests are phony. They would not have allowed Swami Vivekananda to enter their kitchens. Yet he was so proud to be a Hindu."

Adina laughed, but not the swami.

"The Beatles honored you with the song '*Jai Guru Dev.*'" she said. "The Maharishi honored you with a new colony named after you, Shankaracharya Nagar, across Rishikesh. They follow your TM in that colony and around the world. But I don't practice it. Do you approve of my method, Swami ji?"

"Any method that works for you is good. Patañjali said that a couple of thousand years ago. We don't convert anyone to TM. Remember the rule—'Everyone must be free to choose her or his way.' And add to that, this 'Your way is good only if does not hurt others.'"

Then Adina saw a deer running from behind the screen and a tiger was chasing it.

"Swami ji, please save that deer and save yourself," she yelled.

The deer sat in front of the swami. The tiger followed suit and sat next to the deer. Adina saw the swami levitating in the air. She realized that he was indeed an accomplished yogi. Patañjali said this about a yogi's achievement "In his presence there is abandonment of enmity." She took a long sigh of relief and thought of Jim Corbett's tiger hunt. "Thank goodness it is not a man-eating tiger from nearby Rudra Prayag. Everybody is safe."

Adina was moved by this unusual sight. She hummed "*Jai Guru Dev*" and tears began to blur her view. She wiped them and the screen was again empty.

CHAPTER 24

God's Children

Indra, dashaasyaam putraaṇaa dhehi
"Indra, place within her ten sons."

Your nani didn't have to offer a crown jewel to any deity," Nikhil Atri said to Adina. "There is a built-in blessing for the bride at the time of Hindu wedding. The bridegroom tells her not to have terror in her eye and not to be a husband-killer. O Lord Indra! Place within her ten sons."

"Uncle Atri, what is this terror thing?" Adina asked.

"Didn't your dada explain it to you? He was the priest who performed the wedding ceremony for Drishti and Sean with those Vedic mantras."

This evening Nikhil and his wife Kirti were celebrating their daughter Drishti's twenty-fifth wedding anniversary in their home. Adina was invited, a sort of representative for her dada and dadi.

"Dada is funny. He told me that if the bride had ten sons she might go for a drastic action. There will be tension in such a big crowd. The father will have no time to discipline so many kids. Definitely, she would like to kill him."

Nikhil laughed. "Drishti is very happy with her daughter and son. Sean has no problem with these kids. But your dada is correct. India is terrorized by its own population, over one billion people. The Vedic blessing to blossom is really a curse. Did your dada tell you that, after his ceremony, there was a Christian ceremony, too? Sean is an Irish-American Catholic. His priest had kind words when he married Sean and Drishti. He called them God's children. Doesn't your nani think you are some god's child?"

"Uncle, if we all are God's children, then God is a very bad father. If God is almighty, then why did he allow such a big massacre in Pakistan yesterday, where more than ninety Shia Muslims were murdered by some terrorists in a bomb blast? And they are still counting the number of the wounded in and around the mosque. Today there was news that the Shia Muslims have refused to bury the dead bodies. They have placed those mutilated bodies on the road to block traffic. Muslims mutilating Muslims! And yet the victims and the victimizers claim that God is great, that God is with them. Who is speaking the truth?"

"Neither. Otherwise, why are Christians killing Christians, Hindus killing Hindus, Muslims killing Muslims? All of them claim that the Almighty is with them. We all argue for our proofless truths. Gandhi thought God was with him, and his killer thought the same God was—"

"With him." Adina completed his sentence. "That's the worst example of a Hindu killing a Hindu."

"When I was growing up, I thought only Hindus and Muslims killed each other. I was a child when my parents fled to India from Pakistan in 1947. That year Pakistan was created as a new country. Mr. Jinnah, the founder of

Pakistan, told the world that Indian Muslims needed a country of their own. India has more Muslims than Pakistan. Jinnah insulted Muslims, his words indicating they could not live with the non-Muslims of India. We are all living together there and here. President Obama says that the USA is a country of Christians, Jews, Muslims, Buddhists, Hindus, and even non-believers such as your dada."

"Did he really include my dada?" When he frowned, she squirmed. "I am just joking, Uncle."

Both now laughed.

"Yes, he did say that. I am also joking," Atri said. "The president is right. But the first thing the president does is a gross violation of the constitution. He takes his oath of office with his hand on the Bible. One Bible is not enough for him. He places his hand not on one but three Bibles, and not once but four times. This act is reinforcing conversion. This is discrimination against all the other religions. This is one reason that the American Constitution firmly declares the separation of church and state. My advice: Take the oath upon the constitution and the constitution only. This is the only way to give equal treatment to all the citizens. The president is elected by the people of different faiths to follow the constitution, not any scripture. But I know my advice won't count. Every clever politician cares more for the crowd and less for the constitution. Have you ever heard any president taking his oath of office and swearing that oath on the little known Hopi religion?"

"No. Dada would love to include the Hopi spirit."

"*Why not*? Otherwise the Hopi Indians have the right of having a separate country. Their ancestors came in America long before the Europeans with their religions. The Hopis can say, 'If Pakistan is possible, then why not

Hopistan?' Don't the Hopi and Pakistani children belong to one and the same family of humans?"

"What if Jinnah meets Lincoln and asks him this question?" Adina asked with a smile.

"Jinnah should never meet Lincoln. Jinnah's achievement is insulting to Lincoln—"

Their meeting was interrupted as a senior couple greeted the Atris. Adina gently walked the other way. She was moved by what Nikhil Atri said. Her mother broke her family and blamed her own child for that. *Where is God? Dada is right,* Adi thought. If He were there, He would have saved her family. He would not have allowed the justice system to so abuse her father.

Sean and Drishti greeted her.

"Adina! We miss your grandparents. Your dada was our grand priest. He was so young then," Sean said, putting his hand on her shoulder. "I tell you, to be married by an atheist priest is a very unique experience! Have you met our son and daughter? We have raised them as atheists. Your dada's blessings."

Adina tried to smile. "Yes, I have met both of them. Don't you think my dada is a deity?"

"Almost!" Drishti said with a smile. "Adina, your dada warned me when I was required to walk the first seven steps with Sean as a bride, on the altar—"

"Warned?"

"He was actually looking at the guests while addressing me, 'Drishti, don't take these steps if you believe the stereotype that a non-white cannot have a successful marriage with a white.' I walked all the seven steps as I cried. Sean also cried." Drishti wiped her eyes. "We are very fortunate that you are attending our twenty-fifth marriage anniversary. Quite a long time, isn't it?"

Adina just nodded her head. Her lips were trembling. When Drishti embraced her, Adina burst into sobs.

"Adina, look who is here. Do you recognize them?" Drishti helped her dry her tears and then introduced her to the same senior couple that Adina saw a few minutes ago with Nikhil Atri.

"No need to introduce us. We could not help but recognize Adina. My name is Sumita, and this is my husband Abhijit Das. We were your supervisors."

Adina touched their feet, for Daddy had told her how they acted like parents for him. The Das couple had protected him and her when he was kicked out by her mother.

"We will let you talk more about your memories. Meet us over there for snacks soon," Drishti said.

Sean waved his hand. "Yes, we will meet you all over there," he said.

Both moved ahead.

"Daddy calls you my second pair of grandparents. I will call you Dada and Dadi. I am sorry to walk away earlier. I had no idea that I would see you here."

"We just returned from India. You were about four years old when we saw you last. This is a great surprise for all of us! I see your eyes are wet. Are you all right?" Sumita said very softly.

"Daddy dropped me here to attend the marriage anniversary of Auntie Drishti and Uncle Sean. I just met them. They have such a happy family."

Adina broke down again and Sumita hugged her.

Mr. Das caressed her head. "We saw you break down a couple of times when you you were with your father and under our supervision. The first visit was traumatic for you. When he left you secretly after playing with you for four hours, you asked us, 'Where is Dan?' We told you that he would return the next week. You sat on the sofa and sobbed and sobbed. We cried with you. Why did your mother do this? We kept on asking ourselves this after your mother picked you up. You didn't look happy with your mother. Later, she complained that you didn't want to see your nani. You became jittery in her presence, and your mother accused us of being at fault." He took his hand away from her head to wipe his own tears.

"Are you still mad at my mother?"

"One of her lies we will never forget. She reported us, saying we let your father take you home in a green car. While your father spent time with you, it was supposed to be at our home and under our supervision. That was the court order. Your mother complained that you told her that you went to your dad's apartment. We became mad when we received a warning from your mother's lawyer. Your father's green car was in for repairs at that time and he had rented a black car. He never took you out of our sight. We felt humiliated, but you were so little that you could not have said anything like that. The legal system ignored our complaint that your mother and her lawyer lied. The legal system ignored all the false allegations your mother made. The judge did not even reprimand her. Did you know that?"

Adina understood everything he said. She also knew a few other disturbing things from other sources. She wanted to confirm those things from the Das couple.

Why didn't the judge base his judgments on Mr. Das' testimony? He believed the psychologist who ignored the lies of another witness for her mother. *Mom is lucky that she is not in jail*, Adi thought.

Mom coached her witnesses and approached two more people who refused to testify on her behalf. They understood what she was up to. Her lawyer was also lucky because she asked Mr. Das to change his statement. The judge never questioned her integrity. They both could have been reported to the bar.

"In this state, it's all politics, not justice," Mr. Das

said. "You should try to fix the corrupt system when you grow up."

"I am trying right now," Adina responded in a firm voice.

"What are you doing? You are not even thirteen years old yet," Sumita asked.

"Dadi ji, it is a long story, but actually, there are many stories like mine. If all the victims raise their voices, then there will be a change."

"You mean some sort of class action?"

"We will not know yet. I have to wait until I find my crown jewel."

Sumita perked up, suddenly alert. "What crown jewel?"

"It's another long story. Maybe I can talk to you later. Right now, you should have some snacks."

"Yes, let's go there to the snack table and talk more. We love you, Adina," Mr. Das added.

They all went to where the snacks were being served. Adina saw Drishti and Sean with their son and daughter surrounded by guests.

"Drishti, you are a CFO of your company," one guest asked. How did you get time to raise these godly kids?"

"I didn't raise them alone." Drishti laughed. "Actually, Sean took six months off to stay home with our daughter so I could work fulltime in my office. Then, with our son, I took six months off so he could work fulltime. We took turns with every chore. Sean still does laundry, though it is uncommon that a CEO has to do his family's laundry. One thing I share with Sean only nominally. He still drives the kids to school, the doctor…"

Adina walked away, suddenly weary of the conversation. "I am not any god's child," she mumbled. "If I were, I would still be a member of a little happy family, like those two lucky big kids. My mother was not lucky with one daughter. She should have been blessed to have ten sons. They would not have needed my mother's coaching to accuse my father of not spending quality time with them!"

CHAPTER 25

Quest for Equal Treatment

I Have a Dream
(A Speech by Dr. Martin Luther King, Jr.)

Dada had once quoted one of his colleagues who was a historian. "Dreams of equality sleep close to death threats."

Adina knew that some of the greatest leaders in human history were proof of his quote, Lincoln perhaps the most. The cost of the American Civil War in human lives and property was so painful but so worthy in every sense. The country emerged stronger as the United States of America. The opposite example was the partition of India, which cost over one million lives, not to mention the terrible economic costs. Gandhi was a figure in that struggle, and, like Lincoln, he was gunned down. Gandhi's dream failed. Ordinary persons could fail to achieve the dreams of extraordinary persons.

MK Gandhi didn't get the Nobel Peace Prize, but his famous follower Dr. Martin Luther King, Jr. did. Unlike MLK, Gandhi had to fight on two major fronts, one outside the country and another inside. The first was British rule and the second was India's social discrimination. The second was exploited by Mr. MA Jinnah, the founder of Pakistan. Jinnah never trusted Gandhi's fight for equal treatment. He strongly felt that the Hindu majority would never treat the Muslim minority as equals. Gandhi allotted huge funds to help the new Muslim Pakistan. The man who gunned him down was a Hindu fanatic.

Dada had told Adina that Dr. Martin Luther King Jr. went to India in 1959 because he was deeply impressed by how Mahatma Gandhi fought for equal treatment. Adina found a statement by MLK on the Internet about his visit: "Since being in India, I am more convinced than ever before that the method of nonviolent resistance is the most potent weapon available to oppressed people in their struggle for justice and human dignity. In a real sense, Mahatma Gandhi embodied in his life certain universal principles that are inherent in the moral structure of the universe, and these principles are as inescapable as the law of gravitation."

His friend and advisor Bayard Rustin helped him understand Gandhi's fight for justice and human dignity. Gandhi's famous "Salt March" against the British became a model for large protests, and Rustin led MLK to organize an event that had had never happened in the United States capital before. On August 28, 1963, the historic march of blacks and non-blacks, over a quarter of million people, took place. Adina gazed at Dr. Martin Luther King standing at the steps of Lincoln Memorial and concentrated on these words of his seventeen-minute speech:

"I have a dream that one day this nation will rise up and live out the true meaning of its creed. 'We hold these truths to be self-evident: that all men are created equal.'"

She kept on repeating the words "these truths to be self-evident: that all men are created equal."

In her own case, the American judge fatally shot the meaning of equal treatment under the law guaranteed by the US Constitution and fought for by Lincoln and MLK. Her father begged for equal treatment, but he was punished, even before being proven guilty, which he never was. After her mother's allegations were found to be false, there were more punishments for Adi and her father. She was determined to tell MLK her story of his dream's failure.

He appeared on the screen exactly as Adina meditated on his picture at the Lincoln Memorial, as if giving the "I Have a Dream" speech. MLK did not look at her, in spite of her several attempts, but she decided to tell her story, anyway.

When she was finished, she asked him, "Dear Dr. King, did you understand why I have told my story just now?"

MLK didn't look at her, but she heard his words. "That all men are created equal."

"Dr. King, my dada's Indian friend experienced something of what you did,", she continued, after his words. "Let me tell you about Mr. Nathan's experience the same year you gave this speech.

"In 1963, Nathan left Texas. He was fed up with the segregation he experienced during his two years working toward his master's degree in Civil Engineering. In his small way, he defied the humiliating segregation in the South. That's when he realized that his Brahmin parents also practiced segregation against the untouchables in his country's southern state of Madras. How much the untouchables had suffered for thousands of years in India. Mahatma Gandhi finally challenged this painful practice.

"Like Gandhi in India, Nathan broke the laws of segregation in Texas. He didn't have a car while he was student there. He used buses instead. In spite of his black complexion, he would sit in the bus seats reserved for the whites. He also drank from the fountains meant for whites. In theaters, he would watch movies from the seats reserved for the whites. In restaurants, he would sit where only whites were allowed to sit. And so on. But he never thought of Gandhi's extreme attempts. In his Sabarmati Ashram, Gandhi forced a boy from Dada's community of Brahmins to clean the toilets of the lowest caste untouchables. That seventeen-year-old Brahmin boy first hesitated to follow Gandhi's practice, but he was determined to be a Gandhian. That was his reason to join the Gandhi's Ashram. He cleaned their toilets regularly, and later India honored him as one of the notable Gandhians.

"Nathan was lucky. Nobody in Texas questioned his practice of ignoring segregation. At that time, he had no idea that, soon, a man from Texas would become the next president of the USA and sign the historic Civil Rights Act. In 1964, no one had the faintest idea that, forty years later, the Civil Rights Act would allow Obama to realize Dr. King's dream of equality. But Dr. King's spiritual guru was Gandhi. He might have given credit to Gandhi, 'Obama is here because Gandhi was there.'

"After receiving his master's degree Nathan moved to Chicago. There, he roomed with another Indian, Mr. Ganju, who was Dada's friend. Unlike Nathan, Ganju's complexion was white, as he was a Brahmin from Kashmir. Ganju had also graduated in civil engineering. One day Ganju told Dada that he got a job in a Chicago firm. Nathan had also applied for the same job. He had much better qualifications than Ganju. Ganju told Dada that Nathan did not get the job due to the color difference.

"Two years later, Dada met Nathan at his new apartment. He was living with a white woman but had a wife and a son in India. He told Dada that he was trying to test the Civil Rights Act of President Lyndon Johnson. That was the last meeting Dada had with him."

"Dr. King, what do you think of Mr. Nathan?" Adina asked.

MLK didn't turn his face toward Adina but, again, she heard his words. "Free at last! Free at last! Thank God Almighty!"

Then she heard a gunshot, which disturbed her attention. She shut down the computer, out of fear.

In the end, she had one question for Dr. King. Why didn't he thank Lincoln and Gandhi instead of Almighty God? Maybe he knew that, unlike the Almighty, these two had limited might to fight for equal treatment for all and yet the Almighty allowed social discrimination for more than two thousand years in India and two centuries in the USA. In Adina's case, an ordinary judge accomplished more than Gandhi, MLK, and Almighty. He undid all of their work in two weeks. The killers of Lincoln and Gandhi undid that work with two gunshots.

What bothered Adina most was Martin Luther King's hesitation to talk to her directly. Why didn't he express his opinion about Nathan? Nathan admired MLK so much.

CHAPTER 26

Ganga's Tears

Gaŋgaayai namaḥ "A bow to Ganga"
(A prayer mantra for the Ganges)

Adina remembered that the festival of *Ganga Dashahara* was in June. The holiest river Ganga, or Ganges, was worshipped on the tenth day of the bright lunar half in this month. The river's deity was Ganga Devi. Her highest temple was in Gangotri, a few miles below the origin of the river at Gomukh in the Garhwal Himalayas. The other name for this river was Bhagirathi, after King Bhagiratha of Ayodhya, and ancestor of Lord Rama.

King Sagara, Bhagiratha's ancestor, had two wives, Keshini and Sumati, and wanted a son. The king performed several long rituals to please Sage Bhrigu. The sage was pleased with Sagara's penances and granted his wish very generously. Keshini wanted just one child, and she gave birth to Anshuman. But Sumati wanted many sons and gave birth to a gourd that contained sixty thousand sons. They all grew up to be strong warriors.

King Sagara was very happy to have so many princes

in his previously childless family and so performed a horse sacrifice called *ashvamedha*. A horse was released to travel all around, in order to establish the authority of Sagara. Indra stole this horse as he was afraid that Sagara might claim heaven. When Sagara heard that his horse had been stolen, he sent his sixty thousand sons to find it. They reached Sage Kapila's Ashram where Indra had hidden the beast. The princes accused Kapila of being a thief. The sage was disturbed in his meditation by all their noise. He opened his eyes with fire and burned all the sixty thousand princes instantly.

Sagara then sent Anshuman to look for the horse and the princes when the princes did not return. He found the horse and a heap of ash. Garuda arrived and told Anshuman what happened, and he told Anshuman to bring the Ganga from heaven to wash the ashes of the dead princes or the princes would remain in hell for ever.

Anshuman could not bring the water of the Ganga, but finally, one of his descendants, Bhagiratha, prayed to Lord Vishnu, who released the Ganga on the head of Lord Shiva who was meditating in the Himalayas. Shiva contained the very powerful river in his head until Bhagiratha pleased him with long prayers. The lord released a small part of the river at Gomukh where Bhagiratha was waiting in his chariot. The river followed his chariot until it reached the Bay of Bengal. On its way, it washed over the ashes of the dead princes, who instantly went to heaven. Since then it became easy for anyone to be released from all the sins and attain heaven if his or her body was touched by the Ganges water.

Adina concentrated on this story from the *Ramayana*. In that ancient Sanskrit epic, Sage Vishvamitra tells Rama and Lakshmana how their forefather, Bhagiratha, brought the Ganges from heaven. From her dada she knew of the temple of Ganga on its bank at Gangotri, the holiest and highest temple of the holiest river. Even today thousands of believers went there to worship the river's statue, which represents the river as a beautiful goddess. She saw the picture of the goddess and kept meditating on the statue with this Ganga story in her thoughts, But Goddess Ganga did not appear on the screen at all.

The following day, Adina came up with an alternate idea. Dada and Dadi had told her that they knew the temple priest, Pandit Semwal, who was their distant relative. The late priest would have known if any crown jewel from her nani reached the temple. The worshippers there firmly believe that the goddess grants their wishes.

Her meditation on Pandit Semwal worked and the priest blessed her with a raised hand, "Adina, you are our child. Did you know your ancestry is rooted here in these mountains?"

"Yes, Pandit ji. My pranams to you. Dada and Dadi told me about you and your picture. I need your help."

"Tell me what I can do for you."

Adina told her case briefly. Pandit Semwal said that, during his tenure, no such jewel came to the temple. However, he did confirm that even atheists believed the power of Ganga. He told her about India's first prime minister, Jawaharlal Nehru, who was also respected as Pandit ji. "Nehru was not like a traditional pandit, although he was a Kashmiri Brahmin by ancestry. He was an atheist, but he loved the Ganga for his hometown of Allahabad is at the holiest confluence of Ganga and Yamuna. His ashes were scattered on the waters of this confluence."

"Dada and Dadi told me that his two grandsons worshipped the Ganga at the temple."

"Yes, when they were young boys they would come secretly, early in the morning, and request that I pray for them. I have performed the Ganga Puja for them at the

Gangotri temple. They were very different from their atheist grandfather!"

"Did you perform a *Puja* for my dada and dadi, too?" Adina smiled as she asked him this question.

"No. They, too, secretly visited the temple with your father. But there was a death in our family eight days before their visit, and so I was impure to perform as a priest for ten days. They wanted to take a picture of the beautiful statue of Ganga, but I forbade them. There were no pictures allowed then. But here is a picture of the goddess." Pandit Semwal showed the inner sanctum where Goddess Ganga's statue stands in a beautiful posture.

Adina gazed at her eyes. "This picture is slightly different from the Internet picture. Were there any other kinds of restrictions to worshipping this statue?"

"There is a great difference between Ganga and several other goddesses such as Kali. No animal sacrifice is allowed in this temple. Ganga is the symbol of non-violence, but some stupid visitors violate this principle. You are not allowed to catch even a fish in the Ganga. Once I had to interfere in one case of animal sacrifice. Some men from the plains wanted to sacrifice a ram at the Gangotri temple. I forbade them. Then they went up at Gomukh and sacrificed the helpless ram. They ate its meat as *prasad* of Ganga. Meat is not our sacred food. I protested and requested that local officials stop cruelty against animals. The Ganga was brought down by King Bhagiratha to wash away the bad karma of his ancestors and send—"

The priest disappeared from the screen before he could complete his sentence. Instead, the statue of the Ganga became a living goddess.

"Adina, I have heard everything," the goddess said. "Never believe false stories. Bhagiratha never brought me to the earth. His relatives have lived here hardly three thousand years, but I was born in the Himalayas when no humans were yet born. And a woman producing sixty thousand boys in a gourd! The ridiculous joke is that Bhagiratha had a chariot at Gomukh. Even today there is no chariotable road there."

"Ma Ganga. Pranam. Do you really wash away the bad karma of the dead?" Adina asked, thinking of those sixty thousand dead princes.

"Someone must wash away my bad karma. I will give you one example." The goddess merged into the river that was visible below the temple. Her commentary on the river was audible above the noise of the fiercely flowing water.

However, at Tehri, a few miles below Gangotri, the flow was blocked by the outrageously huge Tehri Dam, Asia's highest dam that was recently built on this river. *And it is over a fault*, Adi remembered, *if it breaks the river will wash away the equivalent of more than half the population of America*. She also remembered that scientists were saying that, because of global warming, the river would have no water at all one day, and so there might not be anything washed away if the dam broke.

"The river meets the Alakananda at Dev Prayag, a few miles below the dam," the goddess said. "Its combined water is not polluted as far as Rishikesh, a few miles farther down, but that is not the case at Hardwar, or Haridwar, which means the door of Hara, or Hari, the two gods Shiva and Vishnu. Pollution of the Ganga starts at Hardwar, where people ritually throw the bones and ashes of their dead relatives in these waters, because the dead reach the abode of Hara or Hari through them. Hara or Hari did not create these waters, humans did create Hara and Hari. That's the truth. But gullible people prefer falsehood to truth. Nevertheless, the Ganga at Hardwar looks clean by comparison to when it arrives at Varanasi.

Devout Hindus cremate the dead on its banks and release the bones and ashes into its waters. Some unburned organs float around, even whole dead bodies. Varanasi is the place where the dead loses dignity. Varanasi is the place where holiness is the name of hell. It smells awful there, for hundreds of bodies are roasted every day."

For a few seconds, Adina saw funeral pyres, one after another. Nearby, she saw naked men bathing in the river—*naga sadhus*, nude saints. She shut down her computer.

But she remembered Ganga's words just before the screen went off. "My waters are not worth bathing, are not worth drinking."

Those words are not false accusations, as anyone can see the truth of them at Varanasi, Adina thought.

CHAPTER 27

Narada

Madbhaktaa yatra gaayanti tatra tishṭhaami Naarada
"Where my devotees sing there I stay, Narada!"

Adina now figured that the most likely place for Nani to have offered the crown jewel would be where devotees assembled and sang the chant of Lord God, but there were countless places where devotees danced and sang. Adina had seen the Hare Krishna devotees dancing and singing, and she knew their holy Sanskrit scripture was the *Bhagavata Purana*, where it was written that Lord Vishnu told Sage Narada the importance of *Kirtan*, chanting. Vishnu, they believed, resided with chanters, and to feel Vishnu's presence, Narada carried with him a *vina*, the ancient lute. He never stayed in one place. He was a journalist of Vishnu. His job was to collect news of the universe and report to Vishnu. Narada was unbeatable for investigative journalism and a pillar of Sanatana Dharma, the perpetual religion.

It was said that Narada was cursed to be a journalist. His father Lord Brahma was expecting him to get married and raise a family, but Narada refused to obey his father. He even discouraged his siblings from getting married.

The lord of creation was disappointed and cursed his own son. "You wander everywhere. Don't come near your brothers. You are such a bad influence!"

Narada took this curse very positively, very creatively. *Wandering must be made useful*, he thought. He developed interest in news gathering and, thus, Narada became the first journalist.

Being a journalist was not easy for him. Some liked his news, but some accused him of disinformation. Everybody who accused him misunderstood him, however. He never meant any harm to anyone. The ultimate good of all was his ultimate goal, and he went out of his way to help anyone who lost.

Adina knew, from what her Dadi and Dada had told her, that Narada meant "the giver of what belongs to man."

Adina also knew that Nani used to feel like a loser, and to have a grandchild became her sole goal. Narada would know where Nani might have gone to attend a *Kirtan* chanting and pray for a grandchild.

Adina meditated on Narada's picture with his *vina* musical instrument until the faint sound of the lute began to emerge. The sound resembled Ravi Shankar's *sitar* music, which she had been listening to since she was two years old. Dada told her that Ravi Shankar was the modern Narada, the greatest international musician India ever had.

Adina became calm as the *vina* music became louder. Then she saw a forest of banyan trees. Under a huge tree she saw Narada playing the lute. "Pranam Devarshi!" Dada had told her that Narada was always addressed as Devarshi, the divine sage.

Narada stopped playing the *vina*, stood, and walked

toward her. "Long live my child! You are Adina, I know."

Adina was surprised. "How do you know me, your holiness?"

"I am a journalist. Music is not my profession, but it keeps me in a good mood."

"You mean you also go through moods?"

"Sometimes someone does not like the news I have. Not everybody treats the same news alike. A disagreement leads to a debate, which causes me anger or frustration."

"Yes, I have heard stories of your frustrations."

"Which stories? There are so many stories about me, and not all of them are true."

"You are a celebrity. Dada says that to be a celebrity is a curse. Even your loved ones can demean you by creating incredible stories about you. Only you can tell me which stories are your true stories."

"There are volumes of stories about me. Storytellers keep changing them."

"There are two stories, which are considered to be true, that indicate you were really interested in marriage. But some people, including your father, say you never were. Lord Brahma misunderstood and cursed you."

"What are those stories?"

Adina told him those two special stories: Narada went to the Himalayas, where he meditated for years. His spiritual status became as high as the Himalayas. Wherever he wandered, people would address him as "Devarshi." That they revered him as a divine sage made him proud, but pride was not the virtue of a saint. Vishnu told his consort Lakshmi, "My devotee Narada has ego. We must help him to overcome it. Otherwise, he will lose his respect as Devarshi."

Lakshmi concurred with her lord.

One day, Narada travelled to Ayodhya. King Ambarisha welcomed him into his palace. There, Narada met the king's daughter Sumati. He had never seen such a beautiful woman anywhere. Before leaving the palace he expressed his desire to the king.

Ambarisha told him very politely that he was unable to decide for her, but he invited the sage to attend her forthcoming *svayamvara* ceremony, in which she would choose a suitor for herself. Narada gladly accepted the invitation.

In the meantime, Narada met Vishnu for a special request. He wanted to look as handsome as Vishnu. Vishnu agreed to transform his face, and with his new face Narada attended the "self-selection" ceremony of Sumati. She talked to every suitor. Finally, she chose the suitor who was sitting in the center. He turned out to be Vishnu.

"Sumati, why didn't you choose the suitor who was sitting on the right side of Vishnu?" Ambarisha asked her after the ceremony.

"You mean that monkey?"

The princess laughed. So did the king.

Narada was very dejected. He cried and left the palace immediately. In a nearby pond, he went to wash his face and saw his reflection in the water. He went to see Vishnu immediately.

Vishnu knew why he came back to see him. Before he could say a word, Narada cursed him. "One day you will lose your beautiful woman, too. You will cry like me."

"I am very sorry, but Lakshmi and I wanted to help you, and so we decided to be the beautiful Sumati and the handsome suitor. Marriage is not meant for you, for it would keep you from moving as you must. Now you will move anywhere to engage in investigative journalism. Moreover, you will be genuinely respected as Devarshi. So can you forgive us now?"

"I will forgive you, my lord. But not now! You shall lose your beautiful woman. Then, only with the help of a monkey, will you be able to regain her."

Narada followed Vishnu's advice thereafter and vowed to remain a bachelor.

The *Ramayana* tells of how the avatar of Vishnu, Rama, the famous prince of Ayodhya, was hurt by his own family members. He was going to be the king, but on the advice of his stepmother, his father, Dasharatha, exiled him along with his beautiful wife Sita. While wandering in a forest, Sita was kidnapped by Ravana, the demon king of Lanka, and Rama had no idea of her whereabouts. One day, he met a monkey whose name was Hanuman. This powerful monkey jumped over the ocean, met Sita in a garden, and then returned to Rama. With Hanuman's information, Rama prepared a huge army and killed Ravana. Sita was rescued because of Hanuman's help.

After this *Ramayana* story, Adina told a *Puranic* story of Narada: Once, Narada begged Lord Vishnu to reveal his maya to him. "She has never been revealed to anyone. You are no exception, Narada," Vishnu said to Narada, who was disappointed.

A few days later, Narada wanted Vishnu's help with a project in investigative journalism. Vishnu agreed to help him, and the two friends had to go out for the whole day. On the way, Vishnu became thirsty and asked Narada to bring him some water. Narada ran quickly to the nearby river with his *kamandalu*, a jug.

While he bowed down to fill the jug, he saw some mud in the water, and when he looked for the cause, he saw a beautiful woman taking a bath in the river. She saw Narada, trying to get clear water in the jug, filling it and emptying it again and again. The woman understood his problem. She used her scarf over his jug to filter the water. Narada was awed by her beauty, and they fell in love instantly. They married immediately and settled on the bank of that river, where they built a house.

Not many years later, they had a daughter and two sons. It was a very happy family. But, one day, a big rain storm flooded their house and the daughter was swept away. Narada swam after her. But then he saw his wife trying to save their two sons. He could not save the daughter and so he ran toward his wife, who could not save the two boys and was struggling to keep from drowning. Narada tried to hold his wife as tightly as possible, but a giant wave came and she slipped from his hands.

Somehow, he managed to swim back alone to dry ground. Where his house once stood, he closed his eyes and wailed loudly. Then he felt a couple of gentle taps on his back. He turned around to find Vishnu.

"Lord!" he cried. "Look what has happened to me! I lost my wife, my children, my house. I have no desire to live without them!"

Vishnu finally calmed him down. "Narada! Where is my water? I could not wait for you any longer than one hour."

"What water are you talking about, lord?"

Vishnu laughed. "Look at the jug in your hand."

"You are laughing and looking for water when I have lost everything I owned, Lord Vishnu!"

"I have come here to clear up your confusion. You have lost nothing except your dream."

No sooner had Narada heard these words than he burst into laughter. "I understand your maya, my Lord. Please forgive me for the delay. Here is your water that I collected one hour ago from this river."

When Adina finished this story, she beamed at him., "Devarshi, I admire you. Maya or no maya, you cared for your family. You wanted to save your daughter first. It wasn't your fault that she was swept away. You ran back to save your wife and sons. What a model father and husband you are in this story. Are these real stories?"

"As I said before, all my stories are imagined—"

Adina blinked, stunned. "All of them?"

"Yes, even the ones from the *Mahabharata* or *Ramayana* or *Puranas,* all those stories are myths. Each of these books has various versions. Every narrator uses his own words and the stories change. Even if you ask the same narrator to repeat it, his story is not the same again. Every story is like a river, as its waters are never the same. All journalists know this fact. But I appreciate your intelligence. You understood the messages in these tales."

Adina smiled. "But I still want to know if you were ever interested in marriage?" She repeated her question when she heard no answer. She saw no Narada on the screen, just a forest of banyan trees.

Far to her left on the screen was a small banyan tree under which three well-known musicians were seated cross-legged: Ravi Shankar on the *sitar*, Allah Rakha on the *tabla* drums, and John Lennon chanting his lines: "Imagine there's no heaven, Imagine there's no countries, And no religion, too." The music was so calming that she closed her eyes. She felt no loss for Narada.

Vishnu was nowhere to be seen amongst these real and great musicians. His absence was no loss, either.

CHAPTER 28

Bhairava or Barbarism

Bhairavaaya namaḥ "A bow to Bhairava"
(A mantra for god Bhairava)

Dadi and Dada were not afraid to tell Adina how, in the name of religion, women had been sacrificed like animals. Lord Bhairava used women and animals for the greed of his devotees and became a guard for Lord Shiva. Bhairava had to move wherever Shiva moved. Two favorite residences of Shiva were Kailash and Kashi. The Himalayan mountain of Kailash in Tibet was the ancient Kailasa. Kashi's other ancient name was Varanasi. Bhairava's diet was not identical in these two residences of Shiva. His family also was not identical in these two places. In Kailash he looked after Shiva and Parvati and their children, but in Kashi the women known as *Yogini*, *Shakini*, and *Dakini* became a sort of family for him.

Yoginis were women living by magic, which was associated with their homeland, the land of the Magi people in Iran. The ancient language Magadhi, spoken in Kashi and adjacent Magadha, was the language of the Maga people. The Shakinis were believed to have come from the land of Shaka, eastern Iran, and the Dakinis may have come from Dagistan on the Caspian Sea.

A folk story that Adina heard from Dadi told of the helplessness of these beautiful women. In ancient times, they were forced to live in a strange land. Divodasa, a king mentioned in the *Rig Veda*, ruled in Kashi. He was an ethical man, an impossible dharma for rulers to maintain. His enemies imported sixty-four Yoginis to force him to leave Kashi. These women found themselves in an unfamiliar city like Kashi where they used magic and other strategies to earn their living. Some of them became maids, some saints, some dancers. They failed to mislead King Divodasa and felt remorseful. Then they decided to practice Yoga. The god of Yoga was Lord Shiva, and they became a family of the lord, which included Lord Bhairava, too. Their association with Shiva and Bhairava inspired them to live in Kashi permanently. Since then, people began to worship the sixty-four Yoginis for fulfilling any wish and, a day in the first month of the Hindu year was set aside for Yogini worship.

Even today, people from all over India came to Kashi to pray at the famous temple of Lord Bhairava, which was near the temple of his boss, the famous Vishwanath Temple. Childless women came there to pray or they visited his temple in any city of India. Even small villages had his temples and shrines. He could easily travel to all these places, even where there were no roads, for a big dog was his vehicle. But most of the time he had to be in Kailash or Kashi because his master was Shiva. Shiva loved him so much that he considered Bhairava as his own form. Bhairava also loved his master, but he could make decisions on his own. Adina remembered two folk stories her grandparents told her that showed Bhairava's power, one ancient and another modern.

The famous Bhairava temple of Delhi was believed to have been established by the Pandavas of the *Mahabharata* epic. The cousins Pandavas and Kauravas were ready to fight each other at the Kurukshetra battlefield, and the Pandavas knew that only Lord Bhairava could assure their victory. Bhima, one of the Pandava brothers, was sent to Kashi to bring his statue to Kurukshetra. Lord Bhairava was willing to move with Bhima on one condition, that the first stop of Bhima would be his final stop. Bhima agreed. On the way, Bhima became disoriented and stopped at Indraprastha, which was modern Delhi. Since then Lord Bhairava has a temple there known as the Kala Bhairava Mandir, the Black Bhairava Temple. Delhi was not very far from Kurukshetra. The Pandavas won the Mahabharata War.

The second story was associated with the Mughal Emperor Aurangzeb, who was known for his religious intolerance. He destroyed several major Hindu temples and established Muslim mosques on those sites instead. One mosque he established was next to the Vishwanath temple. He wanted to destroy another big temple that had the statue of Goral Bhairava, or White Bhairava. He ordered his soldiers to demolish the statue before destroying the entire temple. When one soldier went in to hit the statue, a swarm of bees attacked him and no other soldier dared touch the statue. The temple was saved.

Adina understood the power of Lord Bhairava because of such stories, and she meditated on his picture. Instead of Lord Bhairava, however, she saw many beautiful women dancing on the screen. She guessed they were the sixty-four Yoginis. Then more women joined them. She understood them to be the Dakini and Shakini women. But none of these women looked like witches, as described in popular lore. These were very beautiful women.

Adina kept waiting for the *darshan* of Lord Bhairava. After almost an hour, she dropped the idea of his *darshan* and shut down the computer.

One week later, the next Saturday morning, she tried again.

This time Lord Bhairava quickly appeared on the screen, holding a trident in his hand. He was walking in hilly terrain and his dog was following him.

Adina became curious as to why he was not riding his dog. "Lord Bhairava, Namaste," she said softly.

"Long live, my dear child. What's your name?"

"Adina. May I know why you are not riding your dog? Did you come on foot, Lord?"

"No, Adina, I rode him all the way. I am letting him run around and do whatever he wants."

"I am very grateful to you for granting me your *darshan*. Last week I waited almost one hour, but I saw some women, not you. Who were those beautiful women?"

"They must have been Yoginis with Dakini and Shakini women."

"But they did not look like witches as described in popular lore. They were very beautiful women."

"It's sad that you thought of them as witches. They were forced to leave their homelands, but they loved the new people they settled among and were always willing to help them. I could not come last week because I was in Kashi. You thought that I was in my Himalayan residence. Now I am very close to it."

"Where are you right now in the Himalayas?"

"I am now in Pauri in the Garhwal Himalayas. Nearby is a very big temple dedicated to me, and my devotees are worshipping me there right now—"

"You are in the Garhwal region! That's where my ancestors are from. I am very happy to see you there."

"And I am happy to be here. These Pahari people are

very generous. In spite of their poverty, they are offering me a big ram."

"You mean they are killing a ram for you?"

"In Kashi, I was starving for this kind of sacrifice. The Kashi temple offers vegetarian *prasad* for me, but here in the Himalayas, my dog and I are eating our favorite *Prasad*—fresh raw meat of the *bali*."

"These Paharis consider raw meat your *prasad*? I thought Paharis were kind to animals."

"Paharis are honest people. They offer their god what they eat, drink, and smoke. I don't like those religious people who eat meat, drink alcohol, and smoke pot but prohibit all this as *prasad*. Such people are not faithful to their religion. With such double standards, their practice becomes show business."

Suddenly, his dog's distressed whining was heard. "Adina, I will be with you," Lord Bhairava said. "Let me check why my dog is crying." He walked away fast, and then he saw a tiger chasing his dog. The dog was massive but not as massive as the tiger, which leapt upon the dog. But Lord Bhairava pierced the heart of the tiger with his trident. The tiger groaned for a minute and died.

"I saw you kill the tiger and save your dog," Adina scolded when Lord Bhairava came back. "I heard that killing tigers is illegal."

"I killed it in self-defense. Moreover, when I return from that temple, I will offer this tiger's skin to my master. He loves to wear tiger skin," the lord responded as he raised his trident.

"But you wouldn't kill your dog if he hunted a protected deer here, would you?"

"This is the law of the jungle. Your pet is the food for someone else's pet, and someone else's pet is the food for your pet. You may claim to love other animals but you save your pet from them."

Adina felt like a pet herself and in danger. "I feel as if I am my parents' pet. There is danger for many pets, like me, whose parents have double standards. I came to see you to find a solution."

Before she could talk further, she heard the noise of gongs and conchs.

"I think the priest over there is ready for the *bali* of the ram. I have to be present to accept it and fulfill their wishes. I will be back to you and offer my solution." The lord rode his dog to the temple over a wooded trail.

At the corner, Adina could see a temple and, there, a man severed the head of a ram with a dagger in front of a Bhairava statue. Blood gushed out from the severed neck and torso of the ram, and Adina shut the computer down in one click. She didn't care for any favors of Bhairava. *Let those cruel Paharis have his favors. Their god has double standards.*

CHAPTER 29

The Goddess of Names

Naamadevataabhyaḥ namaḥ
"Salutation to the goddesses of name"
(The mantra for the goddesses of Naming ritual)

The family goddess or god might vary from caste to caste. Adina knew this tradition from Dada and Dadi. Her naming ceremony was called *namakarana*. For the naming ceremony Dada had to invite the group of "fourteen holy mothers" after the worship of Lord Ganesha. These holy mothers were respected as the goddesses of *nama*, name, and, among them, the "family goddess" was *Atmakula Devata*. Since she was the most important deity of the family, Adi thought she would know who did what because she presided over the naming of every child in the family. Under that name, she had the records of the name-owner.

On the morning of the eleventh day after Adina's birth, Dada started her naming ceremony. He had to omit certain parts of the ceremony. For example, he didn't include the purification of the child's mother.

Due to the pollution of childbirth, the mother had to

place a mixture of the five holy products, called *pañcha-gavya,* from the cow in her mouth: milk, yogurt, butter, urine, and dung. Pañcha-gavya purifies the mother after she has already taken a bath. The father doesn't need this mixture. For him and the child, however, a bath is essential. After the worship of Atmakula Devata, the father whispers the name in the child's ear.

Dan whispered *Adina* three times in Adina's ear, and then he bowed to the family goddess Atmakula Devata while saying her mantra: "*Aatmakuladevataayai namaḥ*—Salutation to my family goddess."

Adina meditated on this goddess, and the goddess appeared, looking like Parvati. The terrain was hilly. If she were Parvati, she could have used her vehicle, Simha the lion, but instead she walked toward Adina and looked at her with a raised hand to assure her protection.

Dada and Dadi were originally from the Himalayan hills, and so Adina thought she must be their tutelary deity—the family deity of the Badoni Brahmins of Garhwal. She used these associations and didn't question the identity of her family goddess. Who she looked like was not that important for Adina. "Holy Kula Devata," she said. "Please accept my highest regards."

"Hello, Adina. I am delighted to see you. Live long, my dear."

"Mother, I have come to have your *darshan* because you know all about me under my name."

"*Adina, Adina, Adina.* Three times did your father Danin call you gently in your right ear. Your mother Madhu had tears in her eyes. She was the one who preferred this name to all others."

"Oh, I didn't know that there were other names, too. What other names?"

"There were so many. I will give you some right now. Before performing the ceremony, your dada requested everyone to suggest a name to your father. The ritual requires the father to choose whatever name he likes, but all the family members were excited to give you a name they liked the best. The list grew big, but most voted for Jhandi as the flagship name. Jhandi means flag. Everybody understood it as a joke."

"What was the name my nani suggested?"

Adina thought that might lead the goddess to talk about Nani's crown jewel secret.

"Her suggestion was a combination of Madhu and Danin, your parents' names, which made sense, for you are the child of your parents. She wanted Mada or Dama, but everyone thought that when you went to school your friends might tease you: 'Hi, Mad!' or 'Hi, Dam!' Would you have liked to be greeted like that, Adi?"

Adina laughed. "Well, that depends! It's hard to choose the right name." She laughed again.

"In some cases it's not so hard. No one would care for the name 'Osama' if a boy was born after September 11, 2001."

"Not in the USA, but, in Pakistan, Osama bin Laden was a hero."

"You are right. For many, Adolf Hitler is a hero."

"I am glad I am a girl and these insane killers were men."

"You would be surprised how many girls have the names of boys and how many boys have the names of girls."

"That's true. My great-grandfather's name was Girija Dev, but everyone called him Girija. That is our goddess Parvati, and so he had a name that means Parvati. And my great grandmother's name was Vayu, the name of the wind god, the father of the monkey god Hanuman."

The goddess laughed. "Adi, you are smart. You know all this. Your great-granduncle was lucky that he never came to America. His name was Ram. He didn't look like a he-goat."

"But we admire names which come from animals. I have a classmate named Leo. Another classmate's family name is Lamb."

"I understand you know the great figure Leonardo da Vinci. I feel good about the writer Charles Lamb, too. And Ram for Rama is a good nickname. Any name is fine, so long it does not evoke ill feelings. But nobody wants his child to be poor. So, your parents liked Adina, never poor. Live up to your name, dear Adina."

"But some Indian children raised as American kids would not like to live up to their names. Those names are embarrassing. Americans make fun of those kids."

The goddess raised her eyebrows. "Really? Give me some examples."

"I will give the names of my friends. Harshita, Harsh, Meet, Dik Pal. Harshita blames her parents. The parents try to make her happy. In India Harshita means 'the happy one.' That explanation makes Harshita angrier!"

The goddess nodded. "I understand the bad shade of her name. She can modify it slightly as Harshi, and no problem. Any name can be modified a little bit. Check with linguists."

"Linguists cannot stop Hindi poets and singers from adoring a *gori*. But feminists should say that it is politically incorrect to glorify a 'light-skinned' girl in Hindi films. Not just equality of men and women but also equality of all women. I have a relative. Her name is *Shweta*. But her complexion is not *white*. She is black, like the majority of girls in south India. Her mother is from Tamil Nadu. She is not like my Himalayan grandmother who is light-skinned. She is as beautiful as Dadi."

"Ask goddess Kali why girls are not named after her. Why are so many girls named after Lakshmi and Sarasvati? But don't worry! Kids with any name can earn big fame later, whereas those who have good names may bring shame. Meet the next president named Meet, friendly to everyone! No name hurts the chances of your success."

"So how do you define success, Mother?"

"In simple words, success is do better today than what you did yesterday."

"My mother failed to live up by her good name. Instead of sweetness, she wasted her time in creating bitterness for her, for my father, and for me. Name calling cost my parents hundreds of thousands of dollars. Did you think that I would be really rich when I was given my name?"

"Remember, when I say 'today and 'yesterday,' I mean every day's time. Honor time and work every day with discipline, and you will be rich. Losers lose because they lose time and are doomed to live by poor excuses. I said nothing new. All successful people know this simple work ethic. Seek advice from successful people."

The goddess paused and raised her hand. "A warning! Do not accuse others for your wrongs. The process of success starts when you accept your mistakes and correct them. Failures have a tendency to blame others for their failures."

"Are you telling me, Mother?" Adina retorted with a smile. "I am worried if I could live up to my name."

"Don't worry. Nobody can predict the future by the name that a child gets. A child born today could be the president and earn a Nobel Peace prize, another child a murderer and then earn death penalty. But while growing up, their parents might have celebrated their birthdays with big parties, with high hopes."

Adina cleared her throat. "I have to tell you this story. Dada met a young man, Amitabh from Garhwal, in a

New Delhi restaurant. He was a waiter and asked Dada to arrange a better paying job for him. Dada told him to start his own little street restaurant, a dhaba, which he could expand further. Amitabh looked at Dada as if he was joking. Dada told him bluntly that it would be a little hard for him to become limitlessly famous like the Buddha. With his high school education, this waiter knew that the Buddha was given another title, Amitabha, the man with immeasurable aura. He told Dada that he was named after Amitabh Bachchan, not after Buddha. Dada tried to inspire him. He told him, 'If you don't talk like Amitabh Bachchan, you are not Amitabh Bachchan. If you don't look like Amitabh Bachchan, you are not Amitabh Bachchan. If you look like a Pahari, you talk like a Pahari. You can work hard. Start a business of your own.' Poor Dada has never been able to inspire anyone to start any business. But Dada was quite flabbergasted to know that a Pahari named someone Amitabh. Shouldn't it be in your records of famous people?"

The goddess laughed and added her own joke. "I have millions of names in my records. Most Indian children are named after the Nehru-Gandhi children. Go to New Delhi, and you will meet an Indira or a Rajiv or a Sanjay or a Rahul or a Priyanka on every block. Then there is no limit on selecting the names of the Bollywood actors and actresses. Even in Mumbai's poor slums, many children have these names. Their parents hope those children will be as famous someday. They just copy those famous names as they are. No corrections. Several actresses have boys' names. You will find the same boys' names for their slum girls. Worse, a girl is named Lata after Lata Mangeshkar. They joke about that girl: she is capable of singing all ragas in one and the same note, no rhythm required. Mangeshkar's music made easy!"

The goddess and Adina laughed.

After a little pause, Adina sighed. "Can't she change her name?"

"Sure, she can change her name. Many Bollywood actors and actresses have changed their names. But the famous cricket captain Dhoni didn't change his Pahari name. You can change Badoni to Sharma. So many Paharis are ashamed of their Pahari names. But Lata thinks that her parents gave her the right name."

"Actually, she doesn't have to change her name if she doesn't tell anyone that she was named after the famous singer of India."

"That's right. Lata is a beautiful name, short and easy to pronounce. It has no difficult sounds. And it's not a religious name. Anyone of any faith, rich or poor, can have this name. It's a secular name."

"So Osama is fine to choose?"

"Sure. Why should we think that someone was named after the terrorist Osama unless the boy or his parents say so? Osama is as good as Leo. No animal ever created any religion. Only humans are able to be irrational, but it is quite rational if you want to change your name."

Adina laughed. "I will, as soon as I become penniless. By the way, my mother has changed her name. Does name-change change you?"

The goddess chuckled. "Adi! Change happens when you confess 'I was wrong.' Change has a better chance to grow if you plant it in the present tense. If you say 'I will change' you may put a spin on your own words later! But sure, you have the right to change your name. I can recommend a few names."

Adina then heard some scary shouting and saw a human figure yelling at her in one corner of her screen, quite a robust and ferocious male with big eyes. "Recommend my name. I am Ravana, the enemy of Rama. He and his brother Lakshamana demonized me. They assaulted my sister Shurpanakha, and, for revenge, I abducted Rama's wife Sita. Do you think I was wrong? Revenge is normal for any man, or even for a country. Obama took revenge against Osama. America took revenge against Japan in World War Two. How was I wrong?"

Before Adina could respond, she heard shouting coming from the other corner of her screen. "Wait! Don't recommend his name. He was a coward king of the island of Lanka. I ruled a big country from Mathura. My name is Kamsa. Pick my name. Ravana is a suitable name for liars."

Adina mustered her courage. "No, I cannot recommend your name. You deprived Vasudeva and Devaki of their children. The couple was imprisoned by your order. Both were innocent and they were your relatives. You killed their six children, but then came the seventh child, a daughter. She miraculously escaped. So did the eighth child, Krishna. You are really a terrorist like Ravana. No way will I recommend your names."

Ravana and Kamsa began to brandish their swords. "I am going to thrash you like Krishna's sister!"

A lion came from behind and attacked Kamsa, and Ravana ran away. The lion chased him, and, after they left her screen, she heard the roar of the lion and cries of Ravana. She was confused. Could the goddess be Parvati? She might have left her Simha behind. Or it could be another Simha. Lions, like any other animals, don't name themselves. But Adina decided to name this lion Leo and use Simha only to refer to Parvati's lion.

Adina shut the computer quickly for one reason. Leo came back and began to tear out the guts of the wounded Kamsa. Adina couldn't watch Kamsa dying bit by bit again.

The goddess reconfirmed what Dada and Dadi had

told her. A child's name was cultural but the child was natural, nameless. The goddess implied this when she said, "Only humans are able to be irrational." Humans named themselves, as did the whole world of nations, and then they fought. But these names were not their natural identity.

Also, the goddess implied that animals were rational because they didn't use names. Did Leo use any names for his fellow lions? Did the cosmos change if humans referred to Lanka as Sri Lanka? Adina laughed at her questions as she greeted herself. "Hello, Adina!"

CHAPTER 30

The Goddess of Satiety

Jai Santoshi Ma! "Hail Santoshi Ma!"

Adina got excited when for two reasons she saw a series of photos of Santoshi Mata and a description of a Hindi film *Jai Santoshi Ma*. Mata Santoshi was the Mother of Satiety because she provided *santosha,* or satisfaction, regarding any wish of the worshipper.

While babysitting Adina, Nani frequently watched Bollywood movies. Adina remembered well that the film *Jai Santoshi Ma* promoted belief in the Puja of Santoshi. Maybe Nani offered the crown jewel to the goddess.

Mata Parvati was Adina's real ancestral deity. Parvati meant "Pahari." That Pahari goddess was the mother of Lord Ganesha, who was the father of Santoshi Ma. Adina was a Pahari like these three deities and so she felt a close kinship with them.

But Santoshi was never known to the Pahari people until some devotees from the Indian plains told them about her. As a rule, the Pahari people did not take a serious interest in any goddess that didn't require animal sacrifice, for they loved to eat the sacrificed animal's roasted meat as sacred food. The Puja of Santoshi Mata was performed for sixteen Fridays. No regular meals were consumed, and, in fact, just one meal a day. The only foods allowed were hard molasses, chickpeas, and bananas. Sixteen days of such tasteless food was too big a sacrifice for a Pahari. And worse, the Pahari people could not believe that Santoshi Ma was a vegetarian, unlike her grandmother. But Adina's nani was not a Pahari. She would not have any problem meeting this *vrata*'s requirements to achieve her wish.

Dadi and Dada had told Adina about the goddess. One of their devout Hindu friends used to do the Santoshi service. That lady had a daughter and a son, both of them obese. The family doctor wanted them to lose weight before they encountered serious health problems, but the kids were born and raised in the USA and didn't change their regular American diet, refusing especially to give up hamburgers. The parents were strict vegetarians and thought the kids would turn out to be vegetarians someday. Their Santoshi Puja failed, most probably because the kids were not willing to eat that tasteless Santoshi Puja food either.

But the parents put the blame on the kids, saying they lied to their parents. They had secretly eaten a couple of pop tarts just when their mother was reciting the holy *vrata* story of the goddess during the "completion ceremony" on the last Friday in front of the other invited boys. Any sour food was forbidden until the *Uddyapana*, the final ceremony. The two kids continued to gain weight. *Obviously, the goddess was sour with them.* Adi thought. *What a very sensitive goddess!*

Nani would never disrespect any goddess, Pahari or non-Pahari. No devout Hindu ignored this goddess, especially as she had been recognized by Bollywood since

1975. So Adina decided to meditate on the Mother of Satiety.

She gazed on her photo, the same kind shown in the Bollywood movie for the Puja. The photo showed the beautiful young goddess with no Pahari features or Pahari-style clothing. Her light-complexion rightly suggested that she was worshipped more by the women of warm northern plains of India. The goddess was clad in a thin sari with a half-sleeve blouse. A nose ring adorned her long nose and a red *bindi* mark was on her forehead. The four-armed goddess had two weapons in her two hands, a sword and a trident. Most importantly for Adina, she had a beautiful crown on her head.

Adina could not resist laughing because of Dadi's earlier information on the ignorance of the worshippers. If the goddess had her ancestral roots on the border of India and Tibet, then she should have, like other Pahari women, some Indo-Tibetan features. Her thin sari and blouse didn't make sense either. The high-altitude Pahari women had traditionally used a wool blanket as a sari and often covered their heads with a turban. After all, these Pahari deities came from one of the coldest places of the world, the Indo-Tibetan border.

No wonder Bollywood Hindi movies were ridiculed as fantasies. Adina couldn't stop laughing, and so her meditation was doomed on this first attempt.

The next morning, she ignored what Dadi had told her, and, with the strong urge to locate her crown jewel, she succeeded in getting Santoshi Ma on the screen. The goddess looked exactly as in the movie. Nothing like a Pahari woman. And she had a handbag hanging from her shoulder, too.

"Ma, many pranams to you. You look so beautiful."

"May you succeed in your goal. I love you. How do I address you?"

"I am Adina. You can call me Adi. I had difficulty in having your *darshan*. Like me, your ancestry is Himalayan, so why do you look like a woman from the plains of north India? That question made me laugh. I apologize, Ma."

"No need to apologize. My grandmother Parvati is a daughter of the Himalaya, but the Bollywood folks make me look like their local actresses. In Mumbai they have a great celebration of my father, Lord Ganapati, as if he were a native of that city."

"Some Indians wonder why you don't have an elephant's head like your father."

"Those Indians should examine their own heads. My father's original body was created by my grandmother, Parvati, in the image of my grandfather, Shiva, who later transplanted the elephant's head."

"Yes, Dadi told me about the first transplant technology."

"That's the name of my daughter, Technology."

"Oh, you have a daughter. I didn't know. Why doesn't she have a Sanskrit name like yours?"

"She is American. I adopted her there. Some Indian women worship me there regularly, and they recommended that I adopt her. Now almost everybody is worshipping her. Now most Americans put trust in her, not in God. So God is now resting in Yama's abode."

"Yama's abode? What do you mean by that?"

"That you must ask Lord Yama. But tell me why you needed me, Adi."

Adina gave a great many details to the goddess. The goddess nodded, as if she understood everything. However, as with the other deities, Ma Santoshi had no such crown. Nevertheless, she requested that Adina continue worshipping her daughter.

"What do you mean 'continue worshipping' her, Ma?"

"You have already started worshipping her, for most of the information about your parents' case became known to you through my daughter. My *darshan* has been given to you through her blessing. She will fulfill wishes of all with no discrimination. I could not fulfill all of the wishes of my own devotees, and many have lost faith in me."

Then Adina told the goddess how those two kids couldn't control their obesity.

"Adi, their mother was dishonest. Like mother, like kids. She was supposed to eat plain *chana* beans during my worship. Instead she ate *chana chat*, a delicacy full of spices, salt, tamarind, and fried potatoes—all forbidden stuff. But she didn't tell anyone! I wanted to poke her with my trident. Just to let her know that the kids had a digital camera."

Adina laughed.

While Adina was laughing, Santoshi Ma threw away her sword and trident and opened her bag. She showed Adi a small laptop computer and a digital camera. That stopped Adina's laughing.

"Adi, imagine your father's plight without these two gadgets. He preserved important events of his married life. If he had not saved those emails, your mother's lies could have succeeded. Those pictures and videos you mentioned he saved were the saviors of his honor. Now, if anyone trusts your mother, you can show them those emails and pictures. Don't remain satisfied. You can use those records to eradicate this disease of false allegations against the spouse. You don't need Mother of Satiety. You need her daughter, Technology. She has a better record of granting human wishes. Be her devotee. Soon Technology will bring a machine that will reveal human thoughts. Criminal liars will have to face a new criminal justice. Technology will replace your kind of biased judges and psychologists. Technology will succeed in observing equal rights—your parental and grandparental rights, rights of rich and poor, any kind."

Then Ma sighed. After a pause she shook her head. "My real failure can be understood if you watch the 2008 movie *Slumdog Millionaire*. This movie shows how the slums became worse in Mumbai. The 1975 movie *Jai Santoshi Ma* didn't do any good for the slum dwellers."

Adina could not know that Mata Santoshi would be so saddened. She disappeared from the screen, but Adina remembered her instructions: "Check with Lord Yama."

CHAPTER 31

Chief Chitragupta

Citraguptaaya namaḥ "A Bow to Chitragupta"
(The prayer mantra for Chitragupta)

Adi decided that a meeting with Yama's chief-of-staff could be far more useful than the meeting with Yama, the God of Death. The most popular story of Chief Chitragupta was about why Lord Brahma created him from his own body. In the beginning, the creator god Brahma had no wife, and all of his children, including his daughter Sarasvati, came out of his own body and mind. One day Lord Yama complained to the lord of creation, "Pitamaha, I am overloaded with the karmic records of every being. You have to help me in easing my load. Otherwise, many crooks may go unpunished and many innocent unrewarded."

Brahma, the grandfather, or Pitamaha, of all beings, considered the Yama's complaint. He brought out yet another son that was situated in his body, or *Kaya.* Thus some people began to call this *Kaya-stha* or *Kayasthas,* but Brahma called his new son Chitragupta, whose job was to record images, or *chitras,* of all the actions of every being and keep all those images hidden, or *gupta*.

This story was not a random choice for Adina to consider for his *darshan*. She had questions relating to her goals. For example, she wanted to know if he knew what happens to the American children of divorced parents. Divorced parents had to spend more money on their children than the parents who stayed together. Chitragupta might have his own opinion on the matter. At least he would know that the American justice system had no regard for shared parenting.

She meditated on him intensely, and he quickly appeared and blessed her.

"Pranam, Dada told me that you are the keeper of the 'secret records' of all beings. Lord, please forgive me for taking your precious time."

"Yes, I have all the facts and figures of the good and bad karma of all beings. Tell me what you would like to know."

Adina told her story quickly. Chitragupta closed his eyes for a second and then opened them wide. "I am very pleased with you. As an American girl, you have an admirable record. Over eighty-five percent of children from broken homes live with their mothers, like you do. Here are the records of your country. Of the children who do not live with their fathers, thirty percent become suicidal and more than seventy percent are high-school dropouts. More than seventy percent of those in state-operated institutions for juveniles are from this category, as are more than eighty-five percent of adults in prisons for various crimes. If you were a part of these horrible statistics, the blame would be on your mother, who tried to make you a fatherless child by using false allegations against him. Then she said later that she never thus accused him. This is unpardonable. She deserves to be sued, since your father was exonerated. I regularly recommend heavy punishment, for any reckless parents, to the king of fairness, Dharma Raja."

"You mean to Lord Yama?"

"Yama, Lord Death, is my boss. Death maintains dharma, which is law and order, fairness. Yama checks my recommendations with one goal only: dharma. He has the power to overrule my recommendations, and sometimes he does not go through all the details I present to him, for he is overwhelmed. Then I take things into my own hands. Sometimes, I assign this duty to other deities, and humans can also assist me. My load would lessen if you fight for dharma in America, and you will make faster progress if you stop irrelevant talking. Stick to the bottom line if you expect to reach the goal faster."

"What kind of decisions do you make when Death ignores your recommendations?" Adina didn't realize the consequences of her question until suddenly the screen began to show torture. She saw a man crying in pain. He was being surrounded by vultures and hyenas as a group of red wolves was howling and biting him. Blood was oozing from his ears, mouth, and nose. Adina shuddered when she heard the deafening noise of his screams.

"Lord, what is this?" she shouted.

"This is a man who slowly poisoned his wife to death and abandoned his young son," the invisible Chitragupta responded. "The young boy was raised by a couple who had no children of their own. Both husband and wife were on drugs, and they raised the boy with drugs. One day, the boy was admitted to the local hospital where he remained in coma for more than a year. The couple was arrested, but the boy's birth father was not punished for abandoning him. He had started a new family and the members of that family never knew that he had a son. Yama forgot to punish him. So here is my own treatment for this reckless father. He is in the hell called *Raurava*.

This hell is going to increase in noise level until he is disoriented. His son died in the silence of a coma. I am going to change the scene. The noise is going to be unbearable."

Before Adina could object, the next scene was already on the screen. "This hell is called *Kumbhipaka*. See that huge pot? Two women are being cooked in it slowly. Let me bring the pot into your view clearly."

Adina saw two women screaming in pain, their faces burnt and puffed. "Lord! Please have mercy on them!"

Adina heard his response. "These two women are criminals. One is a mother-in-law who hated her son-in-law. Her daughter accused him of child abuse, but the doctor found no abuse of the child, a two-year-old daughter. But a specialist in child development told the judge that there was child abuse and so the son-in-law was not given any custody rights at all. His friends began to suspect him of what he was accused, and indeed, two friends avoided his company and did not allow their children any contact with him. He was legally declared a child-abuser and had difficulty renting a house in any decent colony. One day, he committed suicide. So I am cooking the mother-in-law and the child development specialist here together. I will cook the mother later. But let me show you another hell."

The scene changed, and Adina was looking at a wooded and rocky terrain on the screen. In the middle, she saw a big hole. Before Adina could say anything, the invisible voice declared, "That hole is a dark cave that is huge inside. It's dark and full of filthy air. The name of this dark hell is *Tamisra*. Those two liar friends are gasping for fresh air. They want to confess, but it's too late. Now they can't breathe or talk. They are trying to come out but can't see their way—"

"Lord," Adina interrupted. "How long are you going to torture them?"

"As long as they lived after that man's suicide."

"I hear the cries of men. Where are they coming from, lord?"

"From the neighboring hell, which is darker than *Tamisra*. That is why it is called *Andha-Tamisra*, blinding dark hell. The men you hear crying stoned a woman to death. Let me show them to you from the entrance of this hell."

In the corner of the screen, Adi saw the pitch dark cave and heard the rattling noise of falling rocks.

"Adina, you can't see them. They can't move from within, and each has lost a hand and a leg. That is how we punish them here. Those rocks are falling on them, bleeding them—"

"I have the same question again. How long are they going to suffer like that?"

"I have the same answer. As long as they lived after they stoned that woman to death."

"Won't it be better for you to kill them than torturing them like that?"

"Adina, there is no death penalty in dharma. All these you have watched being tortured have come to us after death. No one dies twice. You meet Death only once. That's the dharma of Death. Not even Death can change that."

Adina understood that Death meant Yama for Chitragupta. "Thanks for your record keeping, Lord Chitragupta. Namaste. It looks like I am ready to meet Yama." She mumbled these words as if gasping for air.

What if Chitragupta continues to show those terrible hidden images? She shut the computer down, but she was surprised at how much anger the karma keeper expressed against the dharma-less justice system of her country.

CHAPTER 32

Yama's Yami Judgments

Yamaaya namaḥ "Salutation to Yama."
(A Sanskrit mantra for Yama)

Because of Santoshi Mata's request, Adina felt obligated to check with Yama, but among Dadi's stories of Yama, she found several in competition for her attention. The easiest icon for his *darshan*, she thought, would be the one found in many temples and books: Yama riding a male water buffalo. Both beings were very dark-skinned, and Yama was wearing a crown and several other things. But the scary thing he carried in one of his four hands was a rope. The god of death used this to strangle a being.

Adina meditated at the dark picture of Yama as shown on her computer screen, but no Yama would appear for *darshan*. She was left with no choice but to use another story of Yama.

One early story in the *Rig Veda* went like this: Yama and Yami, brother and sister, wer twins. Their father was Vivasvan the vibrant, most probably the sun god. The mother's name was Samjña, most probably the symbol of intelligence or consciousness. When the twins became adults, Yami wanted to get married and raise a family. The only male around was her brother, Yama, and so she begged Yama to marry her. He refused her proposal every time. He was against sibling marriage.

The other story was found a little later in an *Upanishad*, and it included a discussion between Yama and a young boy, Nachiketas. The boy's father was mad at him because he would ask question after question. "Now you go to Yama," the father said angrily. "You question me again and again about my motive for charity, but I have no motive."

The young boy was honest and obedient and so he proceeded to meet Yama. He knew that Yama was the God of Death, but the boy was not offended or saddened by his father's rage. He saw his chance to learn more even while meeting Death. He went to Yama's abode, but Yama was not home. The boy waited for three nights, and finally Yama returned and asked for forgiveness. To please his young guest, he granted him any three boons. For the boy's third question, he asked, "Sir, clear the doubt about what happens after death. Some say there is no life after death. Some say there is. This is my third boon."

"Your question is very hard," Yama responded tenderly. "Except for me, no one knows about the hereafter, but I beg you to drop your question. You can ask me for wealth or entertainment or even a kingdom, and I will grant all of these wishes. But do not ask me that hard question."

The young boy became more inquisitive. "If only the God of Death knows about the hereafter, then who could be a better teacher than you? I am your guest and student now. You cannot ignore my request. You have given me two boons already, and now you have to fulfill your promise to give me my third boon."

Yama was very fair and granted the boy's request. "After death, the body dies, not the Atman. The Self or Atman is never born and therefore never dies. After one's body's death, the Self takes another body. And thus there is life after life until the Self attains knowledge. Attaining knowledge means being able to see your Self everywhere and in all. This Self is all. Such knowledge is the key to stop rebirth. To be in the cycle of rebirth is painful. So, keep trying to get rid of ignorance."

The boy thanked his guru Yama for this talk. The God of Death also praised his disciple, a true inquirer. He then happily sent him back to his father.

The father thought that Nachiketas was not really dead but just wandering around for a few days. He never understood how his young child was determined to look for facts beyond the present life.

The ancient Sanskrit book where this Nachiketas story was given was called the *Katha Upanishad,* which translated as "hard meeting." The third question was a very tough one to answer at the short meeting of Yama and Nachiketas.

Adina thought of the bright Yama this time, the son of the Sun god. She meditated and meditated until she succeeded and Yama appeared on the screen. Adina greeted him with the normal *Namaste* gesture of respect.

The first thing she asked him was this: "Lord, why didn't you appear in my first meditation attempt at your *darshan*?"

"Why do you want my *darshan*?"

"Did you ever receive a crown jewel from my Nani?"

Yama looked surprised. "What is that?"

Adina told him her story, and, after listening to her, the death god responded, "No, not I, nor anyone from my home, ever received such a jewel. Now I will explain why you failed in your first attempt."

"That will be a great favor, lord."

"Adina," Lord Yama said, addressing her with a grim voice. "I am really dark. That means it's very hard to see me and my endless knowledge of life and death. I am the Dharma Raja, the king of laws. These dharmas are beyond the understanding of anyone."

"Lord Dharma Raja, my father told me that there are laws of the jungle and there are the human laws. Are your laws the laws of the jungle?"

"Your father is right," Yama replied. "My laws are natural laws, the same as the laws of the jungle. Human laws are cultural laws and vary from society to society, country to country, state to state, court to court, and even judge to judge. My laws are not human laws. However, you find my laws in many places."

"What do you mean by that?"

"In some states like yours, a judge can reward a criminal liar and mistreat an innocent person. Such a judge is far from acting within the bounds of human civilization. It does not matter who is rewarded and who is punished under my law. Hitler and Gandhi do not make any difference to me. I know Hitler tortured innocent people and Gandhi wouldn't hurt even a dangerous ant. In the laws of the jungle, the cruel and the kind are not judged. Only humans judge them."

"Sir, if you are unable to judge kind and cruel, then you aren't a Dharma Raja. My dadi and dada told me that *dharma* means the ethics of right and wrong, but they don't believe in your *karma* myth, do not believe that you or God reward and punish beings by their wrong or right actions. There is no life after death."

"I will end your life and your dada and dadi's, too," Yama said as he moved toward her.

"Right now? All three of us?"

"Right now! All three of you!" His voice was firm and loud.

"Your three boons are lies," Adina shouted back. "No god is able to give and take life."

He quickly threw his rope around Adina's neck. She instantly pulled the rope from her neck and shut the computer down. There was no strangling rope now, just the laptop in her hands instead. There was no Yama either.

Dadi had told Adina long ago about that old Indian ideal that Yama conveyed to Nachiketas: "See everyone as yourself." She knew it was a good ideal but very difficult to practice. Even saintly people couldn't do it easily. Dadi gave the example of a Swami who preached that we should see one and the same Atman or Self in everyone. The only exception he made was Sonia Gandhi.

"She is a foreigner, Italian," Swami ji said that to his followers.

He never told them that xenophobia was caused by ignorance, xenophobia was a sickness. What happened to his mission of the Vedanta philosophy, the oneness of all? Like the previous Vedanta philosophers, he had no concern for the equal rights of women and untouchables of India. Like the American judges who had no concern for the equal rights of parents and grandparents.

So Dadi had three more questions for the Dharma Raja. Doesn't every citizen of India have the right to be a top leader in India? Are there really any foreigners living on Mother Earth? Can you really choke any liar?

There went Dharma Raja. He was unable to choke any liar, and the swami would continue lying. It was a joke that, after death, there would be judgment for liars, too. "We better judge them here," Dadi says.

Adina had totally forgotten her question for Yama: "Is God residing with you?"

CHAPTER 33

Return of the Revenge

Shaṭhe shaaṭhyam "Tit for Tat"
(A Sanskrit Proverb)

Devotees tended to see their gods or goddesses, God included, as ideal figures with no faults. They enthusiastically recommended them for peace and prosperity. Adina doubted such claims because her dadi and dada considered all deities as images of extreme human behaviors, way over the edge. Himalayan people loved meat, so their gods loved animal sacrifice. Animals got no peace or prosperity. But the Himalayan priests claimed that the animals beheaded at a Vedic sacrifice got the best in heaven. Adina thought killing animals was an extreme example of cruelty. The state apex court was kind and courageous to ban it. Otherwise, in India it was easier for the court to ban controversial books than cruel butchering. Nobody said here that the *Vedas* should be banned. Many books legally allowed human beheading. Those books were revered.

Adina was bemused when Dada translated an early *Rig Veda* hymn in which Indra and Varuna brag with self-praises. Adina questioned if gods would really brag like this about themselves.

Dada's response was quick. "Most likely these two top gods drank too much *soma* and ate a lot of steak offered at a big *homa* sacrifice."

Adina laughed so much! Gods, too, could be under the influence and fight for a greater share of the Vedic sacrifices.

But what about their family fights? Besides their politics, gods had families. Not all, but some of the deities Adina interviewed were householders. She wondered if it was a myth that having a family meant a happy household. When most young humans grew into adults, they developed respect for their parents. Godly families were expected to follow this sort of human ideal too. Dada and Dadi never told Adina if there were stories of domestic violence in godly families and so she decided to find out for herself by revisiting some of those families with her thoughts.

She thought of Ganesha, the elephant-headed god to be worshipped first. His father, Shiva, beheaded him when he was just an infant. The moment she thought of this violent abuse of a child, her screen showed a fight between Shiva and Ganapati.

"You accepted a whole lot of *bhang* offered by your weed-smoking devotees. Then you got high and returned home earlier, unexpectedly. Weren't you under its influence when you cut off my natural head? I am going to cut off your head right now," Ganesha yelled at his father Shiva as he wielded his ax.

Shiva also picked up his ax. "How do you dare call me a weed smoker?" he yelled back. "I placed an elephant's head on your top, not in your tummy. Look at your udder, full of fat from the sweet *laddus*. Those free balls were offered by your devotees." He tried to slash Ganesha's long and wide stomach. "I am going to cut your tummy!"

There appeared to be no winner in this fierce fight. Both hurled sharp weapons and accusations at each other, but with no spins. Both were successful in thwarting each other's attack and appeared unscathed.

Nevertheless, Adina kept looking at them, almost petrified. She thought the fight was over and took a deep breath when they stopped momentarily.

But then Ganesha used his long trunk to grab Shiva's neck. Luckily for Shiva, his cobra, who slithered from his master's neck, wrapped itself around Ganesha's trunk. Before the cobra could bite him, Ganesha pushed Shiva backward.

The cobra fell to the ground but it grabbed Ganesha's mouse in his mouth. Before it could swallow the mouse, a peacock, the vehicle of Karttikeya who'd just arrived there, came from behind.

"Go, Ganesha, my brother," Karttikeya encouraged. "Go, get him. He didn't want to raise me. He left me in the care of those Krittika nurses. Go brother, teach him a lesson—"

"Yes, I am your adopted brother, Karttikeya. Shiva adopted me because my natural mother Parvati pressured him. He failed to tell me who my elephant mother and elephant father were."

"Maybe he wants to hide that information from you."

Karttikeya didn't see Shiva's bull, Nandin, behind him. The bull gored Karttikeya so hard that he fell into the recycle bin on Adina's computer. In retaliation, the peacock threw the cobra into the recycle bin. The mouse was still in the mouth of the cobra. Shiva, Ganesha, and Karttikeya entered the recycle bin to regain their animals. They knew that, unlike their father Shiva, the cobra was not a vegetarian.

Adina didn't want to wait any longer. "What if Parvati's lion showed up here to enjoy them with gusto?" she wondered aloud.

Lo and behold, the lion appeared and roared as he heard cries from the bin. He jumped into it. Adina quickly took advantage of the recycle bin on her computer and changed the screen.

She thought that, if this happy family could go wild, then other happy-looking families could also drop their mantle.

Adina's interest, and her focus, now shifted to other deities—to Sarasvati and her father Brahma. They appeared on the screen, quarreling.

Sarasvati thrashed her lute, the *vina.* "I am going to address you as Brahm," she shouted. "You were first my dad. Then you became my husband. I cannot call you 'Dad.' I cannot call you 'Hubby.' You are not a decent being. Your one head says one thing while the other says another. How can you say to me 'Hey, my little baby!' this time and 'Hey, my dear wife!' another time? Get out of my sight."

"Don't get mad at me. I only meant to act in your best interests. I gave you that swan. That animal flies better than any supersonic plane. We both are lucky to have him as our vehicle."

Sarasvati picked up the broken neck of the *vina,* and she began to hit the swan with it so badly that the bird hid in the recycle bin. Brahma went after him but couldn't see him. Suddenly, the swan sent his distress calls from the bin. Sarasvati and Brahma entered the bin too.

If Sarasvati is so unhappy about her marriage, then think of Krishna's eight wives, Adina mused. She considered them, one by one.

Rukmini came on the screen. "Pranam Ma," Adina said respectfully.

"I bless you, my daughter," said Rukmini, showing affection through her beautiful eyes. "What is your reason to meet me here?"

"Ma, you shared Krishna with seven other wives. Were you happy with your marriage?" Adina asked, looking straight into Rukmini's eyes.

"Only in the beginning," Rukmini replied.

"Ma, you look sad."

"So was Satyabhama, the other wife. She told me. But I am sure Radha was the worst victim because she was Krishna's first love."

"How about other girls?"

"You mean the cowgirls, the *gopis*?"

"Yes."

"Why does one of God's representatives need so many women? Why don't people call the situation what it is: women's mistreatment by a male bully? Krishna's devotees have questionable beliefs. They condemn one man for touching women inappropriately and worship another man for kissing women inappropriately. Calling one man a *badmash* and another a *bhagavan*! Such double standards have harmed women, even unto their violent death." Rukmini began to sob. She closed her eyes. Her distinction between an "abuser" and an "avatar" appeared seamless to Adina.

Adina understood her pain. "Someday your pain will be taken away by a UN law. Polygamy is a crime. It is actually slavery for women." Adina wasn't sure if Rukmini heard her words of hope. The screen had gone blank.

Adina now didn't want to meet the other wives of Krishna.

She thought of Indra, who was close to Krishna in his status as a culture hero. The throne of heaven was what he cared about the most, and so he was always apprehensive that some competitor would take his throne. How could he be happy even in heaven with this sort of worry? As soon as she opened the screen again, she saw Indra with his son Jayanta, who was rebuking him.

"Father, you humiliated my mother Shachi. You should have treated her as your wife, the only wife. Instead, you added those *apsaras*. What you call heaven is a high-level harem. Didn't you take advantage of those women?"

Indra didn't say a word in retaliation. Instead, he picked up his thunderbolt and hurled it. Suddenly a big rainstorm came and a bolt of lightning hit Jayanta in the shoulder. He fell into the recycle bin. Shachi seemed to have been agitated by the destructive lightning strikes. She appeared there to seek help from Indra.

He told her what happened, and she screamed in fear. "He was the legitimate heir to your throne. Why did you inflict such terrible pain on him?"

"Let's look for him in that bin," Indra responded.

They too entered the recycle bin.

Adina didn't want to see Indra again, but Shachi's words stayed with her. How could a parent deprive his own child of his inheritance? No family members should be allowed to inflict such pain on their legitimate heirs.

This thought led Adina to remember Kaikeyi of the *Ramayana*. She and her son Bharata began to quarrel on Adina's computer screen.

"Mother," Bharata said in a harsh tone. "You became jealous of Rama because he was my half-brother, but he was the eldest among us four brothers and the legitimate heir of Kosala's kingdom. Why did you exile him?"

"Son, I didn't exile him. Your father Dasharatha did," Kaikeyi responded.

"You are a liar. You advised our father to send him in exile."

"I never said that Rama was not the legitimate heir. It was Manthara who said it."

"Manthara was your housemaid. You were her queen. How could you shift your blame to her? You forced our father to inflict pain on Sita and our brother Lakshamana. Our father couldn't bear the shock of your malicious intent and died as soon as Rama, Sita, and Lakshmana departed for the forest. You are not only a liar, but a heartless woman. I am not going to live with you." Bharata left the screen.

Kaikeyi cried and followed him. "Wait, son! I did everything for your good. Don't leave me alone. Look at my tears!"

A big shout came from behind the screen. "Your tears are destructive! You are a sick woman. Breaking the family is your entertainment. You are not fit to live with Bharata's family. You are a bad influence on the children. How can you sleep alone with your lies? Go to Dasharatha. Lie with him again."

Then Kaikeyi disappeared from the screen.

Adina laughed when she heard these words: "Go to Dasharatha."

King Dasharatha had a fatal heart attack just when Lord Rama left his capital city, Ayodhya, for exile. Going to Dasharatha meant living with Yama, the God of Death. Adina thought of checking on Dasharatha's relationship with Yama. She was scared, but she mustered her courage and Yama appeared on the screen. But he was not alone. He was with a woman.

That distracted Adina from her original intent. "Pranam, Lord Yama. And pranam to the lady with you! May I know who she is?"

"Good luck to you," both of them said, blessing Adina simultaneously.

Of course, that was the appropriate blessing she needed from the death god, Adina thought.

"She is my sister Yami, Adina," Lord Yama added.

"Oh, what a beautiful sister you have. Didn't she want to marry you? Why did you reject her love?" Even though Adina asked it as a query, Yama looked angry.

"Who told you all this?" Yami asked her.

"My dada and dadi."

"I have already decided to kill those two idiots, and soon." He gave her a dirty look and disappeared with Yami.

Adina was very dejected and closed the computer. She left the room and stopped at the entrance door. After taking a deep breath, she looked up and raised her fists. "Down with your death penalty. You will fail to kill Dada and Dadi just like the American judge failed. He allowed them just twenty percent time of my dad's visits with me. Who the hell is he to decide how much time my grandparents spend with me in my dad's house? Dad thought his parents could both have a heart attack at this news, but they didn't. Their regret is that the American judge violated their natural rights and yet he is allowed to remain scot-free. You kill so many beings every second, and you go scot-free! You are the worst terrorist! You don't let a being spend enough time with his fellow beings. You were not fit for Yami. It's fortunate that you are not that woman's husband. You would have killed her. Down with your death penalty! Down—"

"Adina, hey, Adina, are you all right?"

Adina heard a girl calling her from the street facing her room. She went down to greet this friendly neighbor and laughed wildly. "What all divinities do is give sermons with 'dos' and 'don'ts.' If we don't obey their religion, then they punish us. I have been so respectful to them."

The neighbor didn't laugh. Instead, she was awed by Adina's odd behavior, "Divine lives by intimidation. Are you speaking of didactic divine talk, Adina?" the senior girl asked.

Adina didn't respond. She was trying to compose herself, because this time she was taking the death threats seriously.

CHAPTER 34

Recovery

Maa kashchid dukhabhaag bhavet
"Let no one be a victim of pain."
(An ancient Sanskrit prayer)

Today was the anniversary of Adina's father's exoneration. All along he had been aware of the warning that the trial judge had given to Adina's mother: "Don't come up with false allegations again." This awareness had very little impact on his sleeping pattern. Last night was no different than the nights before—he couldn't sleep soundly. *What if Madhu suddenly fabricates another malicious myth? Some compulsive myth makers easily succeed in having myth worshippers. If they don't succeed in incriminating their victims, they deny the authorship of those myths, with no qualms of conscience. They don't care for being ridiculed by nonbelievers, including the courts. Sooner or later, they invent or copycat more false allegations. And worshippers continue to believe their deity, in spite of the failure of several previous prayers.*

One of the failures of such worshippers was the exoneration of Dan. But his fear of being falsely accused again had not faded over the years, in spite of their failure.

One case had recently triggered his fear again. A daughter, the only child of her parents, recanted her story of an incestuous abuse when she became thirteen. An ACLU lawyer became interested in this case. She took it as a *pro bono* case. The daughter confessed to the lawyer how the mother kept on pressuring her to lie about her father when she was six-years old. After her confession, the father was released from jail. His visitation rights were restored by the judge. After so many years of separation, the mother consented to allow the father for his first overnight visit in a motel—the first place where he stayed after his release. When the daughter returned from the motel, the father was put back in jail. The mother complained again about the same kind of molestation. Fortunately, the daughter was now bold enough to deny the false allegations, and the father was quickly released.

Dan met this father in an informal meeting of a support group of men and women who were victims of false allegations. The small size of the group didn't dim his big hopes.

"Every storm begins with a breeze," he said in this meeting. He recommended launching a big campaign, not only for a law to punish pathological liars such as his ex-wife, but also to punish those who legally violate the equal rights of both parents. He also recommended joining a bigger organization. "My interest is in the tougher legislation for gender neutrality, especially in family courts. Due to my personal circumstances, I was looking for a national organization that fights for it. I found one— National Parents Organization. It fights, not just for the cosmetic political correctness of discriminating against one parent in favor of the other parent. Its major fight is for the equal rights of both parents in child custody," he said.

The group supported his ideas.

After the meeting was over, Dan told the other man his story.

"Disgusting," he said to the other father. "I thought of committing suicide. Such was the impact of this kind of defamation. Two independent psychologists with PhD degrees found the court psychologist's analysis full of faults."

"I smell gender bias," the other man said.

Dan nodded. "Nobody asked Madhu and her lawyers how parents' co-sleeping with their babies was tantamount to child abuse. By the way, my tort lawyer sleeps with his son and daughter. Due to his busy practice, he seldom gets another slot of time to socialize with them."

"Your court is removed from such facts of life," the other man agreed. And thank goodness, your court was not hearing the allegations of Al Qaeda against the United States of America."

"Like my thirteen-year- old rebel, your daughter is your best hope," the other man told him as their conversation was ending. "Imagine her questions for your ex. 'Mom, do you still believe that a twenty-two-month old would say that? Why didn't you immediately confess after the doctor said that you made the allegations, not me? Why didn't you save the big money spent to justify the big lie? What if my innocent father would have committed suicide? Did you ever think of my pain?'"

Dan simled at the man's poignant comments. "You're very perceptive. I hope she asks me, too—questions like that could be very helpful. Pain can make a person very productive. You are an example. Thanks for sharing your pain."

"But I am no Buddha. I believe in the path of punishment for those men and women who inflict pain by false-hood."

"The path of gender neutrality is certainly a middle path conducive to social justice," Dan agreed. "I am a lawyer, also no Buddha."

They both laughed and departed.

This morning, he would have liked to sleep a little longer than on other mornings. But he heard the noisy morning mantras of the famous Canadian geese soaring overhead from the lake in front of his house. He got up and watched the formation of a long line of the majestic birds. For a few moments, he went into a reverie. Were the geese communicating something to him?

"Brother," they seemed to say. "Ours is not just one goose family but the whole goose village, flying to our nesting ground."

Dan understood their behavior as well as his own. "Yes, fellows, I hear you. You just said '*Shivaas te pan-thaanah santu.*' Yes, let your paths be safe. Not mine, I can't fly. Yes, I do have great expectations. But now my nest is broken. The very mother goose that was with me broke it. For you that's an uncivilized act. A civilization starts by building one house. The entire civilization could be history if the housemakers become housebreakers. Invaders of a civilization are not always outsiders; they could be insiders."

Dan's small house was just two bedrooms, not as spacious as the house he'd shared with his ex-wife. Sometimes visiting guests had to sleep in the small living room, not on beds but on the floor. Nevertheless, the atmosphere of this house was good for reducing his depression. It was nestled in a corner of a park, surrounded by a variety of trees and plants, many of them shady and luxurious. Especially the rhododendrons, which were in full bloom bearing flowers of assorted colors. The lake too was small, yet big enough to attract these globe-trotting geese and other birds. It was full of big and small fishes. Dan's neighbor was rowing a boat with his son, but not for fishing. Fishing was not allowed.

Dan quickly went in the bathroom. After a good warm shower, he felt good and did some yoga stretches, including some breathing exercises. After a few minutes of meditation, he sat on his balcony with an Indian *thali*, a metal food plate, which he placed on his portable coffee table. The *thali* contained his complete breakfast: buttered toast, an apple, and a few nuts of all kinds. Beside the *thali*, he put his laptop. He clicked his favorite Beatles song "Hey Jude."

Listening to the song, he started sipping his morning mocha while watching the ducks swimming in the green waters of the lake. He enjoyed watching the small family of ducks swimming so gracefully. The family consisted of baby ducklings guided by the mother in the front and guarded by the father in the back. At the same time, Dan was reminiscing, as memories began to flash into his awareness. *Once in a while your imprisoned past is desperate for release*, he thought.

How did you stop our adversary system of justice from allowing decriminalization of a premeditated crime? How did you get a bar to automatically take away the license of those lawyers who deliberately engaged in someone's character assassination? What could you say against a bar that could consider disbarring a lawyer for an inadvertent act and brush off another lawyer's deliberate breach of professional ethics?

As a lawyer, he could not help but ruminate on the travesty of justice.

Any judge knew that, in criminal cases, it was the prosecutor who tried to collect evidence of guilt while the defense attorney found ways to suppress, discredit, or contradict the evidence. While Danin's case was not a criminal case, it was still logical to assume that Madhu who was making allegations of child molestation and domestic violence would request her attorneys to diligently collect any and all evidence to support her allegations.

Instead, Madhu hampered any efforts at collecting evidence while Dan demanded that evidence of his guilt be thoroughly investigated with his full cooperation. If Madhu seriously believed in the accusations that she was making, then she would have demanded that Child Protective Services and law enforcement get involved in their case. Her failure to have the allegations reviewed by competent authorities in a timely manner should have been sufficient proof to the judge that the allegations were false and malicious in nature.

Dan believed that the trial judge had formed an image of a perfect father. The court psychologist had hers. She watched the interaction of Adina and Dan only once in a forty-five-minutes session, also observed by two supervisors. In her opinion, the interaction was very pleasant. For the supervisors, it was superb. How would she know that this had been their interactional pattern? She could have supplemented her forty-five-minute "fieldwork" by watching scores of videos and photographs that Dan had saved. That photographic evidence, partly provided by Adina's supervisors, didn't make any sense to her.

Actually, she had full authority to arrange for any number of sessions in other settings. Instead, she depended on her ready-made pseudo-scientific psychological jargon. Less work, more money—taxpayer's free money. She implied that Danin did not look like her imagined perfect parent. So she recommended Adina's visit with Dan for one overnight every two weeks. She told the court that her recommendation was very fair. Dan's exoneration made her recommendation very unfair.

Another of Madhu's witnesses testified at the trial court that Adina clung to her father very often, and that was not a good sign of a perfect parent. Like the judge, this witness showed his ignorance of the research that showed the natural necessity of tactile contact of parent and child.

These jokers implied that Madhu was a perfect parent. It was highly unlikely that someone with ethical values would consider a court-declared liar fit for a child's healthy moral or ethical development. But an exonerated Dan was required to see a specialist for qualifying as a fit parent. And later the case managers would evaluate him to see if he had improved. They had nothing to do with Dan's exoneration.

And this cottage industry never raised the human rights issue—child's equal custody to both parents, even if one was legally found a vicious alligator.

A specialist in clinical psychology showed that the problem was with the accuser parent, not with the accused parent. Yet, this psychologist didn't perpetuate the myth of a perfect parent. His opinion was ignored, his PhD degree meant nothing. The courts had declared that there was no child molestation of any kind, that there was no domestic violence either. Yet, Madhu claimed again through her lawyer that she never accused Dan. The judge had more powerful legal tools to hit such claims hard. His simple warning looked like a cosmetic paint.

Dan also remembered the advice from a friend. "Why didn't you use some expletives for the judge at the trial?" The friend sounded furious as he uttered some samples. All samples were pure English except one phonetically adulterated Hindi word *thug*.

"Not even that mild Indian word from my mouth. Over my dead body. Just chuck it," was Dan's response.

"I understand why. He would have held you in contempt," the friend said, using the same defense the judge used. "But then you could have said, 'Oh, it was nothing more than an *overreaction* to my painful punishment, your honor!'"

But Dan reiterated his stand. "Over my dead body!"

The friend seemed to be very serious about his advice. "You never heard a disgruntled man who used not only expletives but also a gun?"

The friend was not a lawyer. But Dan nodded his head to indicate that, as a criminal-defense attorney, he very well understood the use of words and guns to commit violence. Offending words were the grassroots of violence. Weapons followed afterward. Even complimentary words could be considered worse than guns, legally.

The judge was more concerned about Danin's being a doting father than he was about the mother who threatened to kill herself with a gun in her daughter's presence. The more Danin analyzed the facts of his case and that of other fathers who had faced similar hardships and accusations as he did, it became clear that the family court was divorced from reality.

How are such incompetent men appointed as judges?

And how about a few of our own feminist organizations behaving fanatically, somewhat like jihadist groups? They perpetuated a negative stereotype by assuming that South Asian males were guilty, based on mere accusations of domestic violence, even when evidence of such an act was lacking. Dan wanted these groups to be investigated because they could gradually and quietly blow up, not only South Asian, but other Asian models of family solidarity. By joining the statewide jihadist lobby, they could force the legislature to pass a law that would not allow punishment of a wife found guilty of false allegations. For this lobby, it didn't matter how the accused husband was punished by those myths, from day one. Dan had a basis to develop this thinking, not entirely reasonable to some, but limitlessly painful to him.

Not only pain, but fear entered that first fateful evening when Dan returned home and found nobody. A common friend, who established a domestic violence organization to protect South Asian women, hid baby Adina from him for several days. Although that friend knew that Dan was a nonviolent and loving individual, she aided Madhu in kidnapping Adina and provided a false statement against him.

Had Madhu's allegations that Dan was a dangerous person been true, then she would have been protecting Adina. However, because Madhu made up the allegations that Dan was a dangerous person, she ended up kidnapping Adina by not disclosing her whereabouts to Dan. The friend ended up aiding and abetting Madhu in kidnapping baby Adina. She had deployed her position of authority in the domestic violence and South Asian community to perpetuate the negative stereotype that Dan was a typically abusive male of South Asian descent. While Dan considered her to be a friend, she stabbed him in the back.

Thus, began his family disintegration with the help of his own wife's well-wishers. These well-wishers were not alone in causing this disintegration. And he was not alone in experiencing this. For many, the wife as the creator figure of the family was a myth like Mother Goddess, courtesy of those fanatic iconoclasts who ran the legal system.

Dan was disturbed by a gentle tap on his shoulder from behind.

"Surprise, Dad! Here I am with a present for you. I have not found the lost precious jewel, but I have found something much better. I want to share it with the whole world."

Adina clung to Danin.

"You are my most precious jewel, but tell me your story," he said. "I, too, would like to share it with the whole world."

"Some wise voices guided me to start my search for the jewel, and somehow I got my jewel."

Adina was eager to tell about those voices, but hesitated because she knew that her father, unlike her mother, didn't believe in them. She remembered how he joked about Darwin once. *'Adi, you know this revolutionary scientist, Charles Darwin, forgot to include the evolution of the divine species. The Greeks had a lot of divine beings, but later lost all but one, God. Darwin should have researched in India the way he did in Galapagos Island. In India the great evolutionist would have found a different line of divine species, multiplying in leaps and bounds. He had no idea that someday, after his death, devout Indians would export a few samples of their divine species to Great Britain. Poor Chucky!'*

"Adi, it's too bad you didn't find the jewel," he said now. "If you had, we could secretly sell it and pay my lawyer, even though she billed me more after I got less visitation," he added with sarcasm. "So tell me what you have found."

"It's a message, a true golden message. You will see when it is uncovered, when it becomes open to everyone."

"When? When?"

"When I am more mature. I just became thirteen."

Danin kept staring at Adina with empty eyes, as if he wanted to fill them with what and how Adina knew what she claimed to know.

She hugged him then burst out in tears. "I want to help other victims and stop all this lying about other family members."

Finally, father and daughter managed to control their emotions.

"Adi, I guess somehow you have found out our full story, but it's not unique. Our story is just the same as many other stories. A lawyer friend tells me that seventy-seven percent of such lies are found to be unsubstantiated. Every such story has victims with this same kind of domestic terrorism. Families go into debt in the process—"

"Some families are wiped out completely while their lawyers earn more money," Adina interrupted, agreeing with him.

"During every election, every presidential candidate brags 'I am for families,' and after the election, the promise is forgotten and domestic terrorism continues to flourish. Bonds between parents and children are broken by parents. Whenever a parent does such disgusting damage, the other parent runs for help to the lawyers, who are only interested in their fees, not the bonds between the child and parent. Only your supervisors helped me to develop my bond with you. I can never repay them for their selfless love. They never believed an iota of what your mother alleged. They reaffirmed my faith in human compassion, trust, and family solidarity."

Dan broke down in tears. Adina brought a napkin and wiped his cheeks.

Dan finally composed himself and took her hand. "I have many other stories of deception to tell you."

"How do you know about these stories?"

"I read some of them on the Internet. The Internet is really a revolution."

Adina looked down with a strange smile. All her

classmates were relentlessly using the Internet and so it was really no big deal for her generation.

"Maybe your mother read some of those stories and decided to reenact them with me," he suggested. "Or she had some friends who passed this infectious disease to her by telling her these tales. We began to notice some sickish changes in her behavior, ever since you were one year old. She must have enjoyed those stories and entertained the thought of living in some kind of heaven with you. These cases show that there is no such heaven, just a broken home."

Dan paused and wiped his eyes. "But Madhu thought that because she was a lawyer she could overcome the sins of less pious liars. She succeeded in manipulating her witnesses, who didn't even take the doctor's report or other evidence, that raised serious doubts about her allegations, into consideration. What happened to decent people? An investigation conducted with diligence and professionalism should have settled the matter for everyone. This is why my lawyer friend wants to tell my story to the whole world. 'Our case is a disgrace to the legal profession,' he says."

Adina raised her face and looked into the eyes of her father. "Why does he say that?"

"He thinks that we all, Plato to Gandhi, say stupid things, but if we present those things in court as truths, then their consequences are cruel. Aided by her lawyer, a mother who also is a lawyer claims that her allegations are true and the court finally finds them to be untrue. If lawyers do such unjust things, then who will fight for justice?" Dan paused and looked into her eyes for a moment. "How can we tell the civilized world that American children need the love of not only the whole village but of both parents? I was found innocent and yet deprived of my daughter's equal company. I got no compensation for my legal fees, no compensation for my defamation, not for my daughter's either. The accuser went scot-free."

Danin went in the kitchen for a glass of water. He drank some and returned to continue his story. "The court treated me like a criminal. The law says you are innocent until proven guilty. But the psychologist of the court who was assigned to your case attempted to cut my bond with you, writing a report that was acceptable to the court's views rather than presenting the facts."

Adina nodded. "I know she blurred the facts."

"It is normal to expect that a clinical psychologist behave with reason and integrity. All she needed was a sense of honesty. The child needs to be bonded with both parents. Are you a true clinical psychologist if you marginalize a parent, an innocent loving parent? You are a phony counselor if you help the break-up of families, just as you are not a true civil engineer if you don't believe in building bridges." He drank more water. "You loved both parents—"

"I do, Daddy! But go on."

"Just after your birth, your mom wrote to a friend: 'How fortunate I was to have a husband like Dan who inspired me the most!' I was proud of her and myself. I have saved that statement. And then I received the totally unexpected order."

"You mean the divorce notice?"

"Yes, seven months after that statement. The order began to sink me. I didn't know how to swim. Finally, in desperation, I packed up my clothes and some important papers along with your pictures that I loved most. Within forty-eight hours I left, as ordered. I had never imagined being homeless. But I give so many thanks to my supervisors who sheltered me! I lived in their homes for months." Dan wiped his eyes. "I was allowed to see you for a few hours per week in their homes and under their supervision as ordered by the court. How many times they watched you sobbing! Some of them heard you saying 'Dan, come home' as you kissed me. I had no choice except to answer, 'Mommy won't let me in.' I couldn't say anything else to a baby. But that was the truth by which I wanted to teach you the value of honesty. And then I had to leave you there without telling you. I heard your cries as I quietly hid myself in my car. Your mother complained that you were afraid of me. Nobody else, even the biased psychologist, ever said that you were afraid of me—"

"Afraid?" Adina interjected.

"Everybody else stated that you were attached to me too much. Madhu also complained in the court, while crying, 'Dan mistreated me throughout our married life.' A big lie, just like her accusation that I abused you! Once you woke up crying and asked me, 'Dan, I want to sleep in your lap just like when I was a little baby.' I picked you up in my arms and rocked you. You were all cuddled up in my lap. Soon you began to close your eyes but opened them periodically and gazed at me. Within minutes, you fell asleep. If I had informed your mother, she would have put a spin on this against me."

Danin burst in tears. "I never cried in court, though I wanted to. No court-appointed individual ever saw me crying. I didn't want to cry for their mercy like a guilty person, because I was not, but they treated me like one from the beginning, and without any evidence. The court never asked me to show the real evidence. I have saved another statement where Madhu considers me her hero. I have saved so many photos and videos of you with me and others. Why didn't the court ever ask me to show any one of those happy pictures?"

"Don't cry, Dad! I understand your pain." Adi wiped his tears with her bare hands. "You never opened up before like this. I am happy that you are telling me the real story yourself. We will tell the world that we are decent people and we will punish deception. Let's celebrate that I have found my crown jewel, and I will tell you later how I know what I know. My job looks complete, but Dada taught me a mantra: 'Consider every complete job incomplete for complete success. The sense of completion blocks further progress.' The congress will call this venture a success, or so I think, when I present my message to them."

Danin kissed her hands. "False allegations eventually get exposed as the deception they are," he said after a brief pause. "That's what Bernard, an Irish-American engineer, told me at a party. He was singing while playing his guitar, and his voice was dramatic, very emotional. I felt like I might cry. After he finished his Irish song, he told me that he saw tears in my eyes. I told him my story, and he said that was his story as well."

"You mean his wife accused him of child abuse?"

"Yes. He told me that his Asian wife was a Catholic like him. Both believed in the sanctity of marriage. Both believed in equal rights for men and women. She even wanted to be a priest. But the bishop felt offended. He thought she was criticizing the church policy. Just like in Hindu tradition, women cannot be priests. They were not allowed to use the *Vedas*. The Arya Samaj branch, however, broke that tradition defiantly, more than one hundred years ago. Do you know about the Arya Samaj?"

"Dada went to an Arya Samaj college. He told me that he supported priesthood for women."

"Yes, we always believed in equal rights for women and men. We have signed petitions after petitions for women's rights. Dada brought that Arya Samaj influence of his student days with him, though he never became a member of the Arya Samaj. His father, my great-granddaddy, never liked the Arya Samaj, hated even the word *Arya* or *Aryan*—"

"A Brahmin priest hating these words! But tell me more about the Bernard story?"

"When Bernard's daughter was almost twelve years old, she solved the problem. She began to understand who was right and who was wrong. She became very vocal. After six years of separation from her, Bernard was finally given equal custody. Now in his retirement, he lives in this town because of his grandchildren. They all adore him, just like their mother. He told me that his experience with the court system was like mine. That judge dismissed his wife's lies as if lying was part of a normal game between spouses. This is why Bernard recommends a jury trial for such liars."

"Dad, I understand what Bernard meant. The judge didn't care about your pain and didn't care about my pain. He is the judge in a state where spanking the child is considered legally harmful. In the same state, he claims that accusing the father falsely in a court of law is nothing more than an overreaction. How much harm would this overreaction do to the child? He didn't even care to raise such a question."

Dan nodded. "He was the one who robbed me of my crown jewel. He took full advantage of the state-sanctioned gender discrimination. Mom's supporters, especially South Asian American feminists, didn't care for this gender discrimination. By remaining silent on court-proven lies of your mom, these supporters don't realize that they have supported her lying."

"Tell me more about South Asian American feminists?"

"These women brought shame to the ideal of the original feminist movement: men and women must be treated equally. They are fixated at some stereotypes and ignore

some facts. One major fact they ignore is that lying is
gender-neutral. They never told your mother that, no matter what happened with her, she has no license to concoct
false allegations. They never told her that, in every civilized country, there are laws against lying. In fact, lying
is considered a serious crime, a punishable crime—"

"Not in America." Adi interrupted.

"Right. A South Asian feminist scholar of culture
dodges the central issue in her written statement against
me. Like a few supporters of Madhu, she really believes
that the religions of your mom and mine are different.
She ignores the fact that your mother and I were married
with a Hindu ceremony in a Hindu temple. Like many
devotees, your nana and nani believed that we were
God's match. Dad doesn't share such a belief. A huge
majority of God's chosen couples end in divorce and
their children tend to be non-believers. Nevertheless, Dad
behaved like a believer in order to cooperate with the officiating priest at the ceremony. The priest was not told
that Dad taught Hinduism. But he was aware of the fact
that Dad was a Badrinath area Brahmin and, therefore,
respected him very much. Later, your mother asked Dad
if the Hindu priest followed everything prescribed by the
Vedas. Dad didn't want to tell her how the priest missed
the standard Vedic mantras of marriage. But she insisted
that she should be told. Finally, Dad did tell her and requested that she never tell her parents, *ever*."

"Ever? Why?"

"Madhu's parents might be shocked. Dad knows that
most Indian priests, not to mention the common men and
women believers, do not know the standard Vedic ceremony. The Vedic Sanskrit is the first Indo-Aryan language, so too archaic, too complex. So priests use easy
non-Vedic Sanskrit mantras, which were written much
later, when Sanskrit was not spoken by common folks

anymore. This is why Dad had recommended the regular American court marriage. He tried to convince them with a different fact, that we both were lawyers and, therefore, needed just a legal marriage instead of a Hindu marriage. Now if you want to put a spin on that recommendation, you can say in the court that my parents criticized Madhu's religion."

Adina frowned. "But such a spin won't work because you accepted Mom as your wife till death. Don't the Vedic and non-Vedic mantras prescribe that promise? Am I saying right?"

"Yes. I firmly believed in the vows prescribed by our common religion. The last vow ends in the promise that we remain friends throughout our lives. After our marriage, my parents and I kept on pleasing your mother throughout. Dadi has saved some cancelled checks. Anyone is welcome to see those checks with Madhu's name on them. They will find that the last check was given as a gift in the same year she filed for divorce."

"Yes, Dadi showed me two checks as samples. Total of—" Adi began to laugh.

"Forty thousand dollars," Dan completed. "And listen to more! In the same year, Dad asked Madhu if she would like him to buy an SUV or a van for her. She preferred a van that could accommodate seven passengers. Why a van? So that her visiting parents or relatives could also join my parents occasionally on fun trips. But then she requested that Dad hold his decision for a few more months. Those months she needed to plan her vicious game."

Adina stared at him, her eyebrows rising to her hairline. "How do you know that she was plotting against you?"

"I know, it because one late evening she told me to wait for what she was planning for my future. From her tone and looks, I clearly understood that the plan was a threat. But I never expected this would happen a few months after she appreciated me in that interview. That night, I realized that for Madhu the last marriage vow turned out to be a lie. She made it false. And that scholar of South Asia thinks my parents and I criticized her religious affiliation. Does she really understand what our religion is about? Instead of writing cover-up statements, why didn't she request Madhu to tell her the whole truth? A true scholar writes after a thorough investigation of facts."

"Are you kidding? Why would Mom confess to her supporters that she lied? She was seeking their support. Her supporters forgot to ask her why, as a lawyer, she was able to accept domestic violence for more than a dozen years of marriage." Adina sighed. "I agree with you. She would be a fool to disclose her appreciation of you in the recorded interview she gave the same year."

"Oh, no problem for her, even if I disclose that interview. She would lie that the interviewer coerced her," Dan said, "I have not been worried so much about coercion as much about charges of domestic violence. You remember, after the court ruling for custody, I used to pick you up from your mom inside a store. The store was equipped with hidden cameras. But once she forgot to bring your jacket from her car. It was very cold outside. She asked me if I could walk with her out to pick up your jacket. I agreed. But as soon as I stepped out of the store, it struck me suddenly that there wouldn't be any cameras where her car was parked. What if she shouted, claiming that I tried to hurt her when she went inside the car to pick up your jacket? I politely told her that I had an extra jacket for you in my house. She didn't insist further. I took a big sigh of relief."

"I know you wouldn't hurt even an ant."

"I shudder, even today. Imagine if such a scenario had taken place! Her supporters would have believed her, especially those anti-male South Asian American feminists. I call them jihadists because they believe in destruction. Construction of the family, a family with both parents happily together, is not a favorite feature of the agenda of feminist fanatics."

"I understand what you mean, Dad."

"The jihadist feminists have a lobby. Politicians are afraid of this lobby. You may even lose your job if this lobby makes too much noise. There is no balanced noise, no respect for freedom of speech. But don't worry. I have a message. Everything will be all right, just as the man said in his song."

"I hope," she said with a smile.

"I always supported your mother, and even some of her friends, whom I didn't realize were jihadist feminists. Then she was able to persuade some of these witches to conjure up many ghosts who would then be used against you and me. The same witches had also the power to transform any lambs into violent phantoms. They have not been able to sacrifice me yet. But those ghosts keep haunting me." Dan paused for a few seconds. "Look at the arrogance and shamelessness of Madhu's latest lawyer. She complained to my lawyer, 'Dan has caused such a financial burden for my client because he continues fighting for more custody. Every time he complains about the allegations which Madhu never made. It was Adina who made those allegations. He must ignore those allegations and move ahead with his life.' Then why is this lawyer charging such exorbitant fees, if she is concerned about Madhu's financial burden?"

"No wonder so many consider lawyers 'blood suckers,' even though your fees fall much below the normal standard."

"So my lawyer didn't even bother to respond to Madhu's lawyer."

"She should have," Adina interjected.

"But I understood why she didn't. The doctor who examined you, Adi, had already stated in his report that it was not Adina, who was saying those allegations, but Madhu. The court psychologist didn't believe Madhu either, even though she blamed me that I always put my priorities first."

"What priorities?"

"No priorities. Just one priority—defend myself. Shouldn't I, when these insensitive legal perverts punished me even when I was found innocent? My lawyer was aware of all these facts. She, most probably, would have responded positively if Madhu's lawyer had added, 'Madhu will now publicly confess and apologize.' Anyways, confession and apology cannot reduce the past pains. Any sensible person would understand what the root cause of our costly fight was."

"I too understand, Dad."

"They knew this very well that eventually you would."

"That's right."

"As a matter of fact, this was a major concern in their complaints. How would Adina be impacted when she grows and knows about the cause? Madhu's first lawyer should have warned her right in the beginning not to mention those myths to anyone."

"I must have heard them when I was not even two!"

"There you go. It was too late to forbid me from talking about them. I was told that I should never discuss those accusations with Adina. And never ever discuss the punishment I got, not only with you but with anybody. It's like a kidnapper asking his victim to not talk to others about how he kidnapped her and humiliated her. My humiliation has been spoken out loud in the court records.

How do you make its sounds unheard, even if you erase or seal them? Ask Madhu's supporters if they heard those allegations just from her artful tears! As Chief Justice McBride noted, 'It is not an easy task to unring a bell.'"

With a momentary pause, he wiped his tears. "Adi, I won't say more now about Madhu's hurtful distortions of facts. I have developed a phobia which I try to fend off by blurting those distortions out over and again in the company of friends. Most friends don't mind, as one of them said, 'Blurting out is better than committing suicide. Many have committed suicide. Check the national data.'"

"I myself have been doing the same with some mystery figures, male and female," Adina confessed. "Telling Mom's mistakes to each of them."

"Them! Mystery figures! I understand now you got a mystery message from them. So what is your mystery message? And who are them?"

"Dad, your friend said, 'from Plato to Gandhi, we all make mistakes.'" Adina ignored his question and instead asked him, "Do you agree with him, I mean your friend? You admire Gandhi, though."

"I should have told you. My friend is not an Indian-American. Just an American, and very much like Plato, he is a fair guy. I agree with him. Unlike the Buddha, Mahatma Gandhi claimed that he had evidence of God's existence. Unlike Mother Teresa, Gandhi didn't doubt God's existence. Gandhi didn't doubt God because his parents didn't doubt God."

"I heard from other sources that Gandhi's parents were idolaters, but not Gandhi."

"True, Gandhi was not interested in image worship. But not all good people have the guts to doubt their parents' beliefs. This is what my American friend thought. I, too, have a lot of good things to say about kind religious people. Some of them would accept my lot as God's will, however, God's will that I be the victim of a liar! But tell me, what is your mystery?"

"Daddy, as I said, I will tell you later. The good news is that I have found something in which I truly believe. This belief will protect homes from break-ins and stop the gangsters who are robbing America of its two crown jewels, Equality and Justice. But let's celebrate my new belief now, and I promise to tell how I traveled in space. Space is our future living. Believe me. Yesterday's myth is tomorrow's fact. That's progress."

"I believe you, Adi. We all are traveling in space, anyways. The Earth keeps moving twenty-four/seven. Where? In space, of course. That's a fact already. We keep moving in space."

"Then let us move out right now to eat lunch and be factual."

Danin caressed her head. "Yes, dear. I am ready to go out for lunch to celebrate and heal. What would you like to eat?"

"Anything vegetarian," Adina replied in a soft voice.

"Of course, we are vegetarians. We have lots of choices, my dear Adi."

"How about Chinese?"

"We eat Chinese a lot. Let's go for Mexican."

She perked up a little bit. "How can I say no to a burrito, tamale, and enchilada? Let's have lots of corn chips and hot salsa, too."

Danin smiled. "Otherwise, I was planning a home-cooked Italian meal for you."

"Dad, you really make good Italian food. Anybody who eats Italian food would think you are an Italian-American."

"Thanks, dear! By the way, you and I look southern Italian, tanned Italians with hazel eyes. I am going to tell you a story. One of my friends was going to Texas from

New Mexico. During the night, he stayed in a motel in the little Texas town of Van Horn. The owner of the motel was an Indian, a Patel. My friend Ron Stein told Patel that his very close friend was also an Indian-American, and Patel asked him for my name. 'Dan Badoni,' Ron answered. 'No, that cannot be an Indian name. He must be Italian. The name sounds Italian. I never heard such a name in India,' the man told him.

"Ron, being a lawyer, wanted to argue with him. 'Look, I have eaten curry dinners at their home. Dan's mother put on a sari. In their family, they speak Hindi with each other. She told me that Badonis are of the central Himalayan priestly-class of Brahmins. I have seen Dan's father performing a Hindu wedding.'

"But the Patel shut him up as he said, 'No matter what you say. Your friend's name is Italian.'

"I love Patels. I have many close Patel friends. When a Patel says something that lends authenticity to whatever he claims. Badoni does sound like Italian, like Baroni, for example."

Adina chuckled. "The question is: Will the Baroni macaroni taste as good as the Badoni macaroni?"

"*Viva Italiano-Americano!*"

Adi Badoni and Dan Badoni, the two phony Italian Americans laughed together.

"Dad, why do our Indian names sound non-Indian?"

"Your dada taught Sanskrit and linguistic anthropology, and your Dadi taught Indian mythology. They selected these uncommon Sanskrit names, but at the same time they are easy to pronounce for most Americans. Dan and Adi."

"I always liked our names," she said, bouncing a little in her chair with a big smile on her face.

"But names must be meaningful in life. If your name is Albert Einstein, then try to understand relativity. If your name is Buddha, find release from stupidity. 'Keep trying,' the Buddha instructs."

"Buddha's voice was the voice of wisdom," she agreed. "Listen to your voices of wisdom. I am trying to hear mine. Thanks. And thanks to Dadi and Dada, my true teachers of myths." Then she asked him the name of religious fools who believe the myths are true. "Dad, what was your word for a religious fool?"

"The word is fundamentalist, but don't tell anyone I said it. Professor Danin Badoni doesn't want to get falsely blamed."

"You said it, Danny boy!"

Both laughed and got up. Dan hugged her.

"Dad, today we talked a lot. It's your exoneration anniversary. I wish Dada and Dadi were here to join us and talk and talk. I want to live with you and with them without the blame," Adi said.

The word "blame" aroused Danin's anger again. Baby Adina loved to sleep, not only with her parents but also with her Dada and Dadi. But the judge was opposed to such natural co-sleeping. That's one of the reasons he had reduced her visits with Dada and Dadi to ten days per year. Couldn't he read the research that shows the majority societies of the world still raise healthier children due to co-sleeping? Danin was so critical of the kangaroo-court judges, who were really politicians in the robes of judges, who were afraid of losing favors of certain groups.

Adina noticed Danin's anguished face. She diverted his attention. "Dad, I have been very worried about the safety of Dadi and Dada, and so I called them a few days ago."

"What was the special reason for your new worry?"

"It was all my imagination."

CHAPTER 35

Revolving Rebellion

Uddyamena hi siddhyanti kaaryaaṇi na manorathaiḥ
"By hard work only are achieved results,
not by fantasies."
(An ancient Sanskrit saying)

Damiano's Bistro was quite far from Dan's house. It was famous for its Italian delicacies, especially its vegetarian offerings. It was always crowded and there was about a forty-five-minutes wait. Nobody seemed to mind the wait here for two main reasons: the setting and the chef.

Perched atop a hill, the Bistro faced a vast lake in the front, serving a spectacular view. Some guests in the waiting line seem to meditate on its blue waters. Today it was a sunny day. The leaves of plush green trees and flowers surrounding the Bistro looked cheerful, courtesy of the sunshine. Many kids, accompanied by their parents, were eating out in the sun. Otherwise, this city was mostly cloudy, very much like its family courts.

The other reason was far more responsible for its reputation. The chef migrated here just after his marriage. The couple was from Naples, Italy. Mr. Damiano wanted to establish a genuine Neapolitan restaurant. Cooking delicious food was part of his family tradition. He had learned to cook the best dishes from his father at a very early age. His dream came true here, though he didn't claim its dishes to be as perfect as his father's. He had to replace, for example, the cheese from buffalo's milk with cheese from cow's milk. Customers could see a note in big black block letters on a wood plaque hung on the front wall of the kitchen, *SORRY! COWS DELIVER OUR MOZZARELLA!* The kitchen was visible from the dining area. This transparency made its cooking credible.

Inside, many customers were watching today's basketball game between the Illinois Bisons and Arizona Stars on the TV. Danin and Adina did not mind waiting because they, too, were enjoying this game. Dan was neutral. He had close friends— big rooters—in both states. "When you have common friends, don't take a side." That was the rule of civility—at least for Dan. So he didn't root for either.

The game was especially intriguing because the Stars' coach was formerly the Bisons' coach. Adina was shocked to see two players from the opposing teams engaged in an especially violent brawl, and the coaches also began to quarrel.

And the noise of the fans! The announcers said that the decibel level was near the record in the *Guinness Book of World Records*. Fans also threw all sorts of objects onto the field during the brawl, and especially as the two players were whisked away. The coaches finally calmed down, after being warned by the referees, and the game began again.

"Isn't it true that the coaches are worse liars than the lawyers?" Adina asked Dan as he drove home after a great meal and a great time together at Damiano's.

"You mean they have double standards because they

teach sportsmanship to their players and yet get into an argument, right?"

"Yes."

"Lawyers and coaches are not the only people who have double standards. I can vouch for the fact that the psychologist who testified at our trial would support equal pay for men and women, but you can see what she did when it was a question of the right to equal parenting for both mother and father. She was not even willing to give me one overnight visit per week with you. And look also at the decision of the judge. He trashed the constitutional rights of grandparents when he granted my parents only ten overnight visits per year, but no such restrictions were placed on your mother's parents. The psychologist and the judge can have such double standards with impunity because they are in positions of authority. Had I violated their decisions, I could have been punished more."

"Yes, they judge by bias, not by logic," Adina said.

Dan patted her hand. "Even staunch religious people have double standards. One of my friends became sick because of the wrong medicine. He called the doctor and the manufacturer 'bastards.' But when his prayers for the same sickness failed he didn't use any expletive for God! Fortunately, he used another doctor who cured him with another medicine. But my friend has changed neither his prayer nor God. Lord God has immunity, doctors don't."

Adina smiled. "Danny boy, waiting for my solution? You have my permission to violate their decisions."

Dan laughed and laughed until he noticed his laughter was affecting his driving.

"By the way," he said then. "What I am telling you, about a double standard on the part of the court, coincides with the opinions of other legal scholars and organizations. Our justice system has double standards. Some courts apply the 'three-strikes' law. But our family courts ignored this baseball-based law. You commit a crime three times and you are convicted. And did you also notice the 'foul-out' rule in the basketball game?"

"Yes, the referees threw four players out of court immediately after they committed five personal fouls."

"Your mother lied many times over. The courts should have stopped her from further foul play. Not only lying, but complaining to the court that I love you more than she does. She claims that you said so. Of course, any jealous mother could say that a father's affection for his daughter is unacceptable. This sort of jealousy indicates mental sickness. But the courts didn't care. I have shared some of those opinions with you before but I kept some to myself which I can now share."

He glanced in her direction for a split second before turning his attention back to the road. "But first I want to tell you there is a secret invitation for you." He pointed his hand toward the glove compartment. "Check the green envelope in there."

She opened the compartment. "You mean this envelope?"

"Yes. This has a secret invitation for you."

Adina opened the envelope. "I see no invitation. Just a page—"

"The invitation starts with the quotes from a few amicus briefs submitted to the higher court in my support. Read them." Dan honked at a motorist who cut him off without signaling.

"Danny boy, never do that. What if he has a gun? Never heard about road rage?" Adina said, then she began to read the quotes aloud.

"'This American state is known for bad family courts...

"'Our national law center stands for justice and equality. We condemn the world-view of this trial judge...

"'The judge is unaware of what researchers say about the advantages of co-sleeping with parents and grandparents. He violated a civil liberty of the parents, who alone have the right to decide whether to sleep with their child. He ignored the cultural values of minorities…

"'The court unlawfully granted the father's parents only ten days per year to visit their granddaughter. The judge believes that restricting the parents will teach the father independent parenting. This family court judge may be unaware that nearly forty percent of households in his state have grandparents and grandchildren living together—"

"Adina!" Dan interrupted to add another lawyer's surprise statement. "'The judge suppressed a declaration by Madhu. Otherwise, she might have been implicated and forced to face the music.'"

But then Dan hesitated to talk about the declaration, as it was too long for now. Also, he didn't want to mention again an amicus brief in favor of Madhu. The worst thing about it was that it had the support of two female Asian American political activists. It claimed that Asian males had a pattern of engaging in domestic violence. The courts had already ruled out domestic violence on Dan's part. Yet this amicus brief brought up that unsubstantiated issue again—just to demonize Dan as a typical Asian American male, a violent wife-abuser.

Dan ignored this absurd amicus brief right now. "Adina, we received much more support after the appellate court upheld the lower court's decisions," he said instead. "My lawyer was upset that none of the judges said one word against your mother and her lawyers, who claimed that it was you, Adina, not they, who accused me with those allegations. Those higher judges should not have upheld the decision of that imposter judge. His decision meant sanctioning criminal conduct. I know that in one American state any accusation found false is a felony and a jail sentence for four years."

"So I could have been jailed if our state had such a law," Adina said with a faint smile.

Dan ignored her joke. "And another crime this imposter judge committed. He tried to suppress the known fact that a twenty-two-month old baby is unable to talk like that. He also suppressed the suffering you and I experienced, due to this premeditated act of your mother's. According to a national organization, inflicting such suffering is an act of domestic violence, and it must be stopped. Rationalizing violence as an *overreaction* to relieve tension is hogwash. This is how many Nazis justified their torturing of innocent men and women. A law school might even use my case to teach human rights violation. Discuss a topic: *How can American courts ignore false allegations as overreactions?* You can suggest your own solution after reading all the recorded details of our case. We can discuss this topic when we get home."

Adina was moved by her father's choked voice and changed the subject. "But where can I read the invitation, Daddy?"

"See the back of the sheet you are reading. The invitation is in big bold letters right in the center of the page!" Now his voice sounded normal.

Adina saw it. "Wow! You mean there is a slumber party tonight? With whom and where?"

"That's a surprise awaiting you at our residence!"

Around six p.m., there was a knock on the door. Adina answered as her father stood behind her.

"Dadiiii! Dadaaaa!" Adina burst into tears as she hugged them each, and they kissed her again and again. Then Dada handed her a pizza box.

"Thank you, Mom and Dad. We had almost ordered pizza at Damiano's for lunch today."

"Dada, it's very heavy and smells awfully good," Adina said, wiping her tears.

"This is a family-size Chicago-style pizza for dinner, and after dinner, we all are going to have a sleep-over," Dadi said as she also wiped her tears.

Adina sat on the sofa in the living room with her grandparents. Dan took the pizza in the kitchen and started preparing tea for his parents.

"Now you know the secret plan for tonight, but tell us how have you been doing?" Dadi asked Adina.

"I have been living in my imaginary world," Adina said, after taking a deep breath.

"No one can avoid living in his or her imaginary world," Dadi said, but she didn't sound uncomfortable. "The imaginary world is part of the real world, but with a difference. Living in the imaginary world is far more costly and dangerous than living in the real world. Mythology and economy are odd bedfellows."

Adina nodded. "My mother's mythology is an example. Her selling of the family assets secretly is another example of economy. Dada calls it 'legalized secret economy.'"

"We have been watching the recent news and efforts to help the victims of the Kedarnath tragedy," Dadi said. "You know what havoc those monsoon floods caused in our ancestral Himalayan region?"

"Yes. I saw the videos of how the Shiva temple of Kedarnath was almost submerged. After a while, the water receded and the damaged temple began to reemerge fully, but more than six hundred pilgrims died there. Later counts showed over one thousand. And many were swept down the holy river Mandakini. It was very horrible scene to watch. Shiva's sons, like Ganesha and Karttikeya, were not seen anywhere there, nor their armies. Finally, Indian soldiers came to the rescue by helicopter."

"Karttikeya could have come on his vehicle, the peacock," Dadi said. "Ganesha could not have reached there upon his slow mouse, and Shiva's bull drowned along with the temple for a while. Maybe the helpless beast thought Shiva would save him. The government lost no time in promising to rescue the lord and his temple within two years. But some staunch faithful rode on *dandi* carriages on the shoulders of local poor men. The riders expected to reap the fruits of their good karma at this cold high altitude temple. They never got any fruits, nor did the poor men get their lowest wages. They perished there together. The government could have taken safety measures before the floods came."

Adina pursed her lips. "Or maybe Shiva thought his immobile bull would rise to the occasion and save them. Can such miracles happen really?"

Dadi shrugged. "Who knows?" she said sarcastically. "And nearby Badrinath was also threatened by the raging waters of the Alakananda. But Vishnu saved his temple and town. Among these two muscular male deities, Shiva looks weaker in the eyes of Vaishnavas, the devotees of Vishnu." She chuckled. "The followers of Shiva like the Ayyar brahmins and the Vishnu followers like the Ayyangar brahmins would be happy to see the destruction of their rival temples."

"Sounds like the feuds between Catholics and Protestants or between Sunni and Shia Muslims," Adina added. "Very violent feuds in Iraq."

"Or even between the nonviolent Digambara and Shvetambara sects of Jainism," Dada said, joining the conversation. "And don't forget the 'Lower Vehicle' and 'Higher Vehicle' divisions of Buddhism. The Theravada Buddhists hate the Mahayana Buddhists for calling their division 'Hinayana' or 'Lower Vehicle' path. I may add the Hindi word *buddhu*, which means *stupid*. Most people of India won't believe me if I were to tell them that it is derived from *Buddha*. So this word should be considered politically incorrect—"

Adina leaned forward, eagerly hanging on Dada's every word. "Thanks, Dada, for this information. Why didn't you tell me earlier?"

"I was always worried about Dadi and I not violating the judge's order not to see you more than ten days per year. It became impossible to do all the things that we wanted to. That judge deprived us of your precious company, due to his blatant disregard, of the laws."

"You didn't really violate any restriction. The judge violated your rights. Why can't such stupid judges be considered criminals?"

"Thanks for not using the word *buddhu* for such judges. These criminal judges are above law. They cannot be tried." Dada frowned and switched to *buddhu* again. "Now let me add a hateful Hindi proverb to *buddhu*. It's '*laut ke buddhu ghar aye*.'"

"Yes, I would like to know, Dada."

"It means 'Mr. Buddhu came back home.' As you know, Prince Gautama left home secretly without his young wife Yashodhara and infant son Rahula. For six years, he wandered here and there for peace. He experienced enlightenment while meditating under a peepal tree. He returned home to tell first to his family and then others that he had found the way to peace while meditating. It is very simple: 'Everyone has to find his own way in his own way.' Those who heard him felt empowered and liberated. So people believed him as the enlightened one, *Buddha*."

Dadi nodded. "The Buddha meant everyone should solve his or her problems in his or her own way," she said. "But the way must be nonviolent. This prince didn't recommend to his fellow princes that they assemble armies. Then fight the war and justify this heinous act. Then make soldiers' wives widows and their children fatherless. Then talk about peace. Some of our national heads are modern princes, who falsely accuse the other nation. Then start a war with a false hope for peace."

"This message applies to individuals, too," Adina said, looking directly into their eyes. "When Gautama returned home, his wife didn't kick him out. She didn't bring witnesses who would hide or evade the facts. She didn't ask her son not to see his father anymore."

"And she didn't denigrate the nonviolent Buddha by calling him a dacoit while shedding false tears of fear," Dadi agreed. "This is what some called the honest Buddha—a thief, *chaura* in Sanskrit. She could have gone to other extremes to destroy her husband's reputation, such as using a chain of false complaints. Buddha preached 'avoidance of extremes' in life. His wife and son liked the 'Middle Path' of Gautama and they became his first disciples. What an honor for him from his loved ones who gladly accepted to travel on his path."

Dada grinned at his wife and granddaughter. "The famous *Mahabharata* saying applies to Gautama Buddha: '*Mahaajano yena gataḥ saḥ panthaaḥ.* The path is that by which the great person went by.' But that Hindi proverb considers the Buddha a fool. Why did he leave home empty-handed if he had to return empty-handed? The proverb meant this question," he explained, "But the ridiculers fail to realize that he didn't return empty-handed. He had left sad, but returned cheerful because he had brought home a solution for his own question: Why life sucks?"

"Yes," Adina said. "Buddha's solution made him an international figure just a couple of centuries before Christ."

Dada smiled at her appreciation of the Buddha. "No

Indian can come this close to Buddha's fame," he said, while raising his hand a little up to show a circle, which he had formed by joining his thumb and index finger for zero or emptiness.

Dadi leaned forward. "But the Indian feminists won't care for any religious man, historical or mythical, famous like Buddha or flamboyant like Krishna. The feminists adore goddess Kali and wouldn't care to rebuild any male deity's temple anywhere in the world. And they are right about those scripture creators who perpetuated the myth of the first female's birth from a male's body. Those male leaders are the ones who made rules for women's slavery. So the feminist movement makes sense. I have an Indian American friend—staunch feminist. She wants to ban a textbook that shows the first Shankaracharya giving sermons to his deciples."

Adina frowned and shook her head. "What is her reasoning?"

"I was just coming to that. In that picture all the disciples of this Shankaracharya are males shown like Brahmins. They all have sacred threads. Apparently, the setting is Kedarnath. All the monks are bare-chested sitting under a tree near the river Mandakini. My friend thinks that the picture represents a decadent culture no matter what the setting is."

"But you and Dada told me that Kedarnath is one of the most beautiful areas of the Himalayas. How can it be decadent? The artist must have a reason to choose that background."

"Yes, there seems to be a reason. As the legend goes, the first Shankaracharya used Kedarnath as his second home. The Shankaracharya slipped down near the Kedarnath temple over the snow and died at the age of thirty-two." Dadi sighed. "Now let's go back to my friend's story. She thinks that Shankaracharya didn't learn much from the Buddha who was born more than a millennium before him. She is right. Instead, he quarreled with Buddhist philosophers of his time. He fought against their Godless philosophy and forgot their egalitarian practice. One of Buddha's chief disciples, Upali, was a *Shudra*. This untouchable Buddhist monk was the first author of the Rules of the Order, the *Vinaya Pitaka*."

"And the Buddha included men and women in his Order," Adina commented.

"You know, near Kedarnath there is the highest monastery of Shankaracharya. It never had a woman or an untouchable head. There goes Shankaracharya's *Vedanta* in practice."

"So, you are implying that the Buddha was not a bigot. Is your friend a Buddhist?" Adina asked.

"No. She is a modern intellectual. No religion. The founders of world's major religions were males. They made the rules. No good for women. That's what she thinks. And I agree with her. But I don't believe in burning or banning books even if they contain rules averse to women's freedom."

"Yes," Dada agreed. "Women have been decapitated for breaking those rules. Though there is a popular ancient story about how Kali killed Shiva in her rage. Later, she realized her mistake that she had killed her own husband and so she revived him. Eventually, an honest wife will always be kind to her husband. And religions would drown if they didn't receive life support from women."

"Just go to India," Dadi said. "It looks like women outnumber men in temple attendance. The temple culture has been so inegalitarian. But the devout women don't get it. They don't give a damn to the feminist movement. If you criticize those women for temple visits, they feel offended. They would like to ban any book written by foreign scholars against India's discriminatory traditions.

But not the *Laws of Manu* which authorizes a woman's father, husband, and son to control her life. Why not the other way around?" she asked rhetorically.

"Mom," Dan shouted from the kitchen, "before our divorce, Madhu controlled my life. She treated me like her chauffeur. And after the divorce, she wanted complete control of Adina. Those false allegations had that intent. Luckily, the state supreme court declared otherwise and highlighted my exoneration: 'These allegations are unsubstantiated.' Thank goodness." He lifted the hot teapot from the burner and carefully placed on a hot pad. "This declaration is a public document. This turned out to be a big slap for Madhu and her witnesses. The state supreme court intended to show the public that her supporters emboldened a person who is now a legally branded liar. Not only Madhu's supporters, but even Adina read this decision on the Internet."

He arranged four empty teacups sort of in a line as he began to pour the boiling tea in each cup. "I am glad Adina and I can have control of our lives. And we will support co-sleeping as needed. No matter what all the courts have said about it and about equal custody. But I am mighty happy that restrictions on your visits were declared unconstitutional by the supreme court." Then he poured sugar and tasted a few drops from a cup with a spoon. *Too much sugar*, he realized. He began to fix the sugary tea problem while he continued talking. "You just talked about women's temple visits in India. For Madhu, there is no need to go to India. Indian temples here are like sacred Indian casinos. Anyone can buy spiritual tickets from them to win women's slavery. But don't you worry. Now Kali has set her feet firmly in American homes. By her grace, thousands of husbands are being crushed with demonic vengeance—"

"By her grace?"

"Yes, Mom. In some states, husbands like me are in jail and cannot see their own children for years, in spite of false allegations. That's what Madhu's malicious intent meant."

"Amazing," Adina said, her eyes widening. "I have seen Indian calendars that depict Kali severing the heads of the demons and sipping their blood. Blood oozing from her extra-large tongue over the dead body of Lord Shiva. Did she really intend to hurt her husband? Most artists do not make it clear in those calendar pictures. I have noticed many artists are male. Their own names often appear at a corner of the calendar picture. The artists clearly suggest that they are true believers of Kali."

"Their belief is justified in a way," Dadi said with a smile. "The Kedarnath disaster proves that nothing can be done against the will of Mother Nature. That is Kali, the dark energy. Dark energy is fact, God is fantasy. Kali is present everywhere. The cosmic soup came out of her. That oozing blood is cosmic soup."

"But, in many of our scriptures, *Shiva* is the creator, as his symbol *Linga* suggests," Dada added. "There are thousands of stories that Shiva saved this, Shiva saved that. Once upon a time the entire universe was going to be destroyed by a deadly poison. Shiva drank it and—"

"Saved the universe," Adina interrutped. "I have heard that story before. But what's your point, Dada?"

"My point is this: a god or goddess cannot save anything, for they are imaginary entities. Adina, you must have heard recently that, near your Dadi's birthplace in Nainital, they sacrificed more than two hundred animals for the Devi. This mass killing of defenseless domestic animals took place after Kedarnath was devastated. I call this sacrifice SAK, short for Sacred Animal Killing. This land of gods is the worst place in the world for SAK. The UN should listen to the decision of the Uttarakhand court, which intended to sack the SAK tradition. The American organization PETA should come here to convert the native SAK people as 'people for the ethical treatment of animals.' People need not to be religious to become ethical."

Dadi laughed. "And people need not be ethical to become religious. So many holinesses are rotting in the hell of jail. "Now let me explain seriously," she said as she stopped laughing. "I had an argument with a few SAK believers. The goddess could not save her husband Shiva from drowning at Kedarnath, I told them, and your Himalayas are not a *Deva Bhumi*. You are doing what many fanatics do. You name your region or country after your god or religion and don't mind the slaughter of the non-believers, the sacrificial animals. Shame on you! Counting the neighboring Nepal, the world will believe that Hindus slaughter more animals than other people do, all in the name of religion. Do really Hindus believe in *ahimsa*?"

"I agree with Dadi," Dada said. "The faithful will continue to pray to saviors who cannot save sinless lives and detest the real saviors such as animal rights activists. I also heard that some weather forecasters had warned about early heavy monsoons. But devotees believe in God's grace, even when they watch the videos of havoc. Over six hundred men, women, and children lying dead, as if sacrificed for Kedarnath," he lamented, "But a leading devout politician says that over six thousand died because some visitors defecated there. Many gullible people would believe her remarks that the atheist visitors were responsible for this tragedy. The media ridiculed her remarks, though."

"Never knew yogis could smell atheist shit," Dan mumbled from the kitchen.

"Did you say something, Daddy? I couldn't hear you clearly."

"I know who she is. As a nun, she wears ochre robes and practices yoga," Dan responded loudly.

"No, no. I thought I heard you talking of smelling something. Anything very special there?"

"The only thing I smell very special here is the *lopchu* tea. Your dada loves the flavor of this best tea of India."

"Thanks, Dan, for adding the *lopchu.* But let me add a comment. She would know very well that yoga follows the non-theistic rational school of *Samkhya.* And one more comment—the state government did not disclose the actual figure of the dead."

"This is why many demanded the resignation of the Chief Minister," Dadi said with a frown, her disappointment clear. "Administrative transparency is still foreign here. But it will come, sooner or later. But the CM alone was not responsible. No sociologist would believe that one leader alone decides all things all the time. Nobody blamed so many gods whose job was to sense troubles beforehand. Then try to remove those troubles as soon as possible."

After a momentary pause Adina shifted in her seat. "I watched a video of a pretty Bollywood actress, the film shot around the time when funds were being collected throughout India for the Uttarakhand disaster relief. The actress was doing the *arti* prayer of Ganesha in a Mumbai temple. One line of the prayer in Hindi went like this: 'Victory to the lord of the world, who removes the troubles of the devotees in a moment.' The video mentioned that the actress boasted about her firm belief in the power of Lord Ganesha."

"She was lucky for she was not one of those unlucky devotees at Kedarnath," Dadi exclaimed. "Lord Kedarnath didn't live up to his name. It is believed that Kedar-khand for Uttarakhand is his eponymous name."

"I agree," Dada said. "This woman had no courage to ask questions. Why couldn't the lord prevent the horrible tragedy of his birthplace, these Himalayas? Did the lord run away to help the poor slums of faraway Mumbai, the city of that actress? The biggest festival of Ganapati is held in this city every year, and I never heard any partici-pant asking Lord Ganapati during this festival why He fails every year to remove the troubles of the slum dwell-ers."

Dadi snorted in disgust. "Gods are not accountable if they fail. They have divine immunity. The US is known around the world as the most litigious country. But have you ever heard that somebody sued God for not answer-ing His devotee's prayers? Devotees don't ask unfaithful questions. Indeed, they hate unfaithful questions. They may be in trouble if they asked unfaithful questions. And if they absolutely have to ask, then they whisper and nev-er write their thoughts. Read about so many tragedies happening in the world due to religious questioning. And God failed to intervene. There isn't such a thing as divine intervention. Are my remarks blasphemous?"

"Dadi," Adina said in shock. "You commit blasphemy and you could be murdered." She shuddered at the thought. "But here is a blasphemy-like case. Ganesha's idols are sold to India by China. Communist China is against religion and it is almost impossible to bring any religion into that country. Isn't China committing a sort of blasphemy?"

"You are so funny. You are really, Adi!" Dadi stretched out her arm to pat Adina's shoulder. "But you make a relevant point. You may call it reverse blasphe-my—non-believer selling religious superstition to a be-liever. However, there is a silver lining in this case. Unlike national border barriers, trade barriers have been removed by Lord Ganesha across the Himalayas. I always thought Parvati made Ganesha with her own body material in our Himalayan region, but now Indians are happily buying Ganesha made in China with Chinese material, far better than Indian material! Missionaries have been exporting their superstitions on a non-profit basis, but atheists are selling them now for profit. Nobody is calling it a blasphemous act, but rather appreciating it as a good export-import business. What a sea change!"

They laughed jointly.

After a momentary pause, Adina broke the silence and mood, too. "I found Dad's devotees: the amicus brief parties and their supporters. I never knew of their existence before."

"Men and women from the universities of California to Harvard, from Washington, DC, to Washington State are supporting equal parenting," Dadi informed her. "Adi, did you note that, among the signers, is a leading anthropologist? And a pediatrician whose best-selling book has been the bible for your parents?"

"And did you remember, Dad?

"What?" Dan asked.

"One of the signers is the leading national organization of women, the majority of whose members are mothers who stand for equal parenting? And we were talking of double standards earlier. Women have been deprived of equal standards, balanced standards."

"But the jihadist-feminist way is not the way to achieve gender equality," Dan said. "Neither is it the way of male chauvinists. A backlash is likely to emerge against feminists from thousands of victims like me. So we need feminists who would encounter this backlash. They should insist that justice and equality are not a matter of double standards. And I will support such feminists worldwide."

"Adina will always need her father's support," Adina said with a smile.

Dadi gently put her hand over Adi's shoulder. "Mothers give birth to men as well as women. Women have to be the natural champions of gender equality." She smiled, "Both of your father's attorneys who fought for him to obtain equal custody were women. So there are fair-minded lawyers and their organizations all over the country. The members of these organizations must have realized your father's case was actually the story of thousands of broken homes in America alone."

"You are right, Mom," Dan interjected, sounding outraged. "The National Parents Organization has correctly called parental alienation *child abuse*. Right now, there are thousands of children like my Adina who are deprived of equal parenting because of ignorant judges, insensitive witnesses, phony psychologists, and greedy lawyers. Any fair-minded person would say that fabrication of a criminal allegation in the name of an innocent child is a crime against the child. This crime was designed to shut out even one chance of co-parenting. Forget about equal co-parenting chances!".

Adina fumed. "And how about equal grandparenting?" she asked, placing her hands on her head and running her fingers through her hair in frustration. "The judge knew that both of you are university teachers, Dada, Dadi. If I spent more than ten days every year with you, would your superior education make me a dumb child? The judge should have researched how much grandparents such as mine could do for a child. Instead, he refused more visits with you. For no good reason, he punished you."

"These court jokers are in the positions they are be-

cause of political favors, not professional qualifications."
Dadi, too, sounded angry. "We are pretty sure they know
that, as parents, we have the right to live with our son
permanently, no matter who is visiting him. And as
grandparents we have the right to visit with you in our
home, no matter who else is with us,"

"Peter is our lawyer friend," Dada said. "He also
thinks likewise about these jokers. They do not make decisions based upon reason but upon rashness. I agreed
with him, Adina. An ice cream seller could visit you
more often than ten days a year, but not your Dada and
Dadi. We couldn't spend a single Christmas with you.
Imagine a tennis coach. He is okay to throw the balls to
you hundreds of times five days a week, but we could not
even tell you a few *Mahabharata* stories on more than ten
days a year. Just a few stories from the second longest
epic of the world." He breathed a long sigh. "You were
playing piano, dancing on the ballet floor, throwing kara-
te chops, and several other fun things which sounded like
fantasies to us."

"Yes," Dadi said. "Such deliberate deprivations can be
legally awarded in America, a country that preaches the
values of equality and justice to the whole world. This is
a country where the child cries out frequently when supervised meetings end, 'I want my dad? Where is he? He
told me he would be back.' And the state says, 'No, he
can't be back.' The state knows that your dad didn't lie
and that your mom did, and still the child keeps sobbing
and sobbing."

Dadi heaved a tired sigh and shook her head in disgust. "And one witness for your mom wrote to the court
that Adina felt a lot better after your dad was denied
regular contact with you," she said. "This witness had
taken dozens of your pictures in playful poses with your
dad, not one time but dozens of times. Liars supporting

liars! The court didn't care for your trauma—the trauma of being separated from your dad. Those witnesses who conducted the supervised visits mentioned that trauma in their testimony. What kind of family values do this judge and his psychologist have?"

"Enough." Dan intervened, sounding possessed by his traumatic past. "What's the point of retelling the same painful stories? We better create new stories, some happy ones. But first let's enjoy the *masala* tea."

He had brought four full tea cups on a tray. He put the rattling tray down on the cocktail table. Adina had already heard about the trauma that she experienced after the divorce, but she was saddened that he could not seem to move past it now. *He keeps repeating the same stories that are really troubling. Now I am learning that from him.*

They all drank the tea and then gobbled the entire pizza. "Eating pizza is our fundamental right," Dan asserted.

"So are donuts," Dada added. "Do you remember, Adi, one of your mother's witnesses complained that your dad fed you unhealthy food, like donuts?"

"I rarely ate donuts when I was growing up," Adi answered without a hitch.

"But that witness confessed in front of the judge that her complaints were based on what she heard from Madhu. A witness must witness, not just hear," Dan added. "Madhu should know the law. The fundamental right of parents to raise their child as they like is protected by the United States Constitution. So I could have given you donuts, but not pot!"

They laughed.

"It's not a laughing matter," he scolded. "Nonconformance of the law could give you the joy of jail. One potential witness was lucky. He practiced internal medicine and smoked pot—*bhang*, I mean. His license could have been taken away if he had agreed to be a witness. By law, a doctor must inform the Child Protective Services if he is aware of that kind of parental abuse of a child. He must have understood the consequences. I wouldn't have reported him, anyway. We have been friends since he came here from San Francisco. His innocent children would have suffered. My child, too."

Dadi looked at him with tears in her eyes. "I hope someday his adult children find out what the Parent Teachers Association of Adina's KG school did for you. It was the best honor for you to be the chair of its legislative committee. I so appreciated the PTA's trust in you."

"And my appointment was voted unanimously, Mom. That day I felt vindicated because all the voters were female teachers. For Madhu and her jihadists, my vindication has no value, though. They would have liked me to be rotting in a prison. Many innocent victims did serve prison time," Dan finished with a deep sigh.

Then came the time for the grand finale of this evening: the slumber party. They all lay down on the floor of the living room, just like in a tent.

"Now we are Henry David Thoreau, Mahatma Gandhi, Martin Luther King Jr., and Cesar Chavez," Dada said, clearly excited. "Right now we have to remember that the judge gave orders against any co-sleeping. Remember when you were six years old, we had almost violated his orders? One evening before going to sleep, we sat on our bed and watched a *Laurel and Hardy* rerun on our laptop. At the end you hugged us all and sang the famous line 'So happy together.' If our circumstances had been good, your mother, too, would have been together. Instead, she walked away to deprive us of this exhilarating experience. We will continue defying the judges who meddle with the private lives of people!"

Adina sat up eagerly. "What if the congress acts?"

"That's a long shot, Adi. The UN must do something for some universal rights of children. Let's hope the leaders of child advocacy groups and the others who have signed amicus briefs for Dan raise hell and the world listens. Punishing innocent children for cultural differences as practiced by their caregivers is domestic violence," Dada responded, his voice gruff.

"That's the position of a legal organization that supports Dad too. He is a victim of a planned act of domestic abuse," Adina said. Then she covered her body with the blanket and whispered, "I will defend the right to sleepover myself. It's my right to co-sleep with my parents or grandparents wherever I choose—one and the same floor or bed. To deny that right to a baby is an act of cruelty. The judge committed a crime. Why didn't I think of having my own lawyer earlier, much, much earlier, instead of when I am thirteen years old?"

"Only if you find an honest lawyer! Otherwise, it's much easier if the judge gives you a rope with which to hang yourself," Danin said.

Adina shook her legs up and down very briskly under the blanket. "You mean to hang around with each other. Right, lawyer boy?"

They all laughed.

"Are you refreshing your tae kwon do?" Dan joked.

"I may need it now to defend myself, Dad," Adina responded. After a pause, she asked, "Dad, how do you know an honest lawyer from the rest?"

"It is very easy in your case! That lawyer should not believe that there ever really existed a twenty-two-month-old baby who could accuse the father and understand that, in this case, the mother believed her own myth."

"I am not an imaginary entity, but rather, a real sacrificial animal—a defenseless domestic animal. I must tell Dada how I really met some divine entities. The same revelations from all of them, again and over. They all denied having my crown jewel. But soon Technology will reveal who lied—"

"Quiet! Dada is snoring," Dan whispered and put his fingers over his lips.

"Let me hum a song line for our *Satyagraha*."

Dan tried to stop her, but it was all in vain. "He knows ours is a true resolve."

"So, I will sing for the success of our resolve for truth." Very softly she hummed the opening words of Freddie Mercury's song "We Are the Champions."

"Continue that Indian's song loudly, my lovely princess," Dada commanded suddenly.

THE END

Glossary

Agni: god of fire

Ahalya: a sage's wife cheated by Indra

Ahimsa: non-violence, non-injury

Akbar: a Moghul emperor of India (14 October 1542 – 27 October 1605)

Amrita: immortalizer, nectar of immortality

Aparna: a name of goddess Parvati

Arti: honoring a deity with lighted candles

Apsara: heavenly nymph

Arundhati: Sage Vasishtha's wife symbolized as Morning Star

Ashish: blessing

Ashvamedha: horse sacrifice

Asura: demon

Aṭhwaṛ: buffalo sacrifice in the Garhwal Himalayas

Avatar: divine incarnation

Baba: holy man, saint

Badmash: rogue

Badrinath: a Vishnu temple in the Central Himalayas of India near the Tibet border

Bagesari: a *raga* named after Vagishvari, the speech goddess or Sarasvati

Bahadur Shah "Zafar": the last Moghul emperor of India (24 October 1775 – 7 November 1862)

Bali: a demon king associated with the Dwarf avatar of Vishnu

Bali: animal sacrifice

Bhagavan: God

Bhairava: a god and assistant of god Shiva

Bhajan: devotional song

Bhang: Indian marijuana, *cannabis sativa*

Bharata: son of Shakuntala and King Dushyanta; son of Kaikeyi and King Dasharatha (Rama's half-brother in the *Ramayana*)

Bhavani: a name of goddess Parvati

Bindi: a color mark on forehead

Brahma: the four-headed god of creation

Brahmaṇḍa: Brahma's egg as the symbol of cosmic beginning

Brahmin: the Hindu priestly class, a person belonging to this class

Buddhi: intellect, intelligence

Chakra: the disk weapon, lit. "cycle, circle"

Chañchala: flaky or unstable woman, a name of Lakshmi

Chitragupta: an assistant of Yama the god of death

Dada: paternal grandfather

Dadi: paternal grandmother

Dakini: a witch

Daksha, Daksha Prajapati: Sati's father, Shiva's ex father-in-law

Dakshina: sacred offering of money, priestly fee

Damau: a tympani-shaped drum

Darshan: viewing, gazing at a sacred object for meditation

Dasharatha: a king of Ayodhya, Rama's father

Devarshi: godly sage, Narada's title

Devasena: Skanda's wife, Shiva's daughter-in-law

Dhol: a bass drum

Dik Pal: (see *Dikpala* below)

Dikpala: protector of a cosmic division, god of Direction,

Dukha: suffering, pain

Durga: a goddess

Dushyanta: Shakuntala's husband and King Bharata's father

Fakir: saint, mendicant

Ganapati: the elephant-headed son of Parvati and Shiva

Ganesha: same as Ganapati

Garhwal Himalayas: the western region of the Central Himalayas of India

Ghazal: a song-poem in Urdu

Ghee: clarified butter

Gopi: cowgirl

Gori: white woman

Graha: planet

Hai: alas!

Hanuman: the monkey god of the *Ramayana*

Harsh: happiness

Harshita: happy

Havana: a Vedic ritual of fire worship

Hiranyakashipu: a demon king killed by the Man-Lion avatar of Vishnu

Holika: a demoness, Hiranyakashipu's sister

Homa: a Vedic ritual offerings of burnt food

Indra: the king of heaven

Ishvara: God

Jaya: victory

Ji: an honorific word after a person's name

Jim Corbett: an Indian British hunter and writer

Kabir: a medieval saint-poet from Varanasi

Kaikeyi: King Dasharatha's third wife and Bharata's mother (Rama's stepmother)

Kali: a black goddess

Kali: black woman

Kamala: a name of goddess Lakshmi, lit. "lotus"

Kamandalu: a jug or drinking pot used by saints

Karttikeya: the six-headed son of Shiva

Katthak: a north Indian classical dance

Kedarnath: a Shiva temple in the Central Himalayas of India near Tibet

Ketu: a mythical planet named for the headless demon Rahu

Khunkhri: a kind of Himalayan dagger

Kirtan: a devotional chorus

Krishna: an avatar of Vishnu, son of Devaki and Vasudeva, hero of the *Mahabharata*

Kshatriya: the warrior class of the Hindu caste system

Kubera: a demon king appointed by gods as their treasurer

Kumbh, kumbha: pot, pitcher

Kumbh Mela: the pitcher fair

Laddu: a sweet shaped round like golf or tennis ball

Lakshmana: a son of King Dasharatha and Sumitra, half-brother of Rama

Lakshmi: Vishnu's wife and goddess of prosperity

Lasya: a female style of dance attributed to Parvati

Linga: phallic symbol of Shiva

Lopchu: a Darjeeling tea of India

Ma: mother

Mahabharata: an ancient epic in Sanskrit

Mahavira: the last founder of Jainism

Mahisha: the buffalo demon killed by goddess Durga

Mahishasuramardini: the murderer of Mahisha demon, goddess Durga

Mahishi: queen

Mai: mother

Manava: man, sage Manu's progeny

Manu: an ancient sage, the father of human race

Mata: mother

Matsya: the fish avatar of Vishnu associated with sage Manu, lit. "fish"

Maya: the magical cosmic force, the mysterious female power of Vishnu

Meet: friend

Mela: fair

Menaka: a heavenly nymph associated with Indra, mother of Shakuntala

Mira: a medieval princess and saint-poet

Mohini: the enchantress, Vishnu's female avatar

moksha: release or liberation from the cycle of karma and rebirth

Nachiketas: a boy who questioned Yama the death god in the ancient *Katha Upansihad*

Namaste: salutation, greeting, lit. "a bow to you"

Nana: maternal grandfather

Nanak: the founder of Sikhism

Nandin: Shiva's bull and vehicle

Nani: maternal grandmother

Narada: an ancient sage known as a son of Brahma and devotee of Vishnu

Narayana: God, Vishnu

Nawab: a title of Muslim kings

Nirṛti: a demoness worshipped as a direction protector

Nṛsimha: the Man-Lion avatar of Vishnu

Pahari: belonging to mountains, inhabitant or language of the hills

Pandit: pundit, scholar, Brahmin

Parvati: a goddess, Shiva's wife, lit. "a mountain woman"

Pashupati: lord of beings, Shiva's title

Pavaka: purifier, a title of Agni the god of fire

Pitamaha: grandfather, a title of Brahma the god of creation

Prahlada: a demon and devotee of Vishnu, Hiranyakashipu's son

Prajapati: lord of progeny, god of creation

Pranam: salutation, lit. "a very special bow"

Prasad: sacred food

Prayag: confluence

Puja: worship

Purana: the ancient scriptures in later Sanskrit

Puranic: belonging to the *Purana* scriptures and tradition

Radha: a cowgirl known as a friend/wife of Krishna

Raga: a scale and mode of Indian classical music

Rahu: a demon worshipped as a mythical planet

Rakshasa: demon

Rama: the hero of the *Ramayana*, king of Ayodhya and an avatar of Vishnu

Ramayana: an ancient epic in Sanskrit belonging to Rama of Ayodhya

Rambha: a heavenly nymph associated with Indra

Ravana: the demon king of Lanka and enemy of Rama

Rig Veda: the first ancient scripture composed in archaic Sanskrit or Vedic

Rudra: a Vedic god, Shiva

Rukmini: one of the wives of Krishna

Sadhu: saint, holy man

Sala: an expletive meaning "bastard," lit. "wife's brother"

Salim Chishti: a medieval Muslim saint

Samkhya, sankhya: an ancient atheist philosophy

Samudra-manthana: a mythological "ocean-churning"

Sangha, samgha: society, group, organization

Santoshi Mata: a goddess, Ganesha's daughter, lit. "mother of satiety"

Sarasvati: goddess of speech, knowledge, music, and other arts

Sati: Daksha Prajapati's daughter and Shiva's first wife who immolated herself

Satyagraha: Gandhi's word for civil disobedience, lit. "true resolve, resolve for truth"

Satya Narayana: Vishnu's title, lit. "True God"

Satya: truth

Satyabhama: one of the wives of Krishna

Shachi: Indra's wife

Shakini: a kind of witch

Shakti: energy, power, cosmic force associated with Shiva as his wife

Shakuntala: King Dushyanta's wife and mother of King Bharata the founder of Bharat "India"

Shankaracharya: a monk who heads one of the topmost Hindu monasteries, the founder monk and philosopher Shankara

Shweta: white

Shiva: god Shiva

Shivani: Shiva's wife, Parvati's title

Shri Ram Sharma: an Indian hunter and writer

Sita: the heroine of the *Ramayana*, Rama's wife

Sitar: a string instrument like guitar

Soma: an ancient plant-based drink to get high

Sukha: happiness, pleasure

Svayambhū: self-born, a symbol for the self-generated cosmos

Svayamvara: a ceremony in which the girl selects her future husband, lit. "self-selection"

Swami Brahmananda: a Shankaracharya of the Himalayan monastery at Joshimath associated with the Badrinath temple and Maharishi Mahesh Yogi

Tabla: a pair of Indian drums

Thali: a food plate

Taraka: a demon

Tilottama: a heavenly nymph associated with Indra

TM: Transcendental Meditation

Urvashi: a heavenly nymph associated with Indra

Vajra: thunderbolt, name of the weapon of Indra, lightning

Valmiki: the sage considered as the original author of the *Ramayana*

Vamana: the Dwarf avatar of Vishnu

Veda: the four *Vedic* scriptures in the earliest Sanskrit, lit. "knowledge"

Vina: a musical instrument like *sitar*

Vinaya Pitaka: one of the first three Buddhist scriptures, lit. "the basket of *conduct* (*Vinaya*) "

Vishnu: a god, lit. "pervader"

Vishvamitra: a sage, father of Shakuntala

Vrata: vow, a fast observed in a worship

Yajña: the Vedic fire ceremony

Yama: the God of Death

Yami: sister of Yama the God of Death

Yogini: a woman who practices yoga

About the Author

Anoop Chandola is a linguist-anthropologist. Before coming to the US, he was educated at the universities of Allahabad and Lucknow. His last two degrees in linguistics include an MA from the University of California, Berkeley, and a PhD from the University of Chicago.

He has taught Indian literatures, cultures, and religions at several universities in India and the US, including Sardar Patel University, the MS University of Baroda, University of California at Berkeley, University of Washington at Seattle, University of Texas at Austin, and University of Wisconsin at Madison. Now he is Professor Emeritus of East Asian Studies at the University of Arizona. He is a member of numerous professional associations including the American Anthropological Association, Association for Asian Studies, Linguistic Society of America, and Linguistic Society of India.

Chandola has published fifteen books and numerous papers. His scholarly books and articles are in the areas of linguistics, music, religion and literature which include extensive interdisciplinary and theoretical analysis. Among his four novels *The Dharma Videos of Lust: The Mysteries of Indian Religions*, published by UKA Press, London, received two finalist awards: "Best Books Awards" of USA Book News and the "National Indie

Excellence Awards." His novel *In the Himalayan Nights*, released in 2012 by Savant Books & Publications (USA), received a Great Northwest Book Festival award. He founded the field of "musicolinguistics" based on coining the term, arguing for its creation and laying a theoretical framework for the discipline.

Chandola lives in Tucson and Seattle with his wife Sudha.